Anticipation

GEMINI
PRESS

ISBN: 9781955858137
Library of Congress Control Number: 2022943840

librapress.com

The ABC's of Romance

Anticipation

Rue Harlow

Prologue

"**I**'ve asked you two here this morning because this situation has gotten completely out of control." Dean Wilkinson looked across his desk at Annabelle Lyons and Marcus Dale with a smile he wasn't feeling. "I'm sure you can understand my concern."

"Of course," said Annabelle.

"Absolutely," Marcus nodded.

Wilkinson gave them another long look, wondering exactly where he should take this. Their recent — and rather *public* — dispute had been causing quite the ruckus, both on and off-campus. But as a wise man once said (Winston Churchill, if someone pressed him for the quote), "A pessimist sees the difficulty in every opportunity; an optimist sees the opportunity in every difficulty."

This moment was an opportunity for sure, assuming the Dean could figure out what to do with the pair of Mountain View University professors who had been going slowly viral for weeks. The professors were young, vibrant, and both good-looking. Marcus had dark features and an easy smile. Annabelle's features — hair, skin, and eyes — were all slightly lighter. But she had the darker smile between them.

Annabelle and Marcus were in the Dean's office because they believed there was a different problem to solve. And until Wilkinson could find a way for MVU to capitalize on the buzz his teachers had been building — apparently by accident — that's where he needed their perception to stay.

"I'm sure you're both aware of the ... chaos you've been causing on campus?" Wilkinson looked at them with a gaze that had been inspiring passion or fear in his students for over thirty years. Where on the spectrum his subjects fell depended on what they had done to end up in front of his desk.

"We're aware." Annabelle nodded.

"We now have students overflowing into *The Science of Love*, ever since word started spreading about your ongoing spat." Wilkinson looked from the class's professor, Annabelle, to its harshest critic sitting next to her.

"I wouldn't call it a *spat*," Annabelle replied.

Marcus doubled down on an earlier argument. "Like I said when I was sitting in this chair a year ago, I think it's irresponsible for this university to teach a course on 'science' when it's all just theory. None of what Ms. Lyons teaches is actual published research."

Annabelle shook her head, looking as though she was keeping a parade of possible responses to herself.

Wilkinson repeated his usual argument. "The word *science* is more figurative in this context."

"I hear you, sir, and I understand where you're coming from, but as the Dean of Arts and Sciences, I hope you don't *mean that*." Marcus shook his head and reset himself. "I'm not trying to be unkind or disrespect Ms. Lyons in my column ... it's not like I'm writing unflattering things about the course itself — I've never even mentioned The Science of Love by name. And yet—"

"You don't exactly need a secret decoder ring to figure out which class you're talking about," Annabelle interrupted. "You can say that *some researchers would have you believe or the cold-hearted analysis of science can't explain* all you want and keep right on pretending that the students at Mountain View aren't reading between the lines, but we both know that—"

Wilkinson raised a hand to stop her. "I've heard your arguments. Plenty of times. We're here today because I hope we can solve this problem together. So, any constructive suggestions from either of you?"

"It would be irresponsible for this institution to stop teaching one of its—"

"*Irresponsible?*" Marcus interrupted her with a scoff.

"Yes," Annabelle repeated herself: "*Irresponsible. I*'ve seen countless young freshman fail my psych courses because they get all caught up with some guy out of nowhere. They get heartbroken, believing that he's their one and only true love. They end up wasting a year's tuition, paying an obnoxious tuition — sorry, Dean, but you know it's true — while learning little to nothing and wasting their time."

Annabelle sighed and finished her argument. "If I can help more young people understand where these emotions are coming from, and that it's not love they're feeling, but rather a chemical and socially programmed formula, then I ... *No* — the University — could really do something great in this world."

"Nope. No way." Marcus shook his head, equally ardent. "Us teachers love a full room, so it's natural that Ms. Lyons would need a little narrative to tell herself. But I would strongly argue the opposite: *teaching our students that love can be reduced to a formula is dangerous to both our present and future.*"

Annabelle rolled her eyes.

But Marcus kept going. "My writing students *channel* their emotions. Those feelings not only strengthen the quality of their work but also make the *students stronger.*" He turned from Wilkinson to Annabelle. "How can you tell young people that love isn't real and then say that you're doing something good for the world?"

"I never said that love isn't real!" Annabelle snapped, seeming even more offended than before. "I said that love is a *formula.*"

"What about true love? What about soul mates? What about the magic of finding that perfect person you are destined to find?" Then, when Annabelle didn't answer: "The person who will be there for you, no matter what, until the very end?"

"And how often does that work out? That's *exactly* what I'm talking about. That kind of thinking can come rolling in like a tornado through a trailer park to obliterate a person's life."

"So dramatic." Marcus nodded in mocking approval. "Sounds like you might enjoy my creative writing class."

Annabelle ignored Marcus and continued her argument. "The idea of *one perfect person* is not only limiting, it's painful. Once a person realizes that they can create that same sense of euphoria with any number of potential partners, that epiphany is incredibly freeing. Only then can a person *plan for love* instead of getting derailed by it."

A low blow from Marcus: "If you can plan for love at any time, then why aren't you in it?"

Annabelle looked slapped. But she quickly recovered, speaking to Wilkinson rather than Marcus. "With more than eight billion people, the world is much too big for me to ignore all critical thinking and simply *believe* in anything as mathematically unsound as 'soul mates.' I do, however, strongly believe in 'mated souls.' And that's what the formula in *The Science of Love* is all about."

Wilkinson raised his hand again. He offered his professors yet another smile, still keeping this friendly. "We need to get our campus back on track. What was once a small story is now quickly spiraling out of control. It was one thing when the Mountain View Daily was covering your feud. Then we were only dealing with students boycotting one class or the other. Annoying, yes, but manageable. With local media now taking an interest in this story, it's time to change the conversation or kill it."

Wilkinson paused to see if either professor had anything to add, then continued when they didn't. "This kind of mess always sours the mood for our most high-profile donors, and MVU needs said donors to pony up some serious funds if we expect to finish those stadium renovations."

"Maybe that money should be going to expanding some of our more serious academic programs," suggested Annabelle. "Instead of yet more money for the football stadium."

"This isn't the time for that discussion," Wilkinson replied.

Marcus nodded, agreeing for the first time that morning, maybe ever. "She's right."

"There are two possibilities here ..." Wilkinson shifted in his seat, gathering himself for the fight. "And frankly, the first option is less than pleasant, involving sabbaticals and unpaid leave."

Annabelle shook her head. "But I didn't even start this. It was when Marcus wrote that scathing piece about my course and how it shouldn't be offered, and—"

"It wasn't 'scathing,' and like I already said, I've never even mentioned your course by name," Marcus retorted.

"It's not hard to figure out the most popular elective course in the entire school, *Mr. Dale!*" Annabelle managed to make *Mr. Dale* sound like a curse.

"None of this would have ever happened if the Dean had just listened to my concerns in the first place. You can 'teach' whatever you want. But you can't call it 'science' and—"

"Enough." Wilkinson silenced the arguing with a raised hand for the third time. They would never get anywhere rehashing the same old arguments. He'd heard this all before. Now it was time for something new. "Nobody has even asked me about option two ...."

"Option two?" Annabelle seemed willing yet confused.

"Option one was us losing our jobs." Marcus helped her.

"Option one involves sabbaticals and unpaid leave." Wilkinson again held up a hand to stop the two professors from responding.

"Option two turns this mess into something that will benefit the university ... But I can practically guarantee you're not going to like it."

Lili

2014

Liliana Travis was dressed like a giant beaver, missing only its head, ready for her life to dramatically change.

Even though the locker room reeked even more like sour socks than usual, Lili was only smelling roses. It had been a long football season — no longer than any other season, but Lili wasn't into football *at all* — and now that it was finally ending, it was time for the final act in her epic plan.

"So ..." Alicia prompted her. "What's the plan?"

"You mean the 'over-plan,'" Runa corrected Alicia.

Lili's two best friends had been with her during every step of this little scheme, just as they had stayed by her side for everything else throughout every noteworthy occasion in high school.

"I don't over plan," Lili defended herself, despite knowing how futile doing so would be, especially considering the crazy amount of thought she had poured into her nutty little endeavor so far.

"Okay." Runa shrugged. "And I bet that *Outlander* show is gonna be *great*."

"Shut up!" Lili laughed, sick of defending that one too. "*Outlander* is gonna be awesome."

Lili had made her two besties get through as much of the historical time travel romance adventure as they were willing to read, but neither of them were as enamored by the genre buster as she was.

Not that she was obsessed at all. Lili didn't get obsessed with anything, including Dominic Moore, no matter what Alicia and Runa said. The Mountain View Beavers' star quarterback was as handsome as he was charming, and Lili had been dying for an actual conversation, instead of the fleeting exchanges in Statistics, he forgot about five minutes after they happened.

Unfortunately, they had little in common. Lili knew she was weird and off-beat. People had been telling her she had a pretty face for most of her life so far, which was a nice way of delivering a compliment without insulting her weight. Not that Lili was fat, but she carried more pounds than most of the sticks and twigs at Mountain View High. It wasn't just a cliché; there was more of Lili to love.

Even though she was happy with herself, Lili still wanted others (like Dominic Moore, specifically) to see her as a catch. She was intelligent, funny, and plenty confident in the proper setting.

Knowing that environment was everything, Lili had leaped on the opportunity to control hers. Claire, the main character in *Outlander*, was always prepared and took charge of her environment. If Lili ever expected to get quality time with Dom, then she had to find a way, just like Claire would. When the Beavers' usual mascot tripped over the tail and broke his leg at halftime during the second game of her senior season, Lili stepped in for Zed Blakeslee and became the mascot herself.

She had hatched the perfect plan. By assuming her role as the Mountain View Beaver, Lili would earn herself an easy invite to Final Down, the epic party that had followed the final game for long enough to have become an official tradition. And there at that party, Lili could woo her crush and finally enlighten Dominic Moore about her awesomeness.

But now that her chance was finally here, Lili found herself at war with a serious case of nerves. Because what if she was wrong?

Dominic Moore might have been the most popular guy in high school, but he didn't seem shallow. Yet, as much as her time spent inside the mascot costume had seemed like an excellent way for Lili to get noticed, it hadn't happened yet.

Maybe because, so far, Lili could only talk to Dom with the mask on. The few opportunities she'd had for a conversation sans mascot so far had seen her either frozen or stuttering.

Lili refused to get in her own way tonight.

"So ..." Alicia redirected them again. "*The plan?*"

"Maybe I just go up and talk to him?" Half of Lili wanted to believe that her directness would be enough, with the other half not wanting Runa to start making fun of her.

"We talked about this." Alicia shook her head. "You need a 'meet cute.' Maybe you could spill a drink on his shirt, then help him to take off that shirt in the laundry room, just peel it right off his body and—"

"I should just go up and talk to him," Lili tried again. "If I can figure out the right thing to say, he'll see how amazing I am."

"How about, *Tell me your name so I know what I should scream tonight*," Alicia suggested.

"I already know his name. Also, eww, no."

"Is there an airport nearby, or is that my heart taking off?" Alicia made another stab at it.

Lili shook her head. "Please stop."

Runa looked at Alicia. "Lili's right. Why can't she just go up and talk to him?"

"Because—"

Runa cut Alicia off and turned back to Lili. "Why did you even need to become the beaver if you weren't going to try and get to know him?"

"I did try," Lili argued. "And I think you get a little too delighted every time you get to say that I 'became the beaver.'"

Runa laughed. "Stop the nonsense. Just march into the party, go right up to Dominic Moore and ask the guy out. Stop trying to come up with the perfect line and just be yourself."

Lili and Alicia traded a glance, rolling their eyes. Runa was sweeter than a summer peach but could be rather clueless when it came to mating rituals. Primarily because for Runa, with her exotic Icelandic beauty, the only difficulty was showing up.

Alicia said, "You don't know how being a girl works because the rules don't apply to you."

"Yeah," Lili added. "It's awesome that you can ask a dude to hook up with you whenever you want, and he'll start drooling all over you like ninety-five percent of the time, but that strategy doesn't work for us."

"I'd say it's more like 80 percent. And you know why it works?" Runa answered herself. "You think guys respond to me because of my blonde hair—"

"And your face and ass and boobs," Alicia cut in.

"—but the real reason it works is that I don't overthink or over-plan over-anything-else. *I act.* And seriously, this is all stupid anyway. It's senior year, and Dominic Moore has been recruited. He's off to college, and everyone knows he has a mongo football career in front of him—"

"I don't think 'mongo' is the word you're looking for," Lili said.

But Alicia seemed to take Runa's argument personally. "Why are you always going on and on about tomorrow instead of living for today? This could be great for Lili! Stop discouraging her from forming an attachment, Ru. *Girlfriend is already attached.* Why shouldn't she try to live this year to its fullest? I mean, I love Jeremy to pieces, but it's not like we'll be together forever." Alicia laughed.

"Can you even imagine? This is *high school*. Lili should be allowed to have fun, and we should be encouraging her."

"Lili can have all the fun she wants. I'm just saying—"

Runa stopped talking mid-sentence as Alessandra walked over to their huddle and announced that it was five minutes until game time. The girls waited as she left, not wanting to talk about *the plan* in anyone's hearing.

"Are you ready?" Alicia asked, dropping the argument.

"As I'll ever be." Lili smiled, drew a deep breath, then donned her beaver head for the very last time.

Tonight, her dreams would all be coming true.

Lili was sweating buckets inside her Mountain View Beaver costume, but the discomfort was easy to ignore, knowing that this was her final few minutes. Hot as it was, she'd enjoyed her time as the Beaver. Making the crowd whoop and cheer to her antics made Lili feel like her weirdness finally had a purpose.

But now, with only seconds left in the game, her tenure as the mascot was about to end. The Beavers were down by five. Lili had gone from dancing in front of the crowd to pacing like one of the coaches, desperate to see if the team could execute a miracle with only seconds left on the clock.

Of course they could. Of course they would. Lili just needed to believe.

Unfortunately, the opposing team had possession of the ball. If the Beavers suffered a loss, that would mean the Final Down would be a consolation party instead of one celebrating a Mountain View victory. Everyone knew that Dominic Moore refused to honor his losses by partying afterward, so that would spell defeat for Lili in addition to the team.

For her plan to work, something needed to happen. *Now.*

Then suddenly … it did.

Rodrigo, a Mountain View player that everyone called 'Refrigerator,' tackled the runner and sent the ball soaring into the air—

Where Dom made a flying leap above a heap of players, all dropping into a pile atop one another, and caught it.

He had three seconds to reach the end zone and claim victory for the Beavers. Lili could already see her dreams coming true, but still, she craved a better view.

So, she ran out from the sideline into the end zone where Dom was barreling toward her.

Lili was jumping up and down like the proudly excellent mascot she was, loudly cheering on the team, its star quarterback, and what would surely be the most serendipitous moment of her life.

Dom got closer and closer.

Her entire world was a blur as he kept getting larger and—

Sudden pain detonated through every inch of her body. The beaver costume felt like it had become a coffin. She opened her eyes and found herself staring at the blue sky past the outlines of her beaver mask with her entire body throbbing.

Something heavy was pressing down on her, making it impossible to recover more than a gasp of her breath.

"Sorry," said the thing on top of her before rolling away and onto the grass.

It was Dom, having won the game after accidentally tackling a mascot that had apparently been standing in his way. The crowd was well past wild and on its way to making her deaf.

Students and players were rushing toward them.

Lili looked around and found herself surrounded by camera phones, the most humiliating disaster of her life now earning its permanence on video. Her humiliation would be uploaded to YouTube before the victory party even started.

But Dom wasn't pumping his fists or celebrating his big win. just yet. His only concern seemed to be for Lili, as he helped her sit up, then ease the enormous beaver head off her shoulders.

"Are you okay?" Dom asked once Lili could finally breathe again.

All that time Runa had accused her of wasting while trying to conjure a perfect opening line, and now her mind was a freshly wiped whiteboard.

She had intended to create the perfect party moment. To orchestrate a meet-cute. To be made-up and in her party dress, not half a beaver costume that was destroyed by that tackle.

After a long and pregnant pause, Lili finally managed: "I'm ... I'm ... a beaver."

Dom grinned, surely not knowing what to make of such an absurd confession.

Then the crowd around him erupted in laughter.

They clapped him on the back, then, with one more grin, he was gone.

And Lili was all alone.

Lili

PRESENT DAY

Lili walked up to Alicia's front door, balancing five cups on a four-cup tray while holding a brown sack filled with freshly baked goodies.

She yelled without knocking. "THE CAVALRY'S HERE!"

Jeremy answered his door with a smile, and then opened it all the way, silently invited Lili inside.

She walked straight to the dining room table and set everything down.

Jeremy plucked the smallest cup from the assembly — a hot chocolate for little toddler Harvey — along with his large vanilla latte.

"How bad is it?" Lili asked.

Jeremy just laughed and gave her a wink. "Good luck."

Then he returned to being super dad, gulping his latte while wrangling socks and shoes onto his toddler in the living room. Alicia and Jeremy's son rarely ever stopped babbling. His current yarn involved superheroes and trolls, from what Lili could hear from the dining room.

The TV was on in the background, but Sid, the Science Kid, apparently had the morning off. A local morning show was currently discussing the weather. Despite the sophistication of the network's doppler satellites and heat maps, conversations about the weather always sounded like two old men sitting on a front porch jawing on just to kill time. The captions were on, even though the show was for grownups because no matter what was playing on TV, Jeremy thought it was wise to give Harvey exposure to the words.

Alicia waddled out into the living room, somehow looking even more pregnant than she had just yesterday. Alicia had been her bestie since kindergarten, and thus Lili had seen her in every possible mood, with pregnancy being the worst of them.

"That mine?" Alicia pointed to the large Americano, clearly marked *Runa*.

Lili grabbed the decaf next to it and held it out to Alicia, unsure if it was safe to say anything.

Alicia rolled her eyes and grabbed her cup. They had been playing decaf vs. caff game for months, but Lili had solemnly promised both Jeremy and herself that this baby would not be contaminated with even a drop of caffeine from *her* coffee shop. What Alicia got from any other source was on her, but Lili had a sneaking suspicion that Alicia's grabs for caffeine were only for show, and she was equally careful with her non-Higher Grounds coffee.

Alicia started ranting while removing the lid, undoubtedly ready to down the still piping brew in a few long swallows. "Being hungover is *way better* than being pregnant. Give me *one* night off from this bullshit, and I will drink circles around Runa."

She took a sip of her coffee, made a disgusted face, then cast a dirty glance at Lili as Runa came stumbling into the living room.

She walked right to the coffee, grabbed the cup that had to be hers, and sipped at the drink like it was liquid ambrosia.

"Did Eleanor say anything about the challenge last night, Runa?" Lili asked. "She was supposed to send me final details yesterday."

"I don't think so," Runa's voice came out in an almost whisper. "But I'm not entirely sure I'd remember either way."

"How much did you have to drink last night?"

"I'm never going to get anywhere in city hall if I'm not willing to knock a few back with the boys," Runa replied after another long sip.

"Old Fashioneds again?" Jeremy inquired from the living room, grabbing Harvey by the ankle as his three-year-old tried to scurry away, still missing his right shoe, though Dad had managed to wrangle both socks onto his feet.

Runa clamped a hand over her mouth and ran to the bathroom.

Lili laughed while pulling out a plate from the cupboard to display her baggie full of freshly baked goods.

Alicia edged closer to the plate of goodies as Jeremy walked over with Harvey, holding his hand.

"Say goodbye to Mommy," Jeremy said.

"GOODBYE, MOMMY!" Harvey exclaimed like he was trying to win a yelling contest. Jeremy kissed Alicia on the cheek, then patted her baby bump fondly, and she visibly shivered.

Then Jeremy and Harvey were out the door and on their way to preschool.

"Why do you hate that so much?" Lili meant Alicia's almost violent reaction to anyone getting even remotely close to her baby bump.

"That's a great question. Why don't you ask me after you get pregnant? We can also talk about the endless parade of people who need you to know that you're 'glowing.' Or the hemorrhoids and constipation. How you can't sleep on your stomach, so life is like fifty bajillion times more exhausting. Maybe—"

"Your husband worships you and is like the nicest guy ever." Lili took a sip of her coffee. "How bad can it be?"

"I can't believe there's still another two months of this prison sentence."

"You're the only mom I know who thinks of pregnancy as a …"

Lili didn't finish her thought because Alicia was no longer paying attention. Her gaze was now turned to the morning show.

She looked back at Lili and asked a question of her own. "What the hell is oil pulling?"

Lili didn't have to explain because the show's guest — an older woman in a Tiffany blue blouse did it for her. "Oil Pulling is an ancient practice that involves swishing oil in your mouth to remove bacteria."

"That sounds dumb," Alicia opined.

"It can kill bacteria in your mouth and improve dental hygiene," argued the woman onscreen.

"So, like brushing and flossing." Alicia looked at Lili, clearly wanting her to agree. She went with it. Alicia's already strong opinions seemed to get stronger with pregnancy, and this morning oil pulling was the devil's work.

Lili pointed at the host, Phoebe Brooke, who now had a mouthful of oil while her guest discussed the benefits. "She looks like she's going to cry."

"Maybe we should tell Runa that oil pulling can cure a hangover."

Lili laughed. "How hilarious is it that Runa can't just tell her mom that the drinks were for work and convalesce at home? She's twenty-six years old!"

"Are you kidding? You'd be afraid of Holder if she were your mother, too."

Runa entered the living room.

Lili and Alicia looked at her, chanting in unison: "*And moving out is wasting money.*"

Runa shrugged on her way to the plate full of goodies. "So what?"

She grabbed a scone and bit into it. Her eyes widened, shaking her head in evident admiration. "The hell do you put in these things." Runa took another bite as she turned to Alicia. "I bet she uses eggs from endangered species or something. This shit is *good*. Best I've tasted outside of Europe."

Alicia grabbed a scone of her own. "When are you going to start selling these in your cafe? Runa's right; these are the tits. Even if you are using endangered species."

"Normal eggs, though they are cage-free. And I don't think girls are supposed to say that things are the 'tits.' It's kinda gross. Also, I've told you a hundred times that I can't sell my scones yet, or any baked goods. Not until I get enough money to make my expansion."

"And we've both called bullshit every one of those hundred times, Lil. You could bake whatever you want to at home, same as already you do, then sell your—"

"And like I always say, that isn't professional."

"At least you'd be doing something," Alicia said.

"I am doing something. And I'll do even more, like *the second* I have the right setup."

"The very second, huh?" Runa said before biting into her scone again.

"How long has she been singing this song now?" Alicia asked.

Lili didn't give Runa a chance to respond. "I'm going to win the Upper Crust Challenge this year. Then I'll have all the money I need to expand my kitchen and do this right."

Alicia nodded. "And I hope that happens, for reals. You know I believe in you. But let's say one of the judges is allergic to awesome, and you don't win, then you should still start selling those damn scones at Higher Grounds."

"I—" But that's all Lili got before her attention was ripped away from Alicia and thrown back at the TV, where Phoebe Brooke was now oil-free and announcing the upcoming segment. Captions were a few beats ahead of the actual words. So Lili knew what the host would say a blistering moment before the words left her mouth.

"—we'll be talking to football legend, Dominic Moore!"

Alicia was already on her way to the TV, intent on killing the show.

"No! I want to see it." Lili walked to the couch and collapsed in the center.

Alicia and Runa came over and sat on either side of her.

After a short commercial break, Lili braced herself as Dominic Moore took his seat in a white leather chair just a few feet away from Phoebe Brooke, with a handsome pot packed with blush-colored orchids raining beauty in between them.

Dom was still gorgeous. Still charming as ever.

Phoebe Brooke thought the same thing. The ex-QB seemed to use more numbers than words, talking stats and what he imagined the odds of a win for the Cave Wolves might be, but the host looked enraptured.

"I keep expecting her to get out of her chair and crawl over into his," said Alicia, only a minute into the interview.

"But notice how he's not flirting back." Runa nodded at the TV. "He obviously knows his effect on women, but he's not playing into it."

Alicia shrugged. "Probably because Phoebe has some oily ass breath."

"So." Phoebe sobered her voice. "Can we talk about the recent scandal that's led to your early retirement?"

"Of course." Dom offered her a good-natured laugh. "I knew the question was coming."

"Marijuana is legal in this state, but you're not permitted to indulge unless it's off-season. Do I understand you correctly?"

"You do." He nodded. "And yes, I was caught with the herb during the regular season."

"There was a rumor that it wasn't just cannabis. That cocaine was also involved. Do you care to comment on that?"

"Drugs can be a real problem when you have a bunch of young men suddenly making a fortune and not really used to dealing with the consequences," he answered in a confessional tone, without addressing the cocaine question. "I apologize to everyone I hurt with my actions. I'm a work in progress, and I promise to do better."

"How many drafts of this crap do you think his publicist wrote for him?" Lili didn't give either of her friends even a second to answer. "He's basically working off the How to Handle Getting Caught Playbook. Fake apology. Using his looks and charm to squirm like a little worm off a hook."

"*Or* ... you're still mad about senior year and are thus unwilling to give the dude any benefit of the doubt," Runa said.

Alicia only added a snort.

"Dominic Moore is from Mountain View," Runa added.

"Oh, like he gives a shit about Mountain View!" Lili scoffed. "He doesn't care about this town or anyone in it. He blew out of our little burg the second he could, and I'm sure he's never looked back. I bet he thinks we're all bumpkins living here in a hee-haw town he's thrilled to have left behind."

"Or Runa's right, and you're still just raw about Beaver Girl."

"I'M NOT STILL 'RAW' ABOUT BEAVER GIRL!"

"And now you've convinced our neighbors." Alicia laughed.

Runa said, "You really need to let that go. It's been eight years."

"People *still* call me Beaver Girl."

"But that wasn't Dominic's fault," Runa insisted. "Titus is the one who posted his video online."

"And it's hilarity's fault that shit went viral." Alicia shrugged.

Lili stood from the couch. "I need to go."

"Now she's mad," Runa said.

"I'm not mad. I just shouldn't have been gone this long. Summer is probably already messed up like half of our regular orders."

"Honey." Alicia reached out and took Lili by the hand, suddenly serious. "Please. Promise me that no matter what happens with the Upper Crust challenge, you'll start selling your baked goods at Higher Grounds."

Lili gave her a tired smile. "I'll do it as soon as I have the right kitchen."

"But that's been your problem forever now." Alicia smiled to soften the blow. "You're always waiting for the perfect moment, just like you did with Dom back in high school. Killing all that time until the final party where you could possibly ask him out. That's exactly what you're doing right now. *Anticipating* isn't the same as *living*."

Runa finally stopped nodding along.

Lili gave them both a hug. "I love you guys and appreciate your encouraging me. But I promise there's a plan here."

Lili left Alicia's, ignoring Runa's whispered comment as she closed the door, "There's *always* a plan here."

"I'm guessing you didn't tell her that Dom is coming back to town," Alicia said.

"I felt like keeping my eyeballs in their sockets and was afraid of her gouging them out if I was the messenger." Runa shrugged on her way back into the dining room for another scone. "Besides, it'll be more fun to let this stay a surprise and watch what happens."

Alicia laughed. "Should I get the popcorn, or will you?"

Dom

D ominic could barely see straight. His head had been throbbing for far too long, and all the deep breathing in the world wouldn't stop it.

But that didn't keep him from smiling wide as he pulled his McLaren up in front of his new favorite building, still draped in secrecy while awaiting its big reveal to the world. Or at least to this sleepy little town.

As hard as it had been driving down to Mountain View from the city after a late night out drinking with the mayor and his teammates, followed by an early morning getting fawned over by Phoebe Brooke, Dom still managed his signature smile.

Of course it was worth it. Dom was back in the town where he'd been born and raised, finally able to give his grandmother the treasure she had been forced to surrender all those years ago.

Fans and the media alike thought that Dominic Moore had blown it. He had his entire football career ahead of him. Two Super Bowl rings and a near guarantee at the MVP for the Cave Wolves this coming season meant nothing could bring Dominic down. Except for the scandal that came out of nowhere dragging him from the zenith of his sport to the basement of professional detention.

He parked and left his McLaren unlocked. This was Mountain View, so it would probably be safe. And part of him hoped that the thing would be stolen and he could go back to get the more reasonable Range Rover he'd wanted, matte black and subtly beautiful. He knew it had been a mistake to take three of his fellow players along for the ride to look at cars. He'd felt the pressure to buy the fanciest vehicle just because he could, and now Dom couldn't even drive the thing without feeling self-conscious. He gave the tire a half-hearted little kick, then entered his grandma's new bakery.

"Well, lookie what we have here …" Dom wasn't surprised to find his grandma in her bakery and was glad to see Titus Stoll, his best friend since seventh grade. They had played high school football together, but Titus coached the Mountain View Beavers these days, shaping young players instead of proudly being one himself. "It's good to see you, man!"

"Two years, you bastard!" Titus clapped Dom on his back as they hugged.

"So that makes me the leftovers?" Louise grinned.

"Never, Louise!" Dom walked over and pulled her into a hug. She hadn't been Grandma since he had moved in with her at seven when she told him that constantly hearing the word "grandma" every day would age her prematurely. If *Louise* was good enough for the world, it was good enough for her grandson.

"I'm glad to see you, Domi. But now Titus will never finish installing my display cases."

"How did she rope you into the free labor?" Dom asked Titus.

He shrugged. "Was the least I could do after what you did for Robbie Lewis."

"That was nothing." Dom shook his head, already uncomfortable with what he knew would be coming if he didn't cut this conversation off at the head.

"Well. Some things just need to be said."

"No big deal." Dom tried again.

So did Titus. He bent under the counter to turn off the Bluetooth speakers that had been belting something from Adele, a sure sign he was about to make this a whole speech.

"It was a big deal, man. When I asked you to look out for Robbie, I guess I didn't know what a big ask that really was. I mean, I *know* Robbie. But still, I figured he'd be more likely to start doing what was good for him once he finally got to where he'd been busting his ass so hard to go, you know?"

"I know." Dom nodded. This was for Titus, not him.

"As a coach, you want to believe the best in your boys." He shook his head, ashamed of himself, even though that was a ridiculous way for Titus to feel. "I'm heartbroken that Robbie let us all down."

"It wasn't your fault," Dom reminded him again.

Louise looked over with a sympathetic expression as Titus continued.

"I'd seen a few worrying things when Robbie was playing college ball, but like I said then, I figured it would all iron itself out, especially with your help." Titus shook his head. "But it wasn't fair to put that on you."

So, they were having this conversation. "Drugs can ruin things for anyone. But, they're a much bigger problem when you've got someone like Robbie who was, suddenly making more money than he's ever seen in his life, with no one ever telling him no. Of course, I tried. A bunch of us did. But there were always too many people willing to let things go. The cost of giving him consequences was greater than the expense of letting Robbie get away with it."

Dom sighed and finished his thought. "I've made plenty of mistakes. Helping Robbie seemed right in the moment. The last thing I want to do is question that now."

"But your career ..."

"Is Robbie in rehab?" Dominic asked, sort of changing the subject.

Titus nodded. "I was talking to Mrs. Lewis the other day. She said he's in rehab and doing fine. A place called Clear Meadows in Chicago. She seems sure he'll be back on the field next season."

"Then it sounds like it was worth it." Dom clapped Titus on the shoulder and left it at that, walking over to give his grandma some attention. "Are you going to show me around?"

"I already gave you a walkthrough."

"On FaceTime. That doesn't count."

"Fine." Louise sighed like she wasn't totally loving the idea of giving him a tour. She walked Dom around the bakery, talking less about its features and more about how she planned to run the place.

"I've got the three things I need," she said in conclusion. "A great oven, the best bread in Mountain View, and killer customer service."

"'Killer customer service?'" Dom repeated. "Aren't you... kinda... sorta known for insulting your customers?"

"Not at all!" Louise slapped at the air. "I'm known for speaking my mind. People like it when you talk to them straight."

"You are direct." Dominic smiled.

"I've been meaning to ask. What made you want to name this place Queen of Tarts?" Titus asked.

"Dom wouldn't let me call it the Busty Baker."

"Her runner-up was Sweet Cheeks," said Dom with a laugh.

"I also liked Buns, but my grandson isn't a fan of double entendre."

"I'm a fan," Dominic argued. "I just think there's a time and a place."

"You're right." Louise nodded. The gesture was already as sarcastic as Dom was sure her words were going to be. "Bakeries are sacred. Like a church. I always forget that."

"Opening is in three days. Are you ready?" Dom asked on his way to pour himself a cup of coffee.

"You look like shit," Louise replied.

"That's not an answer. But it's okay. I feel like shit, so saying that out loud just makes you observant." He filled his cup and took a sip, leaving the liquid on the wrong side of his lips for only a blink before spitting it back out. "This coffee is *terrible.*"

"Not as terrible as your career prospects!" Louise snapped.

Titus laughed. "There might be an opening coaching the Beavers with me if you're interested."

"Maybe in another life." He grinned, about to deliver his incredible news. "It looks like I'm up for a commenting job on SportsBar."

"What's SportsBar?" Louise asked.

Titus answered for him. "It's one of the hundred streamers we're all supposed to be subscribing to now. This one focuses on all things sports."

"If I get the gig, I'll be commentating with Altruence Brown."

"Whoa." Titus raises his eyebrows, not even pretending that he wasn't impressed.

"Who Brown?" Louise wanted to know.

Titus turned to her. "Altruence Brown. He's only a football *legend.*"

"How legendary can he be if I've never heard of him?"

"I've mentioned him plenty of times," said Dom, "but Louise only pretends to like football on my account. If she actually liked the game, she would know that Altruence Brown is my favorite player."

"I don't pretend to do anything. The world can know that I think it's a stupid game for all I care. That doesn't change how proud I am of *you.* I'm glad that *you* know how to throw that dumb thing. But just out of curiosity, do they let people with drug scandals commentate?"

Dominic laughed. "If they eliminated everyone with a scandal in their past, then they wouldn't have anyone left to sit behind the desk."

"You could run the bakery with me." Louise sounded unusually serious.

"I'm not much of a baker." Dom offered her his nicest possible *No*.

"That's crap, and you know it. But even so, I wouldn't expect you to bake. I'm an old woman, and there's much to do around here. You underestimate how much a place like this will take to run and how much I … well, I could use your help. Besides, those abs of yours will be a big draw for the female population of Mountain View. The folks around here are randier than most."

"*Randier*," Titus repeated. "Who says *randier*?"

"People born around twenty years before your mama!" she snapped.

"My abs will be safely covered. Plus, football commentating is more in line with my skillset." Dom took another sip of coffee, slightly curious but mostly hopeful, before spitting it out. "Seriously, if you want this place to succeed, Queen of Tarts will have to serve something better than this swill. Please tell me you have a supplier lined up."

"Nope, I sure don't. But Lili, who works at Higher Grounds across the street, has the best coffee in town. At least, that is according to folks who drink the stuff. Maybe you can use your abs to ask her for her supplier."

"I need a decent cup of coffee to fight this hangover. I'll see what I can do."

"Maybe you should bring some coffee back for us," suggested Titus. "Seeing as we're the ones doing all the work."

"Three coffees, coming right up."

Lili

Lili had only been working the counter for a few hours. Yet, she still managed to pack plenty of interactions into her morning. Lili loved her customers and enjoyed the mental game of trying to remember all of their stories. However, sometimes it felt like she had a thousand open conversations running at any given time in her head.

Today she asked Jennifer Channing about her sick chihuahua. Though Jennifer knew that dogs aren't technically supposed to be eating table food, she always found it hard to deny Buttercup's sad brown eyes and sorrowful frown. The last time she came in, Jennifer confessed that she had made a 'Connecticut-sized mistake' by letting Buttercup finish her avocado toast, not knowing that avocado was a no-no for doggies.

Lili asked Keandre Wilson how his interview went, expecting an eager story about how he'd landed the job, but instead, Keandre had terrible news that bordered on humiliating.

"You know how I had to ask for all those vacation days to do that interview, and having to pay for the plane ticket and hotel? I'm out nearly five-hundred bones before I even sit down to hear that jerkoff telling me that he had 'no intention of hiring me.' That asshat only took my interview in the first place as a favor to my sister. Can you believe that?"

Lili could, but that didn't make it any less terrible. Keandre's story was sad, and it would have depressed her more if not for her getting to play cupid, nudging one of her favorite customers — a painfully shy grad student named Amanda Glover — to sit next to Mike O'Brian, a college senior she had been crushing on forever.

Lili was in the middle of asking Lexi Bowers how she was doing in the literature class that had been "killing her soul" all semester, when she heard the bell above the door ring. As it opened, she looked up to see Annabelle Lyons entering Higher Grounds, armed with her laptop, looking crisply put together like always.

"I swear I keep trying and trying," Lexi said. "I read and annotate and do everything I'm supposed to do, but I always end up using Sparknotes because I get *sooooper* bored of all the monotonous writing in those old books."

"But you're more left-brained, right? You're great at math," Lili assured Lexi while starting on Annabelle's drink. Lili glanced at small bag of coffee beans (poured from the massive sack in back) that had been sitting on the counter, waiting for her to refill the machine. "Think about the literature you have to read as exercise. It's still making you stronger. You're just lifting words instead of weights."

"Thanks, Lili." Lexi smiled, then took her cappuccino to a quiet corner.

Lili slid Annabelle's drink — a small Americano with a dash of half and half, plus one spoonful of foam on top — across the counter just as Annabelle stepped up to it.

"You don't look happy," Lili observed.

"Should I?" Annabelle replied.

Lili gave her the smile she felt Annabelle needed. "You usually do."

"Argh. Have you seen the paper today?"

"No. I get in here too early to catch it. Did you just say *argh*? Is it Talk Like a Pirate Day?"

"That stupid advice column *Mansplanations* wrote ANOTHER scathing review of my class. I really need to stop making my lectures available in audio. I'm sure that's where this creep is hearing them. He doesn't have the balls to actually sit in my class, so he must be eavesdropping on it."

"That's because he knows you'll rip them out of his scrotum." Lili nodded. "But how do you know that it's not someone already in your class?"

"It can't be." She shook her head. "Believe me, I hate what I'm about to say. But it's the truth. Whoever writes *Mansplanations* is an excellent writer. Far beyond anyone registered for my class. I've been through every student file... twice. I don't think a single person is taking *The Science of Love* with the chops to write like that. Plus, the column has been running in the Daily for three years now. That makes my suspect a senior."

"You are *really* bothered by this. Can I suggest some hot chocolate instead of the Americano? A large with whipped cream, on the house."

"You're always the best, Lili." Annabelle picked up her Americano with a smile. "But I think I'll stick with my delicious caffeine. Seriously, what kind of name is *Mansplanations* anyway?"

"I think he's probably just trying to be ironic. Or funny."

"It's definitely not funny.

"At least you're smiling."

"That's because I was thinking about what I'm going to do to this asshat once I figure out who he is."

"Well, it sounds like the game is afoot."

"Why a foot?" Marcus Dale cried out from a nearby table. "Couldn't the game be an arm or an eyeball?"

Lili laughed, not because the joke was funny, but because Marcus was a good guy who always tried hard to make her smile. "The game is an elbow," she said, playing along. "But I suggest we stop there before we get coffee shop inappropriate."

"Is there such a thing?" Marcus asked. "I thought coffee shops were where all the best dirty talk happened."

"Only in sitcoms." Lili shook her head.

Annabelle finished a long sip of her Americano. "It's amazing how much better this stuff can make a girl feel, but I still want to kill the guy."

"Instead of getting mad whenever another one of his columns comes out, why not see it as an opportunity to catch the culprit," Lili suggested. "He has to slip up sometime, right?"

"One would hope." Annabelle turned to Marcus. "Don't you teach creative writing at MVU?"

"I do." Marcus smiled as he stood, then came over and properly introduced himself. "I'm Marcus Dale. I assume you are Annabelle Lyons?"

"I am." She smiled while shaking his hand. "Any chance you'd be willing to look at some student samples for me and maybe compare the work?"

Marcus laughed but didn't answer her question. "Why does this guy's column bother you? Do you really hate being disagreed with that much?"

"I don't mind being disagreed with at all. I believe in my ideas and enjoy a healthy discourse. But you can't have a debate with an anonymous critic, which means that this whole thing has been an entirely one-sided conversation.. Someone who believes in what they're saying shouldn't have any problem having an actual direct dialogue about it. Instead of this ... *bullshit*."

"It looks like you want to say *argh* again." Lili laughed.

"Sorry. I don't mean to get so worked up in your place of business."

"I honestly think it's adorable." Lili smiled to let her know it was all good. "You know ... you don't have to just use writing samples to try to catch him out. You could talk to him directly."

"In my lectures?"

Marcus stood gathering his papers into a neat leather briefcase. "She means you could write to him. He has 'that stupid advice column,' so he must have some way for readers to get in touch."

Annabelle took a breath to reply, then paused before continuing. "Well, now I feel ridiculous for not thinking of that myself. It's genius."

"You're welcome." Lili grinned.

"I'm happy to help anytime. We can compare writing samples or talk about the science of love if you'd prefer. I'm always around Higher Grounds." Marcus gave Lili a wink. "Best coffee in town."

Annabelle thanked Marcus then watched him walkaway, while taking another sip of Americano to reset herself.

"Did he just ask you out?" Lili grinned.

"No." She looked flustered. "He just offered help. Right? No. Definitely no."

Lili laughed, "He's cute."

"Did you see the new episode of *Outlander* last night?"

"Ha! Nice subject change, but I'll let you get away with it. Not yet! So please, no spoilers. You can totally go back to bitching about your mystery columnist if you want to."

"Fair enough" Annabelle gave her a nod. "but he's not *my* mystery columnist. I'm pretty sure he belongs to Satan. And besides, I'm done talking about that."

"We could talk about—"

"Have you ever been in love?" Annabelle interrupted her.

"I don't know that I would call it *love*. I was sort of crazy over someone back in high school, enough that my emotions made me do some really stupid shit. But, guess what? That experience taught me the most important lesson of my life so far."

"And what's that?"

"That I'm strong and powerful on my own. I don't need anyone to—"

Lili suddenly stopped talking, unable to believe her eyes, because speak of the devil, *Was that really Dominic Moore walking into Higher Grounds right now?*

She spun around wildly, wanting to retreat into the back without explanation, but her hand slapped an open bag of coffee beans still sitting on the counter — and sent them skittering all across her tile floor.

"Is everything okay?" Annabelle asked.

"Of course!" Lili lied.

Then she got on her knees to clean the mess, wishing she could melt right into the floor as the nightmare came walking over to her.

Dom

D om's head was still pounding as he entered the coffee shop.
But now, he was also tired from the extra effort required to
seem happier than he was in front of his grandmother and Titus.
They needed to see him upbeat, not emotionally scraping the floor
like he had really been feeling.

Stepping away from The Queen of Tarts, his body was starting to
relax, although the headache was making up for it, steadily motoring
toward a serious migraine.

He looked around the small cafe, assessing the competition. The
place was cute, with soft pastel-colored walls and an assortment of
comfy chairs (none of them matching), but without a display case full
of cakes and baked goods, it was in no way competition for Queen
of Tarts.

He looked over at the big-eyed barista working the bar. She was
talking to a woman with short black hair when she suddenly stopped
mid-sentence eyeing a famous quarterback coming into her shop.

The barista whipped around like a top and smacked a bag of
coffee beans clear off of the counter.

Beans flew from onto the floor and skittered along the hardwood.

The barista fell to all fours and started crawling around, scooping
those fallen beans off the floor and dropping them back into the bag.

Great. It was happening already.

Every eye in the coffee shop should have stayed fixed on the clumsy barista. But the attention on her was already dying. Customers were now looking for the cause of this sudden calamity, and awareness of its source was spreading like a virus.

Whispers and murmurs rolled through Higher Grounds like a wind. Dominic Moore might as well have been naked.

Even after years on the field, in front of cameras, and gracing dozens of magazine covers, the public gaze was an invading sensation he still wasn't used to, or comfortable with.

But at least Dominic knew how to deal with it. He plastered on one of the smiles he kept close at hand and looked around the room, letting every customer (and any surreptitious smartphone cameras) see that he was glad to be back here in Mountain View

He approached the counter, waiting for the barista to finish her cleanup, ready to ward off yet another super fan who would surely only see him for all the things he might not even be anymore.

The barista stood. She was cute ... and sort of familiar, though Dom couldn't place her. Her big brown eyes brimmed with intelligence. Her round face was flushed like the sunrises he saw during predawn practice, and she radiated an energy that felt both confident and loud.

"I hope you usually don't serve coffee off of the floor." Dom said with a slight grin. "No." She clearly didn't think it was funny. "We don't serve anything off the floor. But we have the best coffee in Mountain View if you'd like a cup."

"That's what I've heard, and that's why I'm here. Don't worry about it—" he flashed his well-oiled smile to soothe her agitation "—it happens all the time."

"What happens all the time?" It sounded like the barista was daring him.

"You know ..." How was he supposed to say this? "People are surprised to see a celebrity and—"

"OH! Got it." She laughed. "You know, it was the size of your ego that startled me. The door opened and it was like a tsunami of self-importance just stormed into Higher Grounds. That was what shook me at first. I only spilled the beans after seeing how underwhelming your looks were *IRL*. It's amazing what professional photographers are doing with Photoshop these days."

He shifted on his feet, unsure of what to do or say next. He felt watched, not just by the woman with the short black hair that the barista had been talking to when he entered — now sitting at a nearby table — but by everyone in the place. Most of the customers were pretending that there wasn't a world-famous athlete getting lambasted by the barista.

Or the proprietor.

Of course, this had to be the owner. An employee couldn't talk to a customer like that. Especially not a customer like Dominic Moore, as much as that truth might embarrass him.

"I would love a cappuccino. With an extra shot, please."

The barista looked at him with what appeared to be six dozen thoughts swimming around in her eyes. "Sure thing. Coming right up."

She turned around and made his drink in silence, while a shop full of customers kept pretending to ignore them.

Once finished, she set his drink on the counter without ceremony and repeated his order in a monotone. "Cappuccino. With an extra shot."

He picked it up, took a sip, and felt a sudden warmth through every bone in his body. Not just from the liquid heat, but from the richness of the espresso and its flavorful tango with the milk.

"This is delicious," said Dom.

"I know," she replied.

"Where do you source your coffee?"

"From the ground." Her answer sounded like a joke, but she still wasn't smiling.

He smiled wide enough for both of them. "Seriously. This is *great* coffee. I would really love to know where it comes from. Would it be—"

"I never reveal my sources." The (probable) proprietor was a humorless wall.

"It's not for me." Dom smiled again, this time to obscure his frustration. "Since you clearly have a problem with me." Another little grin, this one to let her know that whatever the problem, it was entirely one-sided. "It's for my grandmother, Louise. She's opening a bakery right across the street." He leaned forward with a conspiratorial whisper. "*And her coffee is terrible.*"

Her face changed. And for a moment, Dominic felt hopeful. He saw something — recognition, compassion, perhaps understanding — but then whatever it had been was suddenly gone from her expression, and she returned to what Dom now identified as feigned indifference.

"I know your Grandma Louise, and I think she's a fine lady, so please tell her that this is in no way personal. But unfortunately, her grandson is a terrible human being. As long as he is in any way associated with her bakery, I'm afraid I'll be taking my sources to the grave."

The proprietor smiled, either like none of what she had said was in any way insulting or supremely pleased that it was. She added a dash of insult to the injury. "And by terrible human, I mean you're like a urinary tract infection with legs."

What the hell?

Dom could only stare back at her in confusion, bowled over by their entire exchange. He had no idea what went wrong or where it had started to slide. Clearly, whatever this was predated his coming into her coffee shop.

She was probably just another unfortunate soul who watched the news too much and had forgotten how to develop opinions of her own. Dom had no idea if she had something against all football players or just him specifically. But there was zero doubt that she had been combative from the start.

The room was still staring. And while most of the people were polite enough to at least pretend that they weren't, a couple of customers had their phones out, ready to record whatever happened next, assuming they weren't recording already.

Dominic was done here. He needed to end this exchange and add this sad little coffee shop to the list of places he would never, ever return to.

He raised his cup as if making a toast. "Are you going to ring me up?"

"It's on the house," she said without a smile. As if her meaning wasn't clear, she added, "I don't want your money."

Dominic dropped a twenty into the tip jar.

He turned around and left the coffee shop, feeling the heat of her staring daggers at his back.

Lili

Lili chewed on her bottom lip while watching Dom leave, pretending that all of her customers hadn't just witnessed the round of pure humiliation that would surely be haunting her for months. The door swung closed, and she marched into the back room without a word.

Amid all the shelves full of supplies, Lili felt safe enough to lose her shit. She paced the small room, running her fingers along sacks of, cursing herself for everything that had just happened.

"I can't believe he just came waltzing back into town like he owns the place! And there I am *again*, making a total fool of myself in front of him. What the actual hell — there's going to be a bakery right *across the street* when I can't even get a *display case*. Even if it is Louise, that's still—"

Lili stopped ranting to herself, stricken with a truth like lightning to her skull: Dominic hadn't even recognized her. They were talking about *him* the entire time because they both knew who *he* was. But he never mentioned knowing her at all.

The only thing Dominic Moore had wanted from Liliana Travis this morning was her source for coffee. And wasn't that hilarious?

Well, to hell with him twice.

Lili walked over to the inventory list hanging on a clipboard attached to the wall just as Summer entered the back room.

"What?" Lili snapped, though none of this was Summer's fault.

"Sorry." She offered the boss one of her ditzier smiles. "We need more beans. The machine is empty."

"Oh. Of course." Lili told herself to relax and reminded herself for what felt like the hundredth time that week that Summer really did try her best, and it wasn't her fault for having such an empty head. She was a freshman in college, and TikTok rotted the brain. Kids these days.

Lili was also still in her twenties and hated herself for even having thoughts that included phrases like *Kids these days*. She didn't have anything against Summer and had to acknowledge that the girl always seemed to be trying. But she was hard for Lili to work with on account of them having so little in common, and thus not enough things to talk about.

"Oh my God. Can you believe that Dominic Moore just came into *our* coffee shop?" Summer said, once again proving how oblivious she could be. "Every girl on campus is just *dying* to meet him now that he's back in town. I bet—"

"You're not allowed to tell anyone where our coffee comes from."

"Why would I even know that information?" Summer asked.

Because you're not an idiot? "Did you hear what he said about his grandmother opening a bakery? We're going to have competition now. That means we need to up our game."

"If the competition is hot and famous quarterbacks, sign me up for a double dose of competition!" Summer laughed, still not getting it.

"No, Summer!" Lili snapped. "If you get all hot and bothered over some guy and let him charm all of our secrets out of you ..."

Summer looked back at her blankly.

"I forbid you from dating Dominic Moore."

Summer laughed again, but this time it sounded uncertain. "You're kidding, right?"

Lili was being ridiculous, obviously, but she still wasn't kidding. "Dating him would be a violation of your non-compete."

"Um ... I never signed anything like that ... and you can't control who I date."

OF COURSE, I CAN'T CONTROL WHO YOU DATE! Lili wanted to scream.

Because obviously, her behavior right now is absurd.

But instead of saying anything else, Lili simply marched back into the customer area, realizing as she did that her exchange with Summer might have been louder than she realized.

Not to mention all that talking to herself.

Looking around at all the customers and imagining what they must be thinking — especially Annabelle and Marcus, who both seemed especially curious about her disaster — Lili figured she might as well go for broke.

"I'm going across the street to check out the competition," she announced as Summer emerged from the back, holding a bag of coffee beans. Lili rested the bag from her hands, set it on the counter, and then took Summer by the arm. "Let's go."

"Who's going to run the cafe while we're gone?"

Lili turned to the room. "Who here knows how to make a coffee?"

Marcus raised his hand with a grin. "I can't make my drinks as fancy as yours, and don't expect any designs in the foam, but I put myself through college as a barista, so for now I can be your man!"

"Great." Lili nodded, taking the bag from Summer and passing them to Marcus. "Marcus is in charge."

She and Summer were on their way to the door.

"Hey!" Marcus called out as she opened it.

Lili turned back around.

"I don't know how to work the register or how much to charge."

"Well then," Lili shrugged, waving to the room at large. "It looks like coffees are on the house."

She was dragging Summer outside before second-guessing herself, barely looking both ways as she trotted — not that there was ever any traffic on Main — across the street and right into the unopened bakery.

There wasn't a bell to announce their arrival, but the trio of people inside all turned around to see who had entered anyway. Dom and his grandma were both there, but so was Titus Stoll, Dom's best buddy from high school and present-day coach for the Mountain View Beavers.

The three of them were staring at her.

Lili's tongue — wagging faster than she could manage it just a few minutes before — was suddenly all tied in knots.

Louise beamed at her. "Hello, dear. Can I help you with something?"

Lili found her smile. "I just heard that you were opening a bakery, and I wanted to officially welcome you to our little corner of Main Street."

"And to check out the competition, right?" Dominic flashed her a combative smile.

Lili ignored him, infuriated by his smirk but knowing she couldn't do anything about it now. He probably mistook her anger for a loss of nerve, when. in reality, Lili was a brewing storm.

Titus broke the moment, walking over to Lili with a grin. "Hey, girl! It's been a while." He pulled her in for a hug. "Thanks again for all the views."

Lili could feel her face flushing. "It wasn't really anything I did."

"You kidding?" Titus laughed. "I still get like two-hundred bones a month just from monetizing that *one video*."

SHIT. Lili saw the light in Dominic's eyes as he suddenly put two and two together. He actually snapped his fingers, to prove he was a jerk.

"Beaver Girl!" And then he started laughing.

Lili felt the anger drain out of her. Instead, she was circling tears. The reserves in her emotional tank had been dipping nearer to empty on the way over here, but now, she was on fumes. Dom had finally recognized her, but not as the woman she was or even the girl she used to be. Instead, he remembered her thanks to the awful nickname she'd been trying to shake ever since that fateful game: *Beaver Girl.*

Louise smiled kindly and took Lili by the arm. "Would you like a tour?"

"I'd love one," Lili replied, keeping her shit together.

Louise led her to the display cases and proudly crowed about Titus' work. It was impressive, the cases painted in ornate swirling patterns at the edges.

"It looks perfect," she breathed, feeling an odd mix of admiration and envy as she studied his work. She tried to ignore the sound of Summer slobbering all over Dominic behind her.

"Oh my God." She might as well have been ten years old. "I am *such* a fan! All of my friends are. We can't believe that you got booted from the team. And for something not even illegal. That sucks, like times a hundred. Isn't there anything you can do? I mean …"

Summer was apparently too dumb to finish her sentence.

Lili looked back to see Dom shrugging in response as Louise led her to the most beautiful kitchen she'd ever seen in real life. Commercial kitchens were supposed to look industrial, but this was French provincial.

"It's gorgeous! And so … *decorative.* Why is it so pretty if no one will ever see it? I mean … that tile work …"

"I'll be seeing it every day." Louise gave Lili another smile.

It was too much. Lili had to smother the obnoxious thunder coming from Summer in the other room, still prattling on and drooling all over Dominic while wrestling with her conflicting emotions. Admiration and envy were engaged in a cage match, with a mounting disappointment in herself that she had wasted so much time waiting for her dream instead of making it happen as Alicia kept constantly encouraging her to do.

Lili had been stuck, trapped in anticipation, waiting for that perfect moment to finally make her move. Now that Louise had this stunning bakery right across the street from Higher Grounds, it was too late for Lili.

She followed Louise back into the front, just in time to hear Summer violating a direct order that Lili had no business giving.

"—tonight if you can make it. His parties are always wild, so ..."

Lili tuned her out.

What Summer did with Dom was her business.

Why should Lili even care?

It was time to start living for herself. Time to say yes to more things than she refused. Time to wake up and do something more than waiting for life to happen.

"Am I invited to the party?"

"Umm ..." Summer looked lost for words. "It's a key party ..."

"Yeah, so?" Lili glared, daring her refusal.

"Do you ... know what a key party is?"

"Of course I do!" She absolutely did not. "Just tell me when and where the key party is, and I'll be there. With ... my keys."

Lili laughed, hoping that she hadn't just said something stupid.

Summer turned back to Dom. "So, do you wanna come?"

He glanced at Lili, feeling he misread her expression because he was emotionally illiterate. He gave Summer a shrug. "Sure."

"How about you." Summer turned to Titus. "Did you want to come too?"

"No thanks." He shook his head while laughing, seeming almost embarrassed by the invitation. "I'm busy."

Lili looked out the window and saw a long line spilling out from Higher Grounds. Either word got out that coffees were free, or

Marcus couldn't keep up with the orders. Either way, Lili was needed across the street.

"Come on, Summer. We're going." She marched out the door.

"Bye, Dom!" Summer offered Dom a hearty wave. "See you tonight!"

"About that coffee source ...!" Dom shouted after her.

Lili turned back as she crossed the street. "To the grave!"

Louise turned to Titus, whispering what Lili only wished she could hear. "Do you think either of them has any idea what a key party is?"

"Nope." Titus shook his head, laughing hard as he walked back over to his paints. "Not a clue."

Dom

✏ ☆ ↩ ✇ ⋮

Column Feedback

Annabelle Lyons <a.lyons@mountainviewuniversity.edu>
To: <submissions@mansplanations.mvdaily.org>

Dear Sir,

As a professor, I always welcome feedback on my courses from my students and on my research when it comes from my peers. However, I do expect that feedback to go through appropriate channels. When you wrote about the "most popular elective course at MVU" in your article yesterday I can only assume you meant my course, The Science of Love.

While I appreciated your perspective, I certainly don't expect everyone to agree with me. The public nature of your article turned it into more of an attack than any sort of constructive criticism.

Do YOU welcome feedback? Because if so, I'd like to give you some privately.

The name Mansplanations is, frankly, stupid. That anyone would want to embrace a term used to describe men who condescend and fail to consider others before opening their mouths is ridiculous to me. Yet, the name is also so apt for your column that perhaps it's because you wanted to go for the most accurate representation of your work?

If so, I applaud you. Well done on choosing the perfect title for your column, you absolute ass.

Kind Regards,

Annabelle

ANNABELLE LYONS
Associate Professor of Psychology
Mountain View University

Dominic felt lost while looking through an assortment of nearly identical-looking shirts. They were all breathable, and he couldn't have cared less about the color, so why had it taken him a quarter-hour to decide on a light blue Nike Playoff Polo?

It could be because there was a football game playing on a TV in the background. Getting lost in a meaningless decision was a lot better than facing the truth that he was no longer participating in a world he'd committed his life to. Same reason he was going to a stupid party when he would prefer to stay home, but doing that meant sitting on the couch and watching the Cave Wolves playing the game without him.

He finished getting ready and then sat on the couch, unable to stop watching a few minutes of the game before leaving. This viewing was for his buddies on the team, not for him. Seeing his boys on the field reminded him how much he wanted them to win. Dom cared about each of his teammates, even though his enthusiasm for football had diminished since his dismissal from the league. And, honestly, maybe even before that.

Dom longed to care about the game like he used to, but he couldn't find it inside himself to muster genuine enthusiasm. It was easier to surrender his career for Robbie's benefit than it should have been.

He picked up the remote and killed the game at halftime, then he stood from the couch and told himself it was time to go, reminding himself that getting out of the house would be a good thing. That whatever a "key party" was, it at least offered Dom the chance to do something different.

Maybe somebody there would see him for who he was, instead of the football player everyone knew about. He was sick of everyone recognizing only his fame and talent without ever seeing his human side. Nobody really knew him, yet everyone seemed so sure they did.

Liliana Travis was probably the worst of them. She started judging him from the second he entered her stupid coffee shop. Or, in truth, she started doing it years ago.

She had been combative with him before a single word was exchanged.

She was probably just upset that Dom didn't recognize her, though he absolutely did, once Titus tweaked his memory. Liliana — or was it Lili? — had been the school mascot his senior year. She was *so much* better than Zed.

Dom had loved watching her. She was always doing these ridiculously adorable butt-wiggling dances, shucking and jiving in front of the packed bleachers as the crowd turned batshit with applause.

That last year in high school was the last time he remembered truly loving the game. Atmosphere had everything to do with it.

And Lili had a lot to do with that.

Plus, she had been funny. Quietly so. In Stats, she used to raise her hand and then tell the teacher she was stretching whenever she got called on, The class seemed to think it was hilarious whenever Mrs. Malakar got thrown off track. For her final presentation, Lili had made a full graph model of Mrs. Malakar's *ummm's* and *aahh's*, charted across the last semester.

Back then, he'd seen her as cool. But apparently Lili just thought of Dom as a dumb jock. Same as everyone else.

He tried to feel optimistic. Told himself that this party could be a chance for the good people of Mountain View — students and citizens alike — to see the real him.

Thinking about it now, maybe Dom didn't want them all to know him. Perhaps it was better for him to be figuring a few things out for himself instead of worrying about what everyone else might or might not be thinking.

He had been a quarterback for so long now, that Dom had no idea what else he could be. He mused that question while driving in silence to the party.

He found a parking spot behind a Prius, just up the street from the party. He hoped nobody saw him getting out of it. His car looked ridiculous parked on an unassuming side street in Mountain View. He should really trade it in for the Range Rover.

Dom walked down to the sidewalk, then triple-checked the address as he approached the home, wondering if he had the right place, considering the series of shockingly phallic lights illuminating a path to the front porch.

And there was Lili, standing on the pathway, looking every bit as unsure as he felt.

"Do you think it's some kind of bachelorette thing?" Dominic asked her.

"Dear Lord, I hope not," Lili answered, shaking her head and almost sounding like she didn't despise him.

Dom gave her a smile, but she was looking over his shoulder at something behind him. The McLaren, judging by her next question.

"Was your Lambo in the shop?" she asked.

He pointed to the Prius. "That one's mine."

"So you're a liar?"

"Why—"

She dangled her keys in his face. A plushy little panda appeared to be mocking him. "That's my car, QB."

"It's just a car." It sounded so weak, even as Dominic said it. "Are you going to bail now?"

She seemed hesitant.

Dom didn't want her to go and leave him at whatever this party was all alone, so he said the one thing he knew might goad her into staying.

He pointed at the panda on her keyring. "Was the store out of beavers?"

For a pregnant moment, nothing happened.

Then her cheeks flushed in a delightful shade of rosé as she lost what sounded like an unintentional laugh before clamping her lips shut as though she'd burped. Instead of answering, Lili turned away from him and practically stomped up the steps toward the porch.

Dominic followed her, first up the path and then into the party.

Inside he saw a set of four bowls sitting on an entry table, filled with key rings, each with a sign above it, painted with various symbols: male-male, male-female with the male circled, male-female with the female circled, and female-female. A fifth bowl had a sign that read, *Surprise me!*

Dominic was finally starting to get what this key party was all about, but judging by Lili's expression, the poor girl was still in the dark.

A hostess approached them. "Do you guys know how this works?"

Lili shook her head.

"Are you straight, gay, pan, or anything else?"

"Um … I'm straight," Lili replied in a trembling voice.

The hostess picked up a bowl — male-female with female circled — and held it out for Lili. "Just drop your keys in here," she said as if that explained everything.

Lili dropped her keys into the bowl, looking even less certain than before.

Dominic followed, dropping his keys into the straight male bowl.

"We will be starting soon," said the hostess while looking pointedly at Lili. "You can head to the kitchen for some drinks if you'd like to loosen up a little."

Lili was standing ramrod straight, her big brown eyes wide enough to park a quarter in each one.

"Come on." Dominic took her by the elbow and led her away from the bowls. "Let's go to the kitchen."

She shook his hand off, but kept following him over to a bar full of drinks.

"What would you like?" Dominic waved a hand across their choices.

"I can get myself a drink, thank you." Then a beat later said, "Something with alcohol."

He laughed, grabbing a pair of wine glasses and pouring. "Pinot Noir. Perfect for … a key party, I guess."

Lili gave him a long and nervous laugh, taking her glass, then a longer sip, looking even more nervous than before.

"Are you sure about this?" Dom smiled: *It's totally cool if you're not.*

"Of course, I'm sure."

Lili was clearly in over her head and looked like she belonged at this party about as much as Dom belonged in a Broadway musical.

"Do you know what this is?"

"Of course, I know what this is!" she snapped.

"It doesn't really seem like your type of thing." *Still not judging.*
"And in truth, it's not mine at all. You want to get out of here?"

Her face was a billboard, blinking in neon and broadcasting *YES!*

"I'm cool," she said.

Dom didn't believe her, but he clearly wasn't about to convince her.

That should have felt like his cue to leave, but he couldn't ignore the sense that they were somehow in this together.

He couldn't stand the thought of leaving her in a bad situation. "Are you sure? Because we could—"

"It's time!" The hostess poked her head into the kitchen and then quickly ducked back out.

He looked into the living room and saw Summer swaying on the other side of the doorway, pretending she didn't care if he noticed her. This was the last place in Mountain View he wanted to be right now, and every cell inside him was sure that Lili felt the same way.

"I'm sure," she said as if proving it to herself. "I even have some key jokes ready for the occasion. Want to hear one?"

"I guess?"

"What's an alien's favorite computer key?"

"Um ... the space bar?" he guessed.

Lili blinked in surprise. "Have you heard that one?"

"I can't even imagine who would have ever told me an alien keyboard joke before, but it wasn't really much of a guess." He pointed to her glass. "Do you want to finish that before we go in there?"

"No. I want to finish this." Then she poured herself a glass of whiskey and downed it.

Dom did the same.

Then they went together into the living room, each of them seeming to follow a dare into this unknown adventure.

The living room was thicker with swingers than Dom had expected. He recognized only two people, not including Lili, the hostess, or Summer, but he counted thirty in total.

Everyone recognized him. And the whispering had already started.

This was already a nightmare. The exact situation he didn't want to be in, with everyone's eyes all over him, and everyone's thoughts hyper-sexualized.

Dom was the prize that he did not want to be.

Most of the women were raking him with their gazes, and not one was even remotely trying to hide it.

The bowls were sitting in a row in front of the hostess.

She smiled at the room and welcomed everyone, before giving a rousing little speech about the tradition of key parties that Dom was barely paying attention to. Instead he was focusing on Lili as a way to ignore all the stares piercing his skin, growing increasingly disconcerted by the look on her face.

He wondered if she knew he was watching her.

"Even though key parties were a bit stigmatized in the seventies, they were always supposed to be about *connecting* with the people around you. This party is a free space to connect with another human — in whatever way feels right for you."

The hostess paused to make sure everyone felt safe before she continued. "There are several talking rooms in the finished basement. It's like an ashram down there; you're going to love it. For those of you who would like to take things further, we have some well-appointed bedrooms and bathrooms upstairs. There is no judgment here; this is a sex-positive safe party!"

Dom exhaled with relief. Even if he left and Lili stayed, at least he would be leaving her in a safe space, but now he might not want to go. If he could stick with conversation and not have to risk another hit to his reputation by being paired with someone who would blab all over social media about whatever happened between them, maybe this night wouldn't be so bad.

He could hear Lili hyperventilating next to him, and he wondered if she might end up doing something she regretted just to prove something that she didn't need to prove. Dom had often seen that behavior on the field, and it never led to anything good. Rookies who let their egos get tangled in proving themselves. It shuffled their priorities and warped their perspective, making it hard to stop before hurting themselves.

And he had definitely goaded her here.

The hostess plucked a set of keys from the male-male bowl.

A tall man with hair like Weird Al Yankovich practically skipped over to the coffee table, dipped his hand into the bowl, then pulled out a Lady Gaga keyring. A heavyset gentleman with a drooping mustache stood with a pleasurable grunt and met Weird Al at the coffee table.

The temporary couple left the living room as their hostess went for the male-female bowl. Of course, Dom's keys came out first.

Maybe it was egotistical to think she'd picked him on purpose, but he was a wizard at stats, and this was simple math.

He went to the coffee table and dug around in the bowl.

A laughing murmur rolled through the room.

"Gotta get a good one," he joked with a smile, searching for the plush feel of a panda bear.

This would be for the best, definitely better than any one of those strangers begging for his body with their eyes, Summer included.

Picking Lili meant saving her from this, so they could both get out of here.

He plucked the panda ring from the bowl and smiled at the crowd.

Lili buried her face in her hands.

Lili

L ili was mortified.

No. That wasn't quite it. Mortification implied shame or embarrassment, even if in deeper shades. And while both shame and embarrassment were appropriate emotions for a moment like this — stuck at sex party, surrounded by swingers — Lili would only half-want-to-die if hit with that reality.

But right now, she wanted to all-the-way-die because Dominic Moore had plucked her keys from that bowl and trapped her in a nightmare.

More like fantasy, argued the most idiotic part of her mind (the part where there was probably a meadow with forty-three rainbows).

Maybe you're the idiotic one, pretending like you didn't wake up to find yourself humping your koala bear while moaning his name after you saw him in the pool sophomore year.

How the hell did she end up in this gonzo situation?

Lili wasn't sure, but it was definitely Dominic's fault.

And Alicia's. And also Runa's. If the girls hadn't chastised her wonderfully normal life, harping on that old falsehood that "Lili never took chances," she certainly would have refused an invitation to this ridiculous party.

She didn't even like *normal* parties, let alone *sex* parties!

SEX. Something Lili hadn't had in over a year.

She wasn't about to break that streak now. At an Orgy. With Dominic Freaking Moore.

But what the hell was she supposed to do? The living room was full of people — *swingers* — eyeing her expectantly.

While Dominic Moore grinned like a monkey.

That's when Lili realized the truth: Dom had done this to embarrass her.

He knew from the start that she had no idea what this stupid party was all about. He saw her panda key when she waved it in his face outside. This was obviously Dominic Moore having yet another hearty laugh at her expense.

Now he was guffawing at her naïveté. Except, that would only happen if Lili allowed it. And right now, she would rather run into a bear cave dripping with honey than let his self-centered, arrogantly oblivious (totally hot) and entitled ass ever land another chuckle at her expense.

Lili walked to the coffee table and said, "Let's go then."

She couldn't read his face as he gave her a nod, but Lili followed him out of the living room, ignoring the murmurs and whispers like chittering insects at night behind her.

She expected Dom to take her upstairs so the torture of a humiliation she would never forget could get started, but instead, he surprised Lili by leading her toward the basement.

The wave of relief as she followed Dom down the stairs was almost euphoric. But as they entered the surprisingly stylish basement, Lili was stricken with the opposite worry.

And the question felt crushing: did he *not* want to have sex with her?

Of course he didn't. Dominic Moore could have sex with whoever he wanted to. He probably had no idea that the panda belonged to her because he didn't see it when she waved it in front of his face —

all that dickhead ever did was think about himself. He was probably thinking about his McLaren looking like the Batmobile or whether he should have taken one of the Lambos. Maybe even—

"It's nice down here," said Dom, looking around. "I've never been in a green room for an orgy."

Lili was surprised to hear herself suddenly laughing.

"At least there are snacks." She pointed to a spread of chocolate, fruit, and wine.

"And alcohol."

Was he trying to get her drunk? So she would be easier? Or so this would be easier on him?

Bitch. You need to stop this.

She dropped her keys on the table and poured herself a glass of pinot to finish what she started upstairs.

"Wow. Did you see that?" Dominic asked.

Lili looked to see where he was pointing and noticed something so (startling ... offensive ... verboten) *taboo.*

Or was it? The world seemed to be changing so fast; what did she know?

"That's a lot of sex toys," she said with a shrug.

"Maybe they bought them in bulk on Black Friday."

"The copy writes itself: *What do our Black Friday deals and last night's Thanksgiving turkey have in common? They know what it's like to be stuffed and jammed into a—*"

"Did you have that prepared?" Dom laughed on his way to the table. It was long and low and covered in toys. Some phallic, some shaped like rings, and many utterly alien to Lili. She didn't know what they were called, let alone what someone was supposed to actually *do* with them.

Lili laughing along with Dom made their moment more surreal. "They really take their themed parties seriously here in Mountain View."

He picked up the biggest dildo from the table and started flopping it around, the head bending toward the floor like its frenulum might be trying to kiss the carpet.

Dom looked over at Lili with a grin but then dropped the dildo like a hot potato when another anointed couple entered the basement and claimed a corner loveseat not too far from the table full of food.

They were already making out by the time Dom walked back over. Why didn't they just go upstairs to start with?

He raised an eyebrow and leaned close to Lili, speaking just above a whisper. "This is *so weird*. I didn't actually know what a key party was."

"Oh my God, me neither." Relief rippled like a current through her body. "This is *insane*."

"I was going to google it earlier, but Titus told me that *key* was like *cool* or *clean* or *epic*. 'The party's gonna be key, man, so it's called a key party.' That's exactly what he said. He also told me that I'd start 'hearing the word *key* everywhere,' now that I knew what it was."

"Domass."

"I'm going to have to find some way to get that asshole back," he said, refusing to acknowledge her clever compounding of his name with an insult.

"At least you had someone to trick you. I had to trick myself."

He raised his eyebrows: *Tell me more.*

"I thought *key* like *answer key*. So maybe we were all going to do some kind of murder mystery puzzle game. Or like, you know, those escape rooms? Where you have to find keys. Maybe we would all work tog—" She took a breath. "I'll stop talking now."

"Please don't." Dom started laughing again.

Then Lili started laughing, a little at first and not especially loud, but the sound swelled as she started laughing harder and harder.

The couple across the room stopped heavy petting long enough to look over at her and Dom with a glare, so they traded tables, going from the food to the toys.

Dom pointed to a small egg-shaped vibrator. "You know, I bet that would make an excellent stirring device."

Lili laughed and kept going. "It's clearly waterproof. Switch it to on, drop that girl in your coffee, and you no longer have to mix in your creamer."

He mimed dropping the vibrator into some brew, then pursed his lips and mimicked the sound: *mbmbmbmbmb*.

Lili picked up a dildo — not nearly as large or floppy as Dom's earlier selection, though there was still plenty of girth for hilarity — and held it to her ear. "A fake telephone for training receptionists," she explained ahead of her demonstration. "Yes ... that's correct ... we do ... of, *of course!* Yes ... yes, thank you for calling Analtech."

"*Analtech?*" he repeated.

"It's a real company," Lili replied, narrowing her eyes at the dildo. "My friend Runa told me about it once when she was reading some article online about companies with terrible names. We laughed for a long time thinking that poor old Analtech must have some very disappointed customers making their way out to Delaware."

"Why Delaware?"

"That's where they manufacture the chromatography plates that Analtech distributes to more than forty countries on six continents."

"I can't tell if you're kidding right now."

Lili shook her head. "I never kid about Analtech."

Dom picked up what she assumed was a cockring. "For napkins?"

"This would make one hell of a cozy." He picked up a sex toy labeled *Pocket Pussy* and looked at it in admiration. "Pop this puppy in the freezer and slide the bottom of your drink right in there."

Lili took her turn by picking up a diminutive-looking butt plug, studying it like she had no idea what it was before turning to Dom, scrunching her face in confusion. "Is this a door stopper?"

By then, they were both laughing so loud that Miss Bossypants, the Hostess, had to come stomping downstairs to ruin everything.

"Just came to check on everyone," she sang upon entering the basement, her attention fixed on Lili and Dom. She walked over to them and whispered like she was doing them a favor. "I was wondering if the two of you might be more comfortable in a private room ... where you won't be tempted to bother others."

"If we were to go upstairs, would we still have access to a wide array of items designed to shove inside our orifices?" Lili asked, totally sober.

"Um ... yes, of course!" The hostess answered her brightly. "There are even more pleasure boxes upstairs."

"Is that the same as a window box?" Dom asked.

Then they were both laughing again.

"I need you two to take this serious!" The hostess was getting more upset. "Please. Follow me."

She turned toward the stairs while Lili and Dom stifled their laughter.

They all stopped after ascending the stairs. "Now—"

But that's all the hostess got before Dom cut her off. "Sorry! We really need to go, you know, do each other!"

He grabbed Lili by the hand and rushed her toward the second-floor stairs.

Lili kept laughing and was nearly hysterical by the time they were racing down the hallway toward a vacant bedroom.

Is this really happening?

She told herself to shut up again. To stop focusing on the future and, for once, just relax enough to have some damned fun.

The bedroom door closed behind them, and her heart was a timpani.

It beat even faster at the sight of Dom ripping sheets off of the bed.

"Umm ... we're not actually going to *use* that bed, right?"

Please say no. *Or yes.* But probably no.

Dom shook his head. "Of course not."

Lili had no idea whether or not she was disappointed.

Yes, she was absolutely dis—

*NO! SHE WAS **NOT** DISAPPOINTED!* "What are you doing then?"

"I'm getting us out of here." He began to tie one corner of the flat sheet to the fitted one.

"You do remember that there's a front door downstairs, right? The one we walked through to get *into* this sex party? I'm pretty sure that the great tradition of key parties doesn't include locking everyone in."

"I'm sure it doesn't, but do you really want to try and get past Mrs. History of Key Parties herself out there?"

Lili hesitated. He had a point, but bedsheets out of a window? What if it broke? What if she fell *on* the great Dominic Moore? What if she froze halfway down.

Dom straightened and looked her in the eye. Like he knew what she was thinking and then said the one thing she couldn't back down from.

"Liliana Travis, I bet you won't climb out the window with me."

"I'll help you tie the knots."

Dom

✆ ☆ ↩ ☑ ⋮

Re: Column Feedback

Submissions <submissions@mansplanations.mvdaily.org>
To: Annabelle Lyons <a.lyons@mountainviewuniversity.edu>

Dear Annabelle Lyons, Associate Professor of Psychology Mountain View University,

Thank you for your email. I always welcome feedback of any kind from any direction. I believe that anything that can be said privately can be said publicly. Otherwise, we are simply feeding into a world where the public and the private are so wildly different from each other that nobody can ever connect because everyone is so focused on the performance they are conducting for the world.

That being said, I don't believe that what you are doing is performative. Instead, you are taking all of your darkest thoughts and sharing them with young minds with absolute abandon.

If you can't take public criticism, you probably shouldn't be in a public role, and you definitely shouldn't be influencing the young minds learning to shepherd our future.

The title Mansplanations was carefully chosen to be used ironically. I'm sure you don't have time to google after all that time spent researching pheromones, so I have included the definition:

Irony is the expression of one's meaning by using language that normally signifies the opposite, typically for humorous or emphatic effect.

In love, there are but bodies and words. It would do you well to remember that.

Best,

Mansplanations

P.S. Speaking of inappropriate titles, let's talk about The Science of Love. While the name of my column is clearly used for irony, yours is a promise you can't possibly deliver on. Love can never be reduced to a formula, and trying to do so negates the true emotions of real people. I've reviewed every lecture of your "science" course, and there hasn't been any real science to speak of.

Dom was having more fun than he'd had in ... not *forever*, but it had been one hell of an awfully long time, and right now, that eon might as well have been forever.

He laughed again, tying the knots next to Lili as they prepared their escape. He looked out the window. They could have definitely climbed down the trellis, but sheets seemed like the more traditional way of breaking out of a bedroom and surely a more fun way for them to share this little adventure.

Watching Lili smiling wide while tying the knots — not to mention all that laughing downstairs — reminded Dom of his glory days.

Not the times when he played football and graced the cover of Sports Illustrated, but when he used to have friends. When he had a life. Lili tying those knots right next to him was a reminder of all the high school hijinks he used to love before football swallowed his life without chewing.

The biggest surprise of the night so far — and Dom couldn't help but keep thinking this on repeat while tying the knots right next to her — was that Liliana Travis had been the best thing about it.

With the two sheets tied to each other and then to the comforter, the temporary couple was ready to secure their escape. Dom tied one side of their homemade rope to the bed, and Lili checked his knot as he lowered the sheet like Rapunzel's hair spilling down from her tower out the window.

"Would you like to go first?" Dom asked.

"You go." Lili shook her head. "I'm not sure I trust your knots."

"That's fair." He shrugged with a laugh and started to climb through the window.

The knots held, and he rappelled to the ground.

Lili went next but panicked halfway down.

"I don't think I can do this." She shook her head, almost whimpering, suddenly paralyzed halfway up the outside wall of the house.

"Just let go. I'll catch you."

"No, you won't!"

"I promise."

"Have you ever caught a tapir before? I weigh about as much as the average tapir."

"I don't even know what a tapir is. But—"

"I'M TOO HEAVY!"

"You're not too heavy, Lili. That's ridiculous. If I can take a head-on tackle from a three-hundred-pound defensive end, I can definitely catch one girl."

"*Woman.*" She barked a manic-sounding laugh. "One who weighs as much as a tapir!"

"Just let go ..."

"To hell with this." Lili shook her head and did the inexplicable, starting to pull herself back up and slowly climb toward the window.

"What are you doing? You're already mostly down!"

"I wasn't even halfway, and now I'm almost at the top again."

Time to try something else. "Yeah, you're right. I can see how this is too much for you. Go ahead and wiggle back through that window. I'll walk over to the fire station and get the fire brigade to bring their tallest ladder so—"

"I know what you're doing, and it isn't going to work." Lili said, descending again and proving the opposite.

She mumbled something under her breath, probably about what a dumb jock he was. But then she hit the ground, and they sprinted off into the night together.

"Ay caramba," she said when they were standing in between his McLaren and her Prius.

"What's with the Bart Simpson?"

"I left my keys in the basement."

"Hmm ... well, I'm not sure we want to go back in there right now, especially after destroying those sheets, differently than everyone else destroyed theirs. Do you have anywhere else you can go?"

"I could go to Alicia's," Lili replied.

Dom was surprised that her answer hit him almost like a disappointment. He was ready to take the couch and offer his bed to her because he didn't want the night to end. Maybe she saw the shade of dismay on his face.

"We could go to a bar?" Lili suggested.

"Great idea." He walked to his passenger side door and opened it for her.

Ten minutes later, they were at the Dirty Habit, a bar Dom had always been curious about growing up. Curious enough that he'd tried to gain entry multiple times throughout his high school career, but the nice old couple that owned the place didn't care how much Mountain View loved the amazing Dominic Moore, or how promising his professional prospects might have been. They weren't about to lose their liquor license by admitting a minor.

"Have you ever been in here before?" Dom asked as they each claimed their stool at a tall yet tiny table for two.

"Of course I have."

"It looks different than I imagined." He kept looking around. "Cleaner?"

"It didn't use to look like this. The Pattersons sold the place a few years ago. Now it's owned by some dickhead from Palo Alto. I guess the bar is like his hobby or something. He drops in every few months and plays bartender. Everyone laughs at him. Dude has no idea. He thinks they're actually laughing with him."

"What makes him a dickhead? Specifically."

"I don't know." She shrugged. "I don't hang out with dickheads."

"Then how do you know he is one?"

"Oh, you can tell a dickhead on sight. Notice I didn't call him an asshole. Dickheads and assholes are *not* the same things."

Their server arrived at the table before Lili could elaborate. Dom ordered a beer, and Lili asked for a glass of rosé. Their server left, and Dom's attention instantly drifted from the differences between dickheads and assholes to Lili's drink of choice.

Rosé? he almost said.

But Dom didn't get the words out because Lili was already on it.

"I don't need to hear your shit, Dominic. Drinking rosé means I won't have a hangover tomorrow morning. Hangovers come with splitting headaches that make it hard to deal with assholes in my coffee shop asking about my sources."

"Not *dickheads?*"

"No." She shook her head. "You are definitely an asshole."

A lull rolled into their conversation.

Dom wasn't sure of the next thing to say next, or even really how he was feeling. Lili thought that everyone was always judging her. He couldn't decide if he found that annoying or endearing. For such a gruff exterior, her underbelly was awfully soft.

Their server returned and set their drinks on the table.

Dom and Lili sipped in silence. Without the sex toys or the sheets or all that talk about dickheads and assholes — which would feel forced to resurrect right now — the energy was back to being awkward between them.

"Why did you come back to Mountain View?" she finally asked. "I mean, apart from the scandal and everything. I know why you're not playing football. But why *here?*"

She took another big breath, then blurted a question that had apparently really been bugging her. "You're rich and famous and can do anything you want, so why come back here and open a bakery?"

"I'm not really back. I'm just helping my grandma get it open, then I'll be off again, and onto the next phase of ... whatever comes next?" He shrugged.

"You don't know what you're going to do?"

"There's a few possibilities. Not sure which will pan out though." He shook his head.

"But you wanted to open a bakery with your grandma in Mountain View before going off to do whatever that is." Lili nodded. "Story older than time."

"Do you know why I lived with Louise in high school?"

"Do you think that everyone always knows everything about you?"

"A lot of times they do," he replied, and it wasn't a joke.

"No. I never asked anyone why you lived with your grandma in high school. Even after all of the long-lost years, it remains one of my life's biggest mysteries."

"My dad died when I was seven, and my mom couldn't handle it. She split. Barely said goodbye. Grandpa was still working as a structural engineer at the time. He couldn't really help Louise to raise another kid that neither one of them had been in any way expecting. She had to give up Sugar Boogie. That was her—"

"*Sugar Boogie!*" She turned to Dom in surprise. "I used to LOVE Sugar Boogie! I totally forgot about that place ..."

"Yeah, it closed when we were both in second grade. Louise gave up her dream of raising me. After Grandpa died last year, I decided it was time to give that dream back to her. The money part was easy, but now that I'm not in the league, and it looks like my immediate future is still being written, I can be a little more hands-on with the project. I can help Louise more than I expected to."

Dom couldn't quite decide what he saw on her face. Lili looked almost glum as he told her his story. Maybe she felt bad for being so hard on him.

Time to change the subject. "What do you think the hostess is going to say when she finds the sheets?"

"I'm sure she's used to weirder shit than sheets hanging out the windows. She'll just think it's some sort of new sex act."

"It's called 'sheeting,'" he suggested.

"Nope." She shook her head. "That sounds like a very unsexy word."

"How about 'roping'?"

Lili turned to him. "Are you kidding me?"

"Okay ... how about 'window hanger'?"

"*Perfect!* Like, 'OMG, that window hanger gave me the BEST orgasms!"

Dom laughed along with her. Until they both fell silent.

"I remember you from high school," he finally said.

"Yeah, as Beaver Girl."

"No. Not like that." He shook his head. "I can picture you as the mascot, but I don't think about the nickname. I mostly remember how you always had the crowd going and how awesome your timing always was. I mean, Zed was fine and all, but that's only because there was nothing to compare him to. But you ... you made the mascot feel like something special."

Dom couldn't tell if Lili wanted him to stop talking or keep going. Her expression somehow pled for both. He couldn't think of what to say next.

He could only stare at her, seeing how pretty she was, thinking about how pretty she had always been, and wondering—

Lili

Why *is he looking at me that way?*
Lili was swimming in and out of reality.

None of this could be true. There was no possible way that Dominic Moore was really giving her *that* look. Not right now.

"So, how about them astronauts?" Lili changed the subject.

"*Astronauts*," Dom repeated like he had no idea what she was talking about.

"Weren't you listening when the orgy hostess talked about the long and storied history of key parties?" He looked back at her blankly, so Lili explained. "It all started with fighter jet pilots training to be astronauts getting closer and ... never mind ..."

Dom was still eying her.

And Lili still had no idea whether she liked that or not.

Maybe she should just go for it. Runa and Alicia might be right. This wasn't really about showing up at some strange party. Lili had never been much of a party girl, and she never would be. This was about Lili capitalizing on the opportunities when they showed up in front of her.

If Lili had never waited for that perfect moment back in high school, she could have slept with Dom back then, instead of spending all of these years wondering about all the *what ifs* and ultimately resenting him.

And sure, he was a stuck-up football player with a McLaren and a pile of Ferraris and rocket ships and like eighteen different houses with pools, plus an apparent drug problem that got him booted out of the game he loved so much he wanted to like totally marry it, not to mention that he was now her competition, like *right across the street*, and how was she ever supposed to compete with that. — but at least it ended up being for a super sweet reason, I mean his *grandma*, that's like totally *awwww*, and exactly the kind of thing Lili used to love about him in high school — it wasn't just about his looks, it had never been about his looks, even though Dominic Moore was (and is) like intergalactically hot (and totally would be as an old man, too), but even hot would never boil her water, Dom had also always been nice to everyone.

He never dated the bitchy beauty queens without a brain in their heads who would have giddily followed him around like a girl-friend-bot if that's what he wanted. Dom had dated the kinds of girls that Lili found it easy to be friendly with.

She had failed to take her chance then. Really, she had never even tried. Anticipated, sure? She'd done that shit on repeat. But had she ever taken the risk? Held her breath and entered the danger on purpose, pushed forward by the promise of something truly unknown — something it hurt to admit that she wanted because not having it would feel like a gutting?

No, she had not.

Maybe Lili could change that now. "You know, I think we had all of our math classes together."

"I don't remember that. Sorry. I do remember Stats, though. You were always messing with Mrs. Malakar. It used to crack me up."

"That woman should not have been teaching."

"I like that you're good at math."

"What? That surprises you? I can't be good at math because I'm a girl?"

"That's not what I'm saying ... I just think it's cool."

"Oh, of course." Lili laughed, feeling like an idiot.

She was supposed to be flirting, not picking a fight. She took a sip of her drink, then delivered a line out of nowhere. "I'm great at algebra ..." Another sip. "I can replace your X, and you wouldn't need to figure out Y."

He needed a moment to process before he smiled. "Are you flirting with me?"

"Maybe."

"That's not flirting."

"Wordplay is flirting," she argued.

"Flirting is fast. You shouldn't have to think about anything for more than a second."

"Oh." Lili nodded. "So, you're not smart enough to flirt with me."

"Whatever, nerd. Do you want a flirting lesson or not?"

"From you? *Not.*" She shook her head, then changed her mind. "Fine. But how hard do you ever have to flirt? Can't you just point to the nearest sports bar and—"

"Feel this." Dom cut her off and gave her a piece of his shirt to rub between her fingers. "What does that feel like to you?"

She looked back at him blankly.

"Boyfriend material," he said.

Lili shook her head with a laugh. "That's terrible. First of all, it's a pickup line, not flirting. Second of all it's like the worst pickup line in the world. A hobo wouldn't let you buy him a bottle of wine with that line. It doesn't even make sense. Your *shirt* is boyfriend material? You didn't ask me to—"

"I know the difference between a pickup line and flirting. I was transitioning our banter away from—"

"OH, YOU WERE NOT!" Lili laughed again. "Why can't you just be direct?"

"I am direct. What about *you*?"

"I'm director!"

"CUT!" he quipped.

Lili laughed. "See. *That's flirting.*"

"Is it, though?" Dom raised his eyebrows.

"More than that stupid shirt line."

"That stupid shirt line was better than your ... equation ... flirting."

"How's this for flirting?" Lili cut to the chase like a better director than Dom. "Are we going to have sex tonight, or what?"

He blinked in surprise. "Are you serious? We just had the chance at—"

"I didn't want to do it there, and neither did you. But I had a crush on Dominic Moore in high school, the same as everyone else who went to Mountain View. So, do you want to *get with this*, or what?"

Then she wiggled her body to let him know it was his for the night if he wanted.

"Was that *get with this* supposed to be your sexy voice?"

"It's my flirty voice. You can hear my sexy voice if we actually have sex."

"Seems reasonable." Dom nodded in approval.

"So, is that a *yes*?"

"Sure." He gave her a smile ten times warmer than the indifference of his shrug. "Why not?"

They asked for the check, then, five minutes later, Lili was luxuriating in a leather seat that made her feel like a cinnamon roll melting in butter. The local radio station played in the background, just low enough that they could barely hear it.

That was fine with Lili; her thoughts were loud enough.

Lili was willing and maybe even eager, but Dom appeared almost hesitant. Probably because he still thought this was like the key party thing, and she was trying to prove something instead of this being what she actually wanted.

But Lili couldn't think of a single thing to convince him.

And still her head was empty on the way to the front porch of a surprisingly modest home Dom must have Airbnb'd for his time in Mountain View.

Her mind was still vacant as he opened the door, and led her inside. He told Lili to make herself comfortable in the living room while he poured them some more wine.

"None for me." Lili shook her head, slow and sultry (she hoped). "That's not what I'm thirsty for."

She started to do a strip tease, but it might have looked more like a seizure when her arm got snagged in her sleeve and sent her toppling down to the floor.

He laughed and scooped her up and into his arms. "You don't have to do that."

"But I want to. Haven't you heard of sex positivity? Loving my body? Luxuriating in my sexiness?" Lili was rambling.

Dominic laughed, which was both sexy and infuriating.

"Okay Big Football Player Man, I bet *you* won't do a strip tease for me."

But Dominic rolled with it. "What if I want to?"

And he already was. He pushed her down in a chair and started dancing, not pulling off his polo so much as peeling it off of his cut body.

Then he shimmied out of his pants (*holymolywhatthehellishegorgeous*), wiggling his eyebrows and strobing through a sequence of hilarious expressions to accompany each of his poses.

Lili couldn't stop laughing.

Dom was laughing too.

"It's weird without the music," she said.

"Good thing you're laughing. Otherwise, I might doubt my performance."

"Here ..." Lili went to her purse, still laughing, and dug inside for some dollar bills before going over to Dom and stuffing them into the elastic of his underwear as he continued to gyrate.

She only meant to grab singles but accidentally tucked a ten in with a one. It was too embarrassing to snatch it back, so she left it.

But once she was back on the couch and watching Dom finish his show, Lili decided that she needed the ten-spot approximately 749 times more than he did and went back to grab it anyway.

That only made Dom laugh harder. Her too.

But the heaving died in the light of her panting, Lili's breath suddenly refusing her anything more than shallow gasps once he was leaning over her.

In his underwear.

His strong arms pulling her against him. His body was so hard, and his skin so soft.

Are you sure? Was the question for her or for him?

It didn't matter with Dom now kissing her, undressing her, making her tingle all over.

His breath in her ear made her shudder.

He suddenly laughed again — it was almost a giggle — and Lili felt permission to do the same.

Her body was alive with laughter and the feel of his hands all over her.

She ran her hands up and down his strong thighs, along his abs, then onto his shoulders as she looked up into his eyes, still laughing as he donned a condom, then laughing even harder as he entered her.

Lili longed to tell him how amazing he felt, moan about the many (countless?) times she had imagined this. Instead she kept basking in the pleasure of their motion and quiet laughter as she pressed her flesh to his.

Lili had never felt more like a woman.

The thought made her laugh even harder because she also felt like a teenager again.

"Why do you keep laughing?" asked Dom, laughing himself.

"It's either laughing or full-on moaning, and I don't know you well enough to moan in front of you," she stammered between breaths.

Dom kept moving with her, making her want to not just moan but scream his name like she always did in her dreams.

"But mostly," she panted, updating her response to his now long past question, "I'm laughing *because this feels soooo good.*"

"You're telling me," he grunted.

And then he couldn't say anything else as the laughter died and their bodies moved together to their mutual release.

But Dom could still laugh though, as he rolled off of Lili and collapsed on the other side of the couch. "That was amazing."

"And hilarious," she added.

Lili

Re: Re: Column Feedback

Annabelle Lyons <a.lyons@mountainviewuniversity.edu>
To: <submissions@mansplanations.mvdaily.org>

Dear Mansplainer Extraordinaire,

Ah, irony. The tool of the weak-minded clown. I never resort to such blunt intellectual instruments because my content does what it says on the tin.

I have a great deal of scientific backing for my own studies, and there are numerous peer-reviewed and published studies the biological factors of love. Take, for example to 2009 study by researchers at UCL (University College London), and University of Warwick, and LSE (London School of Economics and Political Science), which showed that extended courtship enables a male to signal his suitability to a female and enables the female to screen out the male if he is unsuitable as a mate.

In layman's terms (which I'm fairly sure you'll need), this means that the longer a man works on wooing a woman, the more likely he is to be a good match for her.

That is a scientific study that can be applied to my students thusly: don't sleep with a guy on the first date and expect that he'll be a good prospect long term.

Kind Regards,

Annabelle

ANNABELLE LYONS
Associate Professor of Psychology
MountainViewUniversity.com

Lili had never walked to work before.

She kept telling herself that was the reason she felt so ... unsettled?

It wasn't because she was doing the walk of shame. First of all, she had nothing to be ashamed about. What happened last night was her choice and a good one. The fulfillment of a high school fantasy. Her evening with Dom had been fun, and that last little bit at the end before she fell asleep right next to him was actually kind of amazing.

Her stomach still ached from all the laughing, and parts of her body still felt the heat from last night's fire.

But Lili also wasn't obvious. Yes, she was still in last night's clothes, but they were last night's *party clothes*. She had changed before going out, so it wasn't like anyone would know that—

Lili saw how wrong she had been while opening the front door. Summer was waiting inside, already getting the espresso machine setup for the morning rush.

"Why did you ...?" Lili started.

Summer held up Lili's panda bear key ring and declared, "Way to do the walk of no-shame, boss!"

Lili snatched the panda from Summer and snapped at her. "Even if you did have my keys, I asked you to *bring them to me at the shop*. Not let yourself in without me here. Unlocking the door isn't your job and—"

"Okay, boss." Summer kept grinning at her.

"Stop looking at me like that!" Lili felt her cheeks flush. "Why are you looking at me like that?"

Summer shrugged. "I'm not gonna lie, I definitely wanted a slice of that Quarterback cake for myself, but I'm glad you got some."

"Quarterback cake?" Lili repeated.

Summer grinned again, turning from the espresso machine back to Lili. "Was it delicious?"

Lili shook her head. "I don't even know how to answer that."

"Did you know that your face is the exact color of a crab leg right now?"

"You do know that your paycheck comes from my bank account, right?" Lili retorted.

"Sorry, boss." Another grin before she went back to work. "I didn't mean to embarrass you."

"I'm not embarrassed!" She obviously was, and Lili knew that despite her protests, she wasn't fooling Summer, same as she wouldn't be fooling anyone else.

But that was the wrong emotion. Lili shouldn't feel embarrassed because she had nothing to be embarrassed about. The sequence of events was simple. She had been invited to a sex party, attended said sex party, had a great time while at that sex party, and eventually capitalized on that excellent time by ending her evening with a one-night stand.

Lili had sex with a (super) hot (and totally famous) guy (stud) who she had liked (been infatuated with) for a long time (like, at least one-third of her life).

Wasn't that the definition of winning?

Now that she had experienced the great Dominic Moore in all his glory, Lili could finally start rinsing that man from her system. And with Dom gone, she now had more room in her head for the perfect guy.

Lili kept working through the morning rituals required to open her pride and joy, letting that last thought lead to so many others. Ones she wanted because they took her further and further from thoughts about Dom.

It was better to ponder the perfect guy. Nerdy, yet sensible. Definitely not a jock of any kind. Lili's ideal mate would never play football. He wouldn't even *watch* football. The man who would one day gallop in to steal her heart might very well think that the Super Bowl happened in June.

He would value someone who always planned ahead like Lili, and of course he probably wouldn't have perfect hair or perfect teeth or a perfect smile or those perfect square shoulders like Dom had suddenly developed during the summer in between ninth and tenth grade. He also probably wouldn't have Costco abs (six-packs in bulk), or a big, fat—

Wow. Lili really needed to board the first train out of her damn mind.

Unfortunately, she found that impossible.

She tried and failed all morning. By the time Lili was opening Higher Grounds for the day, she had thought about Dominic Moore approximately forty-nine million times. None of her first four customers could have had any idea that her brain was being squeezed like the last bit of toothpaste from the tube. Lili had always been excellent at hiding that.

Her fifth customer was Annabelle Lyons — the psych professor who had a way of peering right into Lili's soul.

"You look extra happy this morning."

"Oh?" Lili took a stab at nonchalance but could already feel the smile claiming her face again. "I may have had a happier night than usual."

"Do tell." Annabelle grinned while raising her eyebrows. "Or you could tell me more about the *Mansplanations* saga instead?"

"You wouldn't believe the nerve of this guy." Annabelle shook her head, now including Marcus in the conversation as he joined them. "The email idea worked, but only if my goal was to get even more pissed off. This dude has an ego like you wouldn't believe."

Marcus placed his order. "Just a drip with a shot of caramel, please, Lili."

"I mean, it's like he can't even listen to a reasonable point or engage in any actual debate. His replies are bordering on ... flowery."

Marcus snorted as Lili prepped the professors' drinks. "You say flowery like it's just empty words."

"Well, it is. It's impossible to win a logical argument when the other side is talking in platitudes and metaphors. Frankly, I'd welcome some actual mansplaining over the fluff. At least that gives me something to argue with."

Lili handed set drinks on the counter.

"Come on." Marcus grabbed both and nodded at Annabelle. "Let's take a look at those samples. We might be able to find this flowery offender."

Annabelle and Marcus moved to a nearby table, pulling out sheets of paper and lining them up. A hint of laughter sparkled in Marcus's eyes, and Annabelle seemed to be lapping it up. Their chemistry was great, but before Lili could ponder the potentially brewing relationship or the secret that Marcus might be hiding, her next customer walked through the door.

Not that Runa was really a 'customer.' She had only paid for her coffee a handful of times, each one after throwing a fit and chastising Lili for never letting her.

Summer was working the till and Lili the bar. But Runa walked right up to the bar, homing in on Lili's expression like dragging a highlighter across her innermost feelings.

"Something's different. You're different. Are you going to tell me what happened last night right away or deflect with some awkward jokes before you finally get to it?"

"You're awkward." Lili started on Runa's usual red-eye — drip coffee with two espresso shots.

"No. I'm direct."

"What makes you think something happened last night?"

"How did the party go?"

Lili stopped and looked at Runa. "How do you know about the party?"

Runa shrugged. "I was there."

"You were there?" Lili would have gasped, but she didn't want Runa to call her Judi Dench.

"It's a sex party. In Mountain View. Why wouldn't I go?"

"I didn't see you there. Not when everyone was in the living room."

"I have a strategy with these things," Runa explained. "I get there early, wait for a guy that looks perfect for me, then pull him directly upstairs."

"What about your keys?"

"They stay in my bag." Runa patted her sensible black over-the-shoulder bag. "I'm not playing the game of chance."

"Congratulations on your key party cheat code. Were we playing hide n' seek, and I didn't know about it?" Lili handed Runa her red-eye.

"I saw your Prius when I left, and there was no way I was going back in there. Once Tami had everyone in the living room, that was my out."

"Who's Tami? And aren't you sort of violating the 'party' part of the key party with your little strategy?" Lili glanced over at Annabelle and Marcus, still talking about the writing samples by the look of things, though Annabelle now seemed to be upset about whatever they were looking at.

"Tami is the hostess and the reason I need a strategy," Runa told her. "She's had a few of these now, and if I have to hear about the history of key parties one more time, I—" She shook her head, couldn't even finish her sentence. "I'm glad you read a book, Tami. It's time to start keeping that shit to yourself. So, let's get to the good stuff. What hunk of bacon was lucky enough to get your keys? Did you make him take you downstairs because you like conversations and cobwebs on your cookie? And did you find the wide array of dildos repellent or arousing once you got down there?"

Lili was tempted to answer as a smart ass, but instead, she told Runa the truth. "It was Dom."

"*No way! You have to be kidding me.*" And then she squealed.

"Keep it down."

"Absolutely not." Runa shook her head. "You should get louder. Please tell me he muffed your ball."

"I don't know what that means."

"A muff is when a player touches the ball without successfully holding it. Your muff is—"

"Never mind."

"Did he sack you?"

"Please stop."

"Did he give you the old Hail Mary? A bit of the tight end? Did he pull you into his line of scrimmage?

"I'm never making you coffee again. I need to work. The woman talking to Summer right now is about to order a vanilla latte."

"If I promise not to make any more football-related sex-puns, will you please tell me what happened, preferably in graphic detail, when it comes to the parts about *Dominic Moore's stir-stick*." Runa whispered that last part. "You can tell me everything while you're working. I'll stick to coffee puns."

Lili shook her head and started on the latte. "We started out in the dungeon—"

"Basement."

"—and, yes, we did have fun with that sex toy table, but not like *that*. We actually … played with the toys. It was … fun."

"Your vocabulary is like crazy great this morning. Super articulate."

"Then we went upstairs and … escaped?"

"*Escaped*?" Runa repeated.

Lili laughed. "We tied sheets together and climbed out the window. Because, Tami. It was fun."

"Apparently, you had fun. First downstairs, then upstairs during your madcap adventure, *climbing out of a window with bedsheets.* Where is the part where you play hide the cannoli?"

"I thought it was only coffee jokes?"

"I couldn't think of any."

"There is no part of this or any story where I 'play hide the cannoli.'" Lili shook her head, handed the vanilla latte to Summer a second before Summer gave her the order, then turned back to Runa. "But yes, Dom and I did have sex. A one-night stand."

"Good. For. You!" Runa was beaming wide enough to have shared him. "And bonus points on it being a one-night stand. Now—"

"Now Dominic Moore is out of my system. This time for good. That means I can start focusing on my plan to find the perfect man for—"

Lili stopped at the sound of Runa's laughing.

"You're doing it again." Runa shook her head. "*Anticipating.* Waiting for the 'perfect guy.' You just started living in the moment, literally yesterday. Why back down now?"

The door opened before Lili could answer. She looked over as the bell jingled to see one of Runa's coworkers at town hall, Eleanor Boothman, entering the coffee shop.

"She's going to want an ice-blended mocha," Lili said.

"And will blab on about some office gossip that I couldn't care less about. Like I don't get enough of that at work already," Runa added.

Lili smiled and started the drink while Eleanor blabbed on about some office gossip that Runa clearly couldn't care less about, wondering if she was glad for the interruption or wanted to finish their conversation.

It would be a minute before they could get back to it. Eleanor wasn't just Runa's coworker, she headed the committee managing town participation in the Upper Crust Challenge. Lili hadn't seen her in a week — a long time for Eleanor to go without an ice-blended mocha — and she was eager to check in.

"Bye, Lili!" Annabelle called out to her with a wave. "I'm off to class now!"

"Does she always report her comings and goings to you?" Runa asked.

"She's just being nice," Lili said, bypassing Summer and handing the drink to Eleanor. "Ice blended mocha. Extra whipped cream." She smiled. "How is everything coming together with the Challenge?"

"It's going great. Couldn't be better." Eleanor handed Lili a ten. "Keep the change — I gotta go!"

"You gotta go?" Runa looked surprised.

"I'm running late for an early meeting." She nodded at the door, then started walking toward it. "Across the street."

Runa and Lili traded a glance. Runa felt it, too.

"I forgot to tell you." Eleanor turned back at the door, and everything suddenly made sense. "We no longer need you to represent us in the Upper Crust Challenge."

"What?" Lili said in disbelief.

"It's nothing personal. We've just been fortunate to find someone a little more high profile."

"You mean a lot more high profile?" Lili snapped, getting angry fast. "Like Dominic Moore!"

"I'm sure you can understand why we would want to capitalize on this opportunity." Eleanor insulted Lili with a smile.

"Lili has been counting on this, Eleanor." It looked like Runa might rip Eleanor's head from her shoulders. "This isn't fair."

"Fair doesn't pay the bills." Another campaign poster smile. "But Dominic Moore will." She held up her ice-blended mocha. "You still have the best coffee in Mountain View! You know I'll be back."

Lili's stomach was still turning as Marcus approached the coffee bar and dropped another dollar into the tip jar.

"It's you, isn't it?" Lili snapped at him.

"I'm sorry?" Marcus seemed surprised.

"Okay, Mansplainer. Please explain why men like to stomp all over everything women try to do?"

Marcus looked caught, but instead of rebutting with an instant denial, he offered Lili a long sigh instead. "Please. Don't tell Annabelle. I'll do it myself, I just ..."

Runa got it. "I've never seen her so feisty. She's clearly enjoying the mystery. Why would we want to take that away from her?"

Lili wasn't so sure, but Summer interjected her thoughts before she could respond.

"The Science of Love has gotten *so much better* since Mansplanations started attacking it."

"I'm not really *attacking* it," Marcus defended himself.

"Fine." She was too defeated for an argument. "Whatever."

"Thanks, Lili ..." He sounded unsure, dropping another fiver into the tip jar before leaving.

"*Well,*" Runa said when Marcus left.

"Well, *what*?" Lili asked. "I won't tell on him. I promised. He did just pay me five dollars for my silence, after all."

"Not that. Are you really going to let Dominic Moore just steal your dream like that?"

No. She absolutely was not.

Lili doffed her apron, threw it on the counter, then stormed out of Higher Grounds and across the street to Queen of Tarts.

Dom

Re: Re: Re: Column Feedback

Submissions <submissions@mansplanations.mvdaily.org>
To: Annabelle Lyons <a.lyons@mountainviewuniversity.edu>

Ah, but if only you could understand the obvious—, that general-izations are the enemy of love. Do you want to tell every couple that ever slept together on the first date that a mutual future is not in their stars?

Or tell young people to manipulate their potential prospects by withholding sex?

Isn't sex, when it's right for a couple, the exact thing we should be using heart and emotion for, rather than boiling it down to scientific studies?

No matter how you dress it up, giving any kind of rules and guide-lines for love severs your students from what they most need in this world: the ability to connect with their own inner compass and follow their heart.

Respectfully,

Mansplanations

Dom couldn't stop smiling.

His expression felt almost foreign. He was used to smiling from his appearances on morning shows to the regular maintenance of his everyday front, toothy smiles were part of his armor. But lately, those smiles had been cardio for his face.

This morning it had felt natural, and he wasn't exactly sure why.

But there really wasn't much of a mystery. Most if not all of his joy this morning came from that stupid key party last night that he hadn't even wanted to stop at, let alone stay at. Especially because of Liliana Travis, a girl he'd not thought of since high school, even though now he wondered why not. He had a great time with Lili last night *because* she was the same girl he remembered. Just as bright, just as pretty, and just as able to make him laugh. Dom couldn't ever remember sex being that fun.

Last night made it easier to feel more hopeful this morning. Not that he expected Lili to fill the hole inside him, but for the first time in a while he believed that the hole even could be filled. Dom wouldn't be sticking around Mountain View any longer than he needed to, and they were both perfectly clear about the *one-night* part of their one-night stand, with a flash discussion about their total lack of a relationship, both last night and again this morning on their ride to Main Street.

Dom pretended he was headed into Queen of Tarts early, so Lili would accept the ride. But then he drove back home and took a piping hot shower, long enough to let the water run cold.

He didn't need Lili to love what she had proven to him. That he might meet someone else in the future that didn't fawn all over him. He entered the bakery two hours later, trying to remember the last time he'd felt so alive.

Louise must have known something he didn't. She started laughing as Dom walked through the door. "How was the key party?"

Oh. "You really should have warned me."

"You know how old I am. How many pranks you do think I have left?" Louise was still laughing. "Did you participate?"

"Sort of." He walked behind the bar, saw the coffee, and wished he'd brewed his own, then poured himself a mug because he was already there.

"What does 'sort of' mean?"

"I went, but then I left." He took a sip of coffee that might have been even worse than yesterday's. Would it be weird if he went across the street? Lili already knew that his grandma made coffee that tasted like beans soaked in sock water. But he didn't want her to think that last night was about anything more than what they had already agreed it was.

"Did you do anything interesting while you there?" She refused to drop it.

"Isn't it weird that you're asking?"

The conversation was cut mercifully short as the door opened, and a woman Dom had been talking to a couple of nights ago while having drinks with the mayor and town hall staff walked into the bakery.

He and Eleanor Boothman had been discussing the possibility of Queen of Tarts representing the town at the Upper Crust Challenge. The contest would be televised, and the more eyeballs on his grandma's desserts, the more likely the bakery would take off. Dom loved the idea of helping Louise spread the word about her new bakery, and understood that any involvement on his part would likely require low effort for significant results.

His only objection was Eleanor. She was the kind of person who drove him totally nuts. Smarmy and gross, she got gropey fast, then progressively worse through the night. Dom finally had to peel himself away from her, barring Eleanor Boothman from his mind and not thinking a single thought about her again until right now as she approached him.

"*Great* news." Eleanor smiled like she was about to sell him something. "Queen of Tarts has been selected to represent Mountain View in the Upper Crust Challenge!"

"Is that news? Didn't you ask me if I could—"

"The Upper Crust Challenge!" Louise exclaimed. "I'm sure that *is* great news! But what is it?"

"You run a bakery," said Dom, turning to his grandma. "How do you not know about this?"

"It's a televised baking challenge. It's on twice a year." Eleanor explained.

"You don't watch TV?"

"I watch TV." Louise snapped back at her grandson. "But only the good stuff. Like Golden Girls."

"Isn't that before your time?"

"I'm a total Blanche."

"The Upper Crust Challenge—" Eleanor cut off the discussion before it went too far off the rails "—is a baking competition focusing on local bakers. They come to a county and invite each town to send one baker to represent them. This year they're coming to Wyndham County, and *Queen of Tarts* will represent Mountain View."

"It's a two-day challenge, with a baker and their assistant." Dom rushed to address his grandma's hesitation. "I'll be yours, of course."

"And what's in it for us?"

"The winner gets fifty-grand, with a matching grand for their town. *When* you win, we're upgrading the park. Just in time for election season, couldn't be more perfect." Eleanor seemed giddy with delight, or maybe with herself.

"Fifty-grand? Aren't these TV things usually a million dollars?" scoffed Louise. "Have you seen my grandson's ridiculous McJagger out front? We—"

"*McLaren*," Dom corrected her, despite the embarrassment.

"—don't need to win a contest, and I'm not sure that entering one is how I'd like to make my television debut." Louise fluffed her hair like that last argument was serious.

"It's just a local—"

"We also get all the exposure we could possibly want for the bakery," Dom kept selling Louise, cutting Eleanor off. "This is a huge opportunity for you. For us. For the Queen of Tarts."

Louise looked at Dom for several long seconds before finally blinking. "Alright, fine. You've convinced me. You can drop the puppy dog eyes. So, what happens next?"

The door opened, and Lili stormed into the bakery.

"Lili. Are you—" Dom started.

"I'll talk to you later!" she snapped at him, marching up to Eleanor and shoving a finger in her face. "I deserve a better explanation than 'It's nothing personal. We've just been fortunate to find someone a little more high profile.' That's bullshit, Eleanor, and you know it! I was promised that spot on the Upper Crust Challenge. I was *counting* on that spot."

"Yes. We had a couple of conversations, but that's all they were. I can appreciate that this is coming as a surprise and that you were hoping to see some extra exposure for your little shop. Unfortunately, I must also remind you that the town's focus is on raising our profile here in Mountain View, not on giving Liliana Travis whatever she wants."

"I didn't even know that Lili baked," Dom interjected, feeling confused.

"That's because you don't know anything!" Lili snapped at him again. "You blew out of this tiny town after high school, and you're going to do the same thing again once this place is open. I want to create something that will last, Domi. Something here—"

"Then do that!" He raised his hands in protest. "I'm not trying to stand in your way here. I didn't know you were a baker, or that you wanted anything to do with this contest. I didn't even know there *was* something called the Upper Crust Challenge until two days ago. How could I? We hadn't even—"

"Well, I'm not going to take it away from Louise now that—"

"Louise doesn't want it," said Louise, shaking her head. "And you're not taking it away because it was never hers to begin with. I didn't know about any of this five minutes ago, so it sounds like *I* would be taking it away from *you*. No thank you, dear." She shook her head again. "I'm not interested in stepping on a preexisting plan."

"It's too late," Eleanor said.

Everyone turned to her, their expressions questioning, bordering angry.

"We've already registered Queen of Tarts in the contest," Eleanor explained. "If we back out now, Mountain View will be forced to forfeit our spot."

Lili, Dom, and Louise all spoke in unison.

Lili: "That's not fair."

Dom: "We never finished our conversation."

Louise: "Looks like we've been hornswoggled, kids."

Eleanor held up a hand. "I came here to deliver what I saw as excellent news. I'm sorry to hear that you all don't feel the same way. I guess we'll all just have to live with that."

She left, and Lili turned her fury on Dom. "This is your fault for being famous! Your fault for always getting whatever you want! Your fault for never giving an actual shit about the people around you!"

"I—"

"You didn't even *recognize* me when we first met—"

"That's because you used to wear—"

"If you say the word *beaver* right now, I swear on the great Shonda Rhymes that I will never speak to you again." Lili glared at him, her nostrils practically flaring.

"Look." He raised his hands again, this time in pacification. "This isn't about me. I was just trying to help my grandmother out. I never even finished my conversation with Eleanor the other night because … I just had to get away from her. There is no dilemma here. As soon as you said that it rightfully belonged to you, me and Louise both agreed."

Lili seemed to soften inside of a moment that could not have been wrenched any tighter.

Then Dom said, "I don't always get what I want."

And Lili snapped at him again. "How oblivious are you? Everything has always just been handed to you because you're Dominic Moore. Not just in high school but in life. Why else would a dumb jock get to jump to the front of every line with his enchanted fast pass? You don't even know how to bake a cookie — no problem, *just smile at the camera!* Maybe lift up your shirt and show the world those chiseled abs!"

"Lili, I—"

"Ruined your career with drugs, and now you're trying to ruin everyone else's?"

Dom had been tackled hundreds of times in his career, but he'd never been hit so hard.

Louise stepped forward. "I've been watching this, wondering where and when it might be my place to—"

"Please, Louise. Don't." He shook his head and turned to Lili, hoping to somehow correct this, still baffled that it was happening at all. "Lili—"

"I don't want to hear it, Dom. I'm sure whatever you say will sound great, but it'll only last until the next time the world wants to fawn all over you. Then you can walk away again."

She stormed toward the door, turning to get in her final word. "Bet you can't pull your enormous head out of your perfectly sculpted ass!"

Lili left Queen of Tarts, but Dom's attention went nowhere.

"Are you okay?" Louise asked.

"I'm great, actually."

And it wasn't a lie. Dom was, of course, disappointed to hear that Lili thought of him as a dumb jock. But that wasn't a discovery. He'd sort of known it before her last declaration turned disquiet into fact.

It hadn't bothered him then.

Not that it bothered him now, exactly.

A sense of intrigue had been stirred inside him. Until Lili marched in here this morning, she was an attractive girl from the past who knew how to make him laugh. But the angry passionate woman who had just told him off, though, was new and exciting.

Now he wanted to prove how wrong she was about him.

And show Liliana Travis *exactly* who Dominic Moore actually was.

Lili

Little Harvey's third birthday party was one week later.

Jeremy was playing Dad the Magnificent as usual, this time alternating between some impressively fluid dance moves — not because the motions themselves were impressive, but because he was doing them as a gaggle of children boogied in between and all around his legs — while flipping burgers.

The children all loved him. Alicia adored him even more, though she defied anyone to prove it with evidence. A few of the older kids — mostly siblings — were splashing in the pool, with the oldest among them making cannonballs in a line. An inflatable obstacle course loomed over everything, but the entire backyard was dressed for the occasion, including a pair of his and hers piñatas, swinging from a low branch on their plum tree.

The obstacle looked fun if you were under the age of ten or weighed a third of what she weighed — a thought which led Lili right to her favorite thing at the party: a full-on sundae bar, though it was only pretend ice cream thanks to a soft-serve machine, the bar was still packed with *all of the fixings*.

Sitting just to the side of that sundae bar was Lili's pride and joy, and she couldn't wait to indulge in it on this Saturday afternoon.

Her contribution to the party, and the most talked about, from what she'd heard so far- the cake.

The cake Lili had made for Harvey was beyond fabulous. Practically magical. The best she had ever made, no doubt. Maybe not in taste — the inside was vanilla, though her version was a crowd pleaser — but certainly in its intricacy. She couldn't sculpt like the Cake Boss or anything, but Lili was constantly improving, every time she tried.

She felt almost guilty thinking about it, but her dinosaur cake was outstanding. A forest green base upon which a small herd of dinosaurs was grazing. A rock plateau sat off-center, with smaller dinosaurs drinking from the pebble-lined river, running from up top to a river that circled the bottom. Lili kept thinking that she should have taken a few more pictures and wondering how many she could get right now without being obnoxious.

"Pleased with yourself?" Alicia asked, catching Lili quietly congratulating herself.

"Sure am," Lili admitted.

"You should be." Alicia nodded in approval. "Now, tell me that I have permission to hate all of this."

"Pregnant women should be able to opt-out of any life event they don't feel up to. One-hundred percent of the time. No questions asked. Is that right?"

"I'm so glad you're here." Alicia put an arm around her. "Now, can everyone else leave?"

"It's for Harvey. And just look how happy he is!"

"He's *three*. He won't remember any of this." Alicia waved her arm around the backyard. "Have you seen that obstacle course? This is ridiculous." She shook her head. "It's because Jeremy's an even bigger kid than Harvey."

"It's fun."

"It's expensive, and a lot of work. Shouldn't we be saving that effort for when he's old enough to remember?"

"I didn't know it was either/or." Lili shrugged.

"You know what I mean." She laughed.

"You could just admit that at this age it's all for Jeremy, and be okay with that. I mean, look at how happy *he* is." Lili nodded at Alicia's husband, keeping all of the children amused by entertaining himself.

"He is too adorable." Alicia shook her head like that was a bad thing.

"Maybe—" Lili stopped.

"What is it?" Alicia asked. "Oh."

She saw the same thing as Lili: Dom strolling right into Harvey's party, almost like he was invited.

"Why is he here?" Lili asked. *Accused?*

Alicia shrugged. "I think Jeremy invited half of Mountain View. It's not too big a surprise that our hometown hero made the cut. Why do you care?"

"Because that 'hometown hero' hasn't been a part of this town for a long time!"

"What does that—"

"ALICIA! HONEY?" Jeremy suddenly yelled. "Can you help me for a second? We've got a five-star poo-splosion over here, and the burgers are mission-critical."

"I'll be back," Alicia told Lili.

But Lili couldn't have cared less. She was already walking over to Titus and Dom.

"You need to leave," she said.

Titus looked at Dom.

Dom looked back at Titus: *It's cool.*

Titus nodded. "Guess that's my cue to go and try my luck with Runa again. Maybe the 900th time will be the charm?" No response, so he added, "Well then, I'll leave you all to it."

"You need to go," Lili repeated once she and Dom were alone.

"I was invited, same as anyone else here."

"I was here first."

"What kind of argument is that? Did you call dibs on this party? Are we in kindergarten?"

"Damn right, I called dibs on this party!" Like she wasn't being perfectly stupid and totally unreasonable. She refined her argument. "I have more of a right to be here than you."

"Oh yeah? And how do you figure that?"

"Not only am I the birthday boy's mom's best friend, I'm like a second mom to Harvey myself. Since I've *been here* for his entire life."

"I've been friends with Jeremy since the second grade, and arguably it makes more sense to have old friends get to know your kid at this kind of event. Like you just said, you've been here for his entire life. You're not really selfish enough to keep little Harvey from seeing his Uncle Dominic, are you?"

"You're not his Uncle Dominic."

"Look, Lili. I'm sorry you have beef with me, but I'm not going anywhere anytime soon. So if you want to be free of my presence, then you can either leave the party or, you know, *not* talk to me."

Then he stood there, like Lili was the one who needed to go.

The most infuriating thing about the moment, in which she stood frozen in front of Dominic Moore with her hands on her hips (not really, but that's definitely the way any witness would have reported it to the court) was that he totally had a point.

So after another few moments of puffing her chest and holding her stare, Lili finally flinched and retreated inside the house to find Alicia in Harvey's sitting room, rocking back and forth with the birthday boy in her lap.

"I can't believe him!" Lili fumed, darkening a tender moment between mother and son. "How could he come back to town after leaving for so long, then decide to open a business that will be my biggest competition, *right across the street?* Dominic Moore is suddenly everywhere I want to be!"

Lili looked at Alicia, waiting for her bestie to offer some comfort.

"You need to stop acting like a big, giant baby," she said instead.

"Am not."

Alicia rolled her eyes. "Plenty of other people have come back to town without you reading them the riot act or thinking they deserved to have it read to them."

"That's not true." Though it sounded sort of true. "Like who?"

"It's true like a bunch of times over. And how about Zed for one?"

Oh yeah.

"Nobody in Mountain View would have ever thought that *Zed* would be the go-to personal trainer for moms with more money to spend than sense, but he totally made it, and I heard you tell Zed how proud you were 'on behalf of Mountain View,' *like you spoke for the entire town.* Twice."

"That was different," Lili argued.

"How?"

"Because you're making me feel like even more of a failure!" She answered a different question entirely, and one Alicia hadn't asked.

And now Lili wanted to cry.

But her best-friend wouldn't allow it, though. "Might I remind you that you started Higher Grounds all on your own? And your cafe is *thriving*. If you can't handle a little competition, then maybe you shouldn't have a business. If your little coffee shop isn't everything you want it to be, the only person who can change that is you. Who's the most spectacular woman I know?"

Lili shook her head, not wanting to say what she knew Alicia wanted her to, but under the heat of her piercing gaze, Lili couldn't help herself. "I am."

"That was hardly convincing." Alicia shook her head, still rocking back and forth with Harvey on her lap. "But I suppose I'll allow it."

Of course, Alicia was right. Lili had been acting like a baby, throwing her little temper tantrum instead of actually doing something about the situation.

"I know I can find another way to get the money for my bakery expansion. I had just put *so much* hope into the contest."

"I still don't see why you can't 'expand your bakery' by baking at home ..."

"Nope." Lili was tired of repeating herself. "I'm going to do it right. It'll just take a little bit longer."

Alicia sighed.

"Shouldn't the mother of the birthday boy be out there, you know, with the birthday boy?"

"Can't I just hide in here until it's all over?"

Lili shook her head. "Not with Harvey."

Alicia relented then they went back outside together.

Lili went right up to Dom, but after her conversation with Alicia, she was approximately one-quarter zen. "I just wanted to wish you the best of luck in the Upper Crust Challenge."

Looking up into his eyes, Lili was *thrilled* with herself. Even without a kid of her own, she was the most grownup out of all the grownups here. There should be some sort of first-place trophy for how adult she was about all of this.

But apparently Dom had no designs on being a grownup himself. He glanced from the obstacle course back to Lili. "I bet you won't run the obstacle course."

"Maybe that's because the obstacle course is for kids," she replied.

He shrugged. "So I bet right."

Lili wasn't okay with Dom betting right, being smug, or generally existing at Harvey's party, so she slipped off her heels and started running the course.

But then Dom was suddenly running right beside her, and despite him being too big for the course and Lili running as fast as she possibly could, he annoyed her a hundred times more than he already had by beating her to the finish line.

He waited for on the other side of it, laughing.

"Whatever." Lili shrugged. "I bet you won't eat a burger with everything on it — from the sundae table."

Oh, but he did: double cheese with strawberry sauce, sprinkles, Oreo crumbles, and fudge.

He dipped his feet into the pool and ate every bite, with plenty of *mmmmms* to let all the onlookers hear how delicious it was. He finished with a flourish, wiped his mouth, and nodded at the water as he stood.

"I bet you won't jump in the pool ... with all your clothes on."

"Easy." Lili walked over to him.

Dom was barely upright when she got there, so it was a breeze, shoving him into the water.

She jumped in after him, then they were both laughing as they surfaced.

He pulled out his phone and held it above the pool. "I hope it still works."

"I hope you didn't have any baggies in your pocket." She laughed even harder.

But Dom didn't join her. Instead, he looked confused.

"You know, baggies with your drugs," she clarified.

He still wasn't laughing. Or even looking at her. Instead, Dom was shaking his head, wading over to the edge, and pulling himself out of the pool.

Then Lili was alone.

Dom

Re: Re: Re: Re: Column Feedback

Annabelle Lyons <a.lyons@mountainviewuniversity.edu>
To: <submissions@mansplanations.mvdaily.org>

Dear Sir,

Have you met any young people recently? Following their heart inevitably means following a cocktail of neurotransmitters telling them that the person in front of them right now is theirs forever.

Have you ever sat with a sobbing twenty-year-old who was just ghosted by the guy she thought was THE ONE?

I have, and I can tell you from experience that there's nothing more comforting to a young person facing the first blush of love than knowing that they are not alone. That their feelings are normal, and that their intensity comes from biological responses that contributed to man's success on this planet.

By giving my students both the understanding of the biological precursors to love AND the formula for its creation, I'm giving them reassurance that they will find true love over time.

Kind Regards,

Annabelle

MOUNTAIN VIEW
UNIVERSITY

ANNABELLE LYONS
Associate Professor of Psychology
MountainViewUniversity.com

Queen of Tarts opened with a bang.

The first few pops of attention came courtesy of Dominic Moore and all the curiosity and admiration generated by Mountain View's most famous export. But the second wave, and every wave after that, had more to do with his grandma's amazing baked goods.

Unfortunately, as much as customers loved the Queen of Tarts' cakes and pastries, the lousy coffee quickly became a serious problem. Complaints weren't coming in nearly as often now, but that only proved how big of an issue it was. At least grievances around the joe were straightforward and therefore, easy to deal with. Whispers were so much worse.

Louise's bakery was getting a fast reputation, for mouth-watering baked goods and a caveat: *don't drink the coffee.*

"Would you stop giving my coffee bar all those dirty looks?" Louise interrupted his thoughts. "It's not *that* bad."

"It tastes like bad plumbing."

She shook her head, admonishing him. "I spoiled you too damn much. You don't even know what suffering is, making that big of a deal out of my coffee. So what if it's not gourmet! Is it made with beans? Does it have caffeine?"

"People want more from their coffee, Louise. Especially at a bakery."

"Then maybe you should be nicer to Lili and—"

"I *am* nice to Lili."

"Great. We need another prep session for the challenge this afternoon, and I was hoping you'd invite her. It should be easy since you're so nice."

"Why?" Dom didn't like this.

"Because next on the list of baking practices is meringue, and nobody meringues quite like Lili."

"Is meringue a verb?"

"The girl at my book club once had a lemon meringue pie that Lili brought in, and you would think she had sent George Clooney to service them—"

"Louise!"

"The girls are still talking about it to this day. And no less than they'd be talking about George Clooney."

"Do I have to invite her?"

"No." She shook her head. "I'll leave it totally up to you. But I'll also remind you that I didn't have to feed or clothe you or give you a bigger bedroom than mine when you started hulking out."

"That's not fair. You're—"

"I'm not trying to be fair, Domi. I'm trying to get Lili to help me with my meringue."

"Why can't you ask her?"

"Because I should be able to ask my grandson to do that for me. And he should be able to walk across the street and have a conversation with that delightful girl without letting his pride get in the way of doing the right thing for his grandma. The *smart* thing."

"She believes the news." He pouted. "Just like everyone else."

"Well, what do you expect?" She pierced him with her gaze before she continued. "Do you think the poor girl is psychic? You can't be mad at Lili for believing the news if you're unwilling to tell her the truth. Cover for Robbie all you want; that's your decision to make, but get used to people assuming those stories are true without being bothered when they judge you for it."

He grumbled something to Louise that he was already trying to forget while crossing the street. Even if she was right, Dom still didn't like the result. Especially when Lili looked over as he entered her shop and didn't seem especially happy to see him.

Not *unhappy*, exactly. More than anything, Lili appeared more indifferent than Dom deserved. She was the one who had said something judgmental instead of simply thinking it.

He was even more convinced she didn't want him there when she started to chat with the customer in front of him, clearly stretching the encounter to avoid dealing with the football player she was still furious at.

"Keep trying, Keandre. Someone is going to see how great you are. How many resumes did you hand out today?"

"Too many. Sure you don't need any extra help around here?"

"I wish," Lili shot Dom a nasty look, "but it's looking like my competition might try and put me out of business."

Keandre's look at Dom clearly said *Good luck, man* before the younger man moved off, leaving the baller to his fate.

"No." Lili shook her head as he approached the counter.

"No, what?" Dom honestly didn't know.

"No. You can't have my source."

"I wasn't going to ask about your source. I just wanted to order a cup of coffee. I couldn't stand the thought of drinking another cup of roasted despair over at Louise's."

"What would you like?" Again, indifferent.

"Just a plain drip. Please." He smiled.

She smiled back. Kind of.

Lili turned her back to Dominic, poured him a large cup of regular coffee, and returned to the counter. "It's on the house."

"I can pay for my cup of coffee."

"Of course, you can." She nodded. "That'll be a thousand dollars."

"Can't I just pay what it says on the menu?"

"Free or a thousand dollars. Totally up to you."

"If I pay a thousand dollars, will you be insulted?"

"Almost for sure."

He picked up the cup. "Thanks for the coffee."

"No." She shook her head again.

"Why do you keep saying no to things I'm not saying? I wasn't going to ask for the name of—"

"I know you well enough to see that you were about to ask for *something*."

"I was." He smiled wider. "I was hoping you would come over and help Louise meringue. That's a verb, in case you didn't know."

"Óchi."

"I'm sorry?"

"Don't be. That means *No* in Greek. I thought you might like to learn something along with your rejection."

"Very funny."

"Not really. I can do much better."

"Look. I know you hate me, but my grandmother could really use your help on this. Please. Don't make me beg you."

"Are you willing to beg me? Because I've gotta admit, the rich and famous — is it *world* famous? How big are you? Globally, I mean?" She shrugged. "International uber stud and all-around American Hero, Dominic Moore suddenly willing to beg for some down and dirty meringueing, I gotta say—" she fanned herself dramatically "— that's enough to get this girl here agreeing to just about anything ..."

"I seriously can't tell what kind of answer that is."

"It's a yes. I will help. But to be clear: I'm helping Louise because she is an awesome lady, and I can't imagine the trauma she must be stuffing into the darkest recesses of her mind after having raised you."

"I'm so glad I asked," said Dom with a sigh.

Lili

Lili had always liked Louise a lot and was looking forward to making meringue with her.

She just didn't want Dom to know. He was too damned smug about everything, using that big fat smile and all those giant white teeth to get his way. But making meringue was fun, and Lili's was killer. She was happy to teach Louise and didn't see doing so as any sort of competition. She loved baking with others and saw strengthening her competition as raising the bar for herself.

Lili arrived at the appointed time with a vat of coffee.

Louise looked elated to see her. "I feel like I got the Martha Stewart of Meringue to come help me!"

She pulled her into an enthusiastic hug, then handed Lili a list:

Baking Categories in the Upper Crust Challenge

- Cakes (layer cakes, cupcakes, snack cakes, roulades ... even cheesecakes?)
- Candy (caramels, chocolates, gummies, misc. confections)
- Cookies

- Pastry (shortcrust, filo, choux, flaky, and puff)
- Custard
- Frozen and combined desserts

Lili shook her head and handed it back to Louise. "I don't envy you having to do choux pastry. That's my nightmare."

"Why is that?"

"It always cracks or doesn't rise. *Every time.*" She shrugged. "I just can't get the hang of it, and no amount of YouTube tutorials or baking shows are going to fix it for me."

"Maybe I can help." Louise squeezed her shoulder. "What choux pastry is for you, that's what meringue is for me. Just so you know what a help this really is. I'm having these little panic attacks, not just because I never seem to know what I'm doing when it comes to meringue, but because I'm just *positive* that meringue will end up getting selected for the final dessert."

Lili grinned at her. "Then let's get you ready to nail it."

Ten minutes later, they were each several sips into their coffees, with the project's ingredients spread across the table. Lili was an excellent teacher, and Louise an eager student.

"Meringue is a ton of fun once you know what you're doing," Lili assured her.

"And clearly I didn't." Louise laughed.

It was true. They had to start at the very beginning, with Lili explaining some of the basics she took for granted. Like to never use packaged egg whites to make meringue. Of *course for* Lili, but Louise didn't know that the pasteurization process could prevent egg whites from forming a stable meringue.

"Never overheat your egg whites. And when whipping, always start your mixer on medium-low to medium speed. Beat until foamy, then turn it up high … like this …"

And then Lili showed her.

"If the egg whites are beaten too quickly at the start, your foam will be weak, and that will keep the foam from stabilizing." She shrugged. "Then your meringue is a little like a leaky balloon."

Lili kept delivering tips to Louise as they worked: adding a small amount of cream of tartar or vinegar before whipping to help stabilize the foam; never using plastic bowls (they can retain a fatty film that might deflate an otherwise amazing meringue); humidity turns a meringue chewy, so always avoid making it on humid days; and a dozen other bits of solid advice that Louise took in with rapt attention.

The learning went both ways. Lili had picked up some of her cooking from books and online articles, but it had mostly come from watching people making culinary magic on video. She'd never been lucky enough to have a hands-on instructor like Louise working right alongside her. She showed Lili how to shred almonds and make macaroon dust. The conversation turned to shelling chestnuts, and Louise seemed almost unreasonably excited.

"Easier than most people realize! You just cut a half-inch gash on the sides and drop 'em in an omelet pan. Allow a half-teaspoon of butter to each cup of chestnuts. Shake that pan over the fire until the butter's all melted, then into the oven for five. Shell 'em with a tiny knife and let 'em melt in your mouth."

Lili had tried chestnuts roasted over an open fire one unfortunate Christmas Eve a few years ago. They must have been very different than the ones her teacher seemed so excited about.

Louise was easy to like, and she obviously felt the same way about Lili. Soon enough, their conversation turned personal. Lili wasn't sure how Dom wiggled into their conversation, only that she suddenly realized they were talking about him.

"He really was the sweetest child," Louise continued. "There was this one time we went to the zoo ... Domi was eating animal crackers from a box, and he got really insistent all of a sudden that we give this janitor he saw sweeping up a few feet away one of his crackers. Domi said that he could tell the man was hungry because he didn't have a grandma to take care of him ..." She shook her head. "It wasn't even what he said, but whenever I remember that look in his eyes, I want to start crying. He was always such a compassionate child."

"Do you think it was all the money or the environment that changed him?"

Louise looked at Lili. "*Changed?*"

She swallowed, not wanting to insult Louise, but it wasn't like she was saying anything that hadn't been on the national (international?) news. "Dom never took drugs in high school ... at least not that I ever heard about. So ..."

"Domi doesn't take drugs now." Louise shook her head. "He never did."

Lili raised her eyebrows.

Louise lowered her voice, even though they were alone in the bakery. "The cops pulled him over when he was driving that Robbie Lewis to practice. *Robbie* had a little weed on him, but worse, he had an even smaller amount of cocaine. Robbie freaked out, and went "batshit inside-out" according to Domi. No doubt about it, that kid would have been booted from the league for good if the news came out. But Domi just grabbed the drugs off of him without even thinking. Don't ask me how I feel about it ..."

"Why would he do that?" Lili asked in mild shock, not sure if she believed the story Dom had delivered to a grandmother he didn't want to disappoint.

"He did it because Titus asked him to look after the boy. Robbie Lewis went to high school here in Mountain View, you know."

"Of course, I know that ..."

But it made her wonder. Lili had always thought of Dominic Moore as a guy who got out of Dodge the second he possibly could, and never looked back at the podunk town he probably wished he never even came from.

Louise painted a completely different picture.

Lili didn't want to believe any of it because then she would have to start feeling ashamed of herself. It was better to have faith in the more likely reality, that the golden boy was using his charm and his stature to wiggle out of responsibility, just like he had been for his whole entitled life.

Lili had questions, but she didn't get to ask even one of them before the Prince of Everything Himself came in and interrupted them.

The mood shifted immediately. The vibe between Lili and Louise was instantly different, and she couldn't quite decipher the energy she felt wafting off of him. Probably more indifference.

"You're just in time," Louise said to him.

"In time for what?" he asked.

"In time for your baking lessons."

"Why do I need baking lessons?"

"Because we're going to be partners in the Upper Crust Challenge, and you could use the help?"

"Why—"

"*Because.*" She cut him off. Something passed between Louise and her grandson that she didn't understand, though Lili found it amusing to watch.

"Maybe that's a bad idea." Lili shrugged, making it obvious that she was only playing. "Dom is probably a lost cause. Teaching him might be a hopeless endeavor."

"Anything you can do, I can do better."

"Eliminate feats of physical strength, and those words make you a liar."

"I bet you would teach me to use salt instead of sugar just to sabotage the whole thing," said Dom, while Louise kept watching their banter.

"I'll take that bet."

Dom shook his head. "That wasn't a real bet."

"I'll tell you what … let me give you a real bet, and I'll give you baking lessons."

Dom looked again to his grandmother before slowly nodding his head. "Lay it on me."

"I bet that you won't do an entire shift at Queen of Tarts … in nothing but a thong. Is that *real* enough for you?"

Then something impossible happened.

"You're on," said Dom with a grin.

Dom

What did I agree to?

Dom stared at himself in the mirror, unable to believe his own stupidity.

Really, this had little to do with intelligence. He had let Lili goad him into the stunt, and he still couldn't quite understand why. There was just something about her that made Dom want to prove himself, even more than usual, and in some of the most ridiculous ways.

But the strangest part had been doing it in exchange for baking lessons that Louise knew he definitely did not need. He'd been helping her in the kitchen since his seventh birthday. She was up to something. He just hoped it wasn't matchmaking, or she'd be sorely disappointed.

Louise's motivations didn't matter. Baking lessons from Lili had their own appeal, even if he was trying hard not to acknowledge that truth. But was the price of admission worth it?

His reflection didn't lie: this was really happening. He was actually going to be serving customers in a thong that read *Kiss the Cook* on its extremely revealing front.

And the worst part? He had been the one to pick out the thong. Unlike the bet itself, that part hadn't been hoisted upon him. Dom thought the thong was hilarious when he saw it in the store. Now it was a viral video waiting to happen.

He drew a deep breath, then stepped out into Queen of Tarts.

Louise started guffawing. "Oh my … the ladies in this town …"

She was having a hard time catching her breath. This already promised to be the longest day of his life. He wished it was over, so he might as well start.

Lili stood off to the side, watching it all with a smile, followed by fits of occasional laughter.

The first customer was the easiest due to her acute inability to not stutter. Her mouth kept flapping open, but not a single word ever left it. Just a wide array of sounds, from mumbles to something that rolled around the edge of a moan.

Dom gave the girl a brownie on the house and told her to have a great day.

The second customer was a carousel of double entendres, making the rounds from "Do you have any cakes with soggy bottoms?" to her most obnoxious entry: "I heard you should leave it in for ten minutes or so."

Dom was the one full of mumbles during that exchange.

By the time he was finished with the third customer — a tall blonde who was somehow the most hilarious of the first three interactions on account of her playing it perfectly straight, as though Dom was still fully dressed and helping this nice woman select her dozen cookies — the line was out the door and snaking halfway down Main Street.

Louise came over to Lili, cackling. "This was the best idea — I don't know how you managed it."

Lili shrugged. "Boys are dumb."

"They sure are!" Louise laughed harder. "We can probably forget about the Upper Crust Challenge — Domi's abs are the best advertising this place could ever have."

"I'm not sure that abs and baked goods go together," Lili argued.

"People aren't logical when it comes to abs like that."

"He's your grandson. Isn't—"

"Blood don't make you blind, honey."

"You better not get used to this!" Dom called over to them after finishing with his seventh straight customer. "This is a one-time thing only. No way I'm—"

Dom stopped talking, and all three of them turned toward the commotion up front. Eleanor Boothman had apparently been trying to get inside for a while. Still, the crowd in the doorway thought she was trying to cut in line and had collectively barred her from entry.

But determined as she was, Eleanor eventually burst through their barrier with flailing arms and a loud declaration that she was here on, "OFFICIAL BUSINESS!"

Dom sighed, somehow feeling even more naked than he already did while walking to the other side of the counter, then over to see what Eleanor was going on and on about.

"You need to shut this down!" she commanded as Dom approached her.

"You mean shut down the bakery?" He looked around at the crowd and then back at Eleanor like she might need a couple of orderlies in white coats to take her away. "Because I think that might cause an actual riot."

"No." She shook her head and then waved a hand up and down his body like a magician's assistant introducing a new trick. "You need to shut *this* down. It's indecent exposure."

"I've read all the town rules, and there is nothing against wearing a thong in public. This would only be a violation if the business owner had an issue with it, and I can assure you, that isn't the case here." Dom turned around, cupping both hands around his mouth as he yelled several times louder than he needed to. "Hey, Grandma!"

Louise glanced over at Lili with a grin, then came walking over.

"Do you have any problem with me serving your customers in a thong?" Dom asked when she got there.

Lili giggled in the background.

"This place is called Queen of Tarts," said Louise, "Right now, my display case still has a Between My Red Velvet Sheets and a Peanut Butter Perversion for sale, but the Caress My Carrot cake is already gone. Do you think I care about Domi's little—"

Dom: "It's not *little*."

Eleanor: "I'm not sure you're understanding the issue."

"—show and tell. What am I not understanding?"

"Regardless of what you think is appropriate, I am concerned about this little display not only being incredibly disruptive to the community but a clear public nuisance and—"

"It's not little," Dom repeated before making his actual point. "What's the big deal, Eleanor? Look around, it's just a line of people. A few even have their babies or kids, and no one else seems to be bothered. It's like I'm at the beach."

He shrugged: *See, no biggie!*

But the gesture seemed to further upset her. Eleanor's face became redder, even more flustered. "You might have been comfortable with all the scandals in your previous career, but if you expect to get any respect in this town, and trusted to represent us here in Mountain View for the Upper Crust Challenge, then I'm afraid you'll have to behave in a much more dignified manner."

"Dignified according to you?" Dom challenged her. "And you're the one who asked me—"

"Dignified according to the traditions of this town."

"If we don't represent Mountain View, then wouldn't the town have to pull out of the contest entirely?"

"Well, yes, but—"

"And it's important to you that Mountain View enters the Upper Crust Challenge so you can get your park funds before the election. Am I right?"

"I think you're missing—"

"No, Eleanor, I think *you're* missing the point."

Dom paused, using the expectant moment to look around the bakery again, silently noting everyone observing their argument, especially aware of Lili in the background, waiting for him to lose their bet, and unwilling to let Eleanor's personal problems spread like a virus through the bakery.

"You're the only one who has an issue here," Dom continued. "I'm not breaking any rules, and I'm sorry to tell you that I won't be backing down. If you want to trash Mountain View's chances because you don't think it's appropriate for me to spend a few hours serving delicious baked goods in a thong, well, I guess that means you'll have to withdraw and then explain your decision to the folks here in Mountain View."

The air conditioner ticked on in their silence, and the hum was suddenly deafening. Eleanor delivered a defeated sigh several long seconds later before opening her mouth as if for a tirade.

But then she spun around and stomped out of the bakery instead.

Once the door had fully shut behind her, the Queen of Tarts erupted in applause. Dom glanced over at Lili, working to interpret her expression. She seemed both irritated that Dom had gotten his way and pleased that at least he was using his powers for good this time.

"Great job not losing the bet, Dominic," she said on her way out the door. "I'm going back to work."

He stayed in the thong for the rest of the day, and throughout every interaction — from sidesplittingly funny to completely indifferent — Dom imagined himself telling the story to Lili. They had to close the bakery early because they were all out of everything except the coffee no one wanted. He was glad for the extra time and eager to get back into his clothes, but not before taking Lili's empty vat back to High Grounds. Hopefully, he could tell her about his day and a few of the more outrageous encounters. Going through those stories while still in a thong made what was already funny that much funnier.

He found Lili sitting at a corner table with Alicia and Runa, surrounded by penis balloons and sipping drinks from penis straws.

"What's all this?" he asked, gesturing at the decor.

"Runa just got back from a bachelorette party, and I guess she felt like she had to steal *all the penises*." Lili waved a hand across the abundance of shafts.

"The women there didn't really know what to do with them." Runa shrugged and giggled. "I always know what to do with them."

"What?" Dom looked sideways at Lili. "They didn't think to use them as fake phones for receptionists to train with?" He shook his head. "Amateurs."

Lili laughed, but her friends' uncertain smiles belied the truth that they weren't in on the joke.

"What are we drinking?" Dom nodded at the blush-colored liquid rising like veins in their straws as the girls kept sipping.

"Runa and I are drinking rosé," Lili reported, "and Alicia has sparkling cider."

Alicia clearly wasn't happy about this. "It's inhumane that pregnant women can't drink when they are *clearly* the people who deserve to be drinking the most. At least at this table."

"Mind if I sit?" Dom asked, pointing to an empty chair.

Lili shook her head. "No, thank you."

"Why not?" Runa looked him up and down. "It's still like a low-rent bachelorette party, but Dominic Moore makes it a lot less crappy than the one I just came from."

"Thanks," he said.

"I'm with Runa," Alicia nodded. "But I think he should do a striptease first."

"I don't do stripteases. And besides, I'm pretty much already naked."

Runa disagreed. "You could *definitely* be more naked."

"I'm not a piece of meat, you know." But then he winked at Lili, her face already reddening. He changed the subject to temper her embarrassment. "So, how about that baking lesson? Our bet went further awry than expected, especially after Eleanor stopped by. Surely I've earned a lesson from the Master of Meringue."

"Is that who she is?" Alicia asked, looking over at Lili.

Runa laughed, still sucking on her straw.

"Fine," Lili agreed. "But we have to do the lesson in my kitchen, with all of my equipment."

"What's wrong with doing it across the street?" he asked.

"Louise has a gorgeous kitchen, but none of my stuff is there." It looked like she needed to say something else before she was satisfied. "And I'm just not used to baking there."

"She means 'Stan' isn't there," Alicia seemed to tell on her.

Lili's face was suddenly even redder. "*Shut up.*"

Dom looked from Lili to Alicia. "Who's Stan?"

But Runa stopped sipping to answer with a guffaw. "Stan is her boyfriend."

Boyfriend?

"I can't believe you're going to let him put his hands all over Stan." Alicia shook her head in disbelief.

"I feel like I'm missing something," Dom admitted.

Alicia and Runa traded giggles.

Lili kept getting redder. "It's my mixer, okay?"

"Okay," Dom said.

"Lili is always waiting for the perfect guy," Alicia explained, "but she spends an awful lot of time with that mixer ..."

"She won't let anyone touch it," Runa added.

"*Him*," Alicia clarified.

"Please stop," Lili begged.

"I can't wait to meet Stan." Dom laughed. "Just text me the *when*."

He stood from his seat then walked to the door, looking back when he got there, with a butt wiggle worthy of the great Magic Mike himself, laughing as the ladies catcalled and whistled after him, first while he was still in Higher Grounds, then all the way across the street to Queen of Tarts where his clothes were mercifully waiting.

Lili

✆ ☆ ↩ ☑ ⋮

Re: Re: Re: Re: Re: Column Feedback

Submissions <submissions@mansplanations.mvdaily.org>
To: Annabelle Lyons <a.lyons@mountainviewuniversity.edu>

It's not that your points don't have merit. I've sat with a sobbing twenty-year-old going through heartbreak, so even the frontlines of love are not a mystery to me.

You, however, are leaving out another part of the equation.

What about soul mates?

What about the feeling of being so completely seen and understood by another person that you know that this is the individual you were destined to be with?

What about fate?

Lovingly yours,

Mansplanations

P.S. Please note the restraint displayed by not making a joke out of the word cocktails in your email.

Lili felt electric, scurrying around the house before Dominic got there, but the current was less excited than nervous. 2097 Maplewood was her pride and joy, yet the home that usually felt spacious enough now seemed to be closing in around her.

She owned property in her twenties. Not a lot of people could say that.

But Dominic Moore could too, plus a whole lot more. Dom would probably enter her 1236 square feet in disgust, seeing Lili's biggest accomplishment in life so far as a claustrophobic shack. His mansions probably all had golden bidets and cashmere toilet paper. He probably washed his face with purified water from a crystal faucet and boiled his pasta in Evian. Lili would bet that his living room was bigger than her entire house, including the backyard.

Dom wasn't used to using a side table as a dining table, or sitting with his knees both pointed to one side in the bathroom because there wasn't enough room for the toilet. He would probably set one foot inside her "custom" kitchen and forever think Lili insane for choosing that space over the luxury galley he'd bought for his grandma.

But as Lili looked across her kitchen counter, surveying the ingredients waiting for her and Dom to get their hands on, she felt nothing but pride.

Seeing it with fresh eyes now, there was zero mystery as to why Lili had chosen her kitchen over the stunner at Queen of Tarts. Yes, the other space was bigger and more elegant, outfitted with every accouterment imaginable, all stainless steel or state of the art.

But this was Lili's home, and she loved her kitchen.

Every inch of her small space had been designed with intention. She'd expanded the original galley when she bought the house into the dining area, making plenty of room for full-sized appliances and prep space. Until this moment, Lili had never questioned her choices, and she wasn't about to let Dominic Moore make her feel differently now.

There was a knock on the front door.

Stan, the flame red eight-quart KitchenAid stand mixer that she would never trade-in for a fancier model, got a pat on his head as Lili reassured him. "Don't worry. You're still my main man."

She opened the door with a flourish, and a dramatic sweep of her hand across the (tiny) living room, presenting her place as the palatial estate that it wasn't.

"Welcome to Travis Castle. Please be careful that you don't fall inside the moat."

Dom smiled and stepped past Lili into the house. She expected him to smart off about the size of her supposed citadel, but he kept any wisecracks to himself. Surprisingly, he seemed to be looking around with genuine interest.

After a moment of taking it all in, he sighed with what sounded almost like appreciation. "Your space is really warm." He nodded at the couch. "Is that as comfy as it looks? I could definitely fall asleep to some Netflix on that."

Lili was suddenly more lost than she wanted to admit. She had no idea if he was making fun of her right now. Was warm a synonym for tiny? Or comfy a nice way of saying old? Was he hitting on her with a reference to *Netflix and chilling* on her couch, or making fun of her and laughing inside right now?

She looked at him, found his face open, and decided to give him the benefit of the doubt. Lili was being unfair. His words were kind, and his manner gentle. Dom always looked great, so today was no exception, but he was also coming across as more relaxed than Lili had ever seen him.

She led him into the kitchen.

He gave the room another appreciative once-over but kept any and all comments to himself.

"I've been looking at the list from Upper Crust, and I think that beyond making meringue, I can be especially helpful when it comes to baking straight cake. Louise is a powerhouse when it comes to decoration, so your role will likely be to focus on getting the basics done while I work on the more complex aspects of your ... What?"

Dom was wearing the ghost of a smile, some undefinable smirk he refused to explain. "It's nothing." He shook his head. "Please. Continue."

Lili wasn't sure that she liked his smug expression, even though it was totally adorable, but they had a job to do so she might as well get started.

"We'll be covering the basics today. Remember how we had Stats together?"

"Of course. Mrs. Malakar. That woman shouldn't be teaching."

"If my baking is Stats then yours right now is—"

"Algebra?"

"—long division."

"Harsh." Dom nodded to himself.

"You understand basic numbers—"

"Thanks for your confidence in me."

"—so that's like your simple ingredients." Lili swept a hand across the table, quickly naming each one before reminding him (probably for the first time) that dry and wet ingredients should be kept separate. She pointed to the eggs, butter, and cream. "I've had these out for a couple of hours now so they can reach room temperature before

I start using them. That makes it easier to mix everything evenly and helps us get a more uniform texture."

Dom gave her another quiet little smirk, but Lili ignored that too.

She started prepping a bowl and ordered Dom to butter the pan and turn on the oven. There was a smooth grace to the way he worked that Lili couldn't help but admire, and he seemed intent on hearing every word out of her mouth, but he wouldn't stop smirking. Lili couldn't stop wondering whether she wanted to rip that grin off his face or French kiss it off of him.

"Now we get to the math," Lili went on with her lesson. "I said long division because, by the time you get there, you already know addition, subtraction, and multiplication. It's not that cooking requires a lot of math; it's that numbers never lie. In math, the wrong numerals will always lead you to the wrong answers. If you get your measurements wrong while baking, your desserts won't ever taste as delicious."

"How strong do you think this math analogy actually is?"

"We're starting with sugar cookies. A simple recipe that's all about measurements."

"All this constant talk about measurements ..." Dom shook his head at her. "I'd swear you had a foot fetish."

"Jesus, Dom." She shifted on her feet, still no idea whether or not he was flirting. "Aren't you like a stats wizard or something? You should like this."

He shook his head. "Never said I didn't."

"Before spooning flour or powdered sugar into our measuring cup, we'll fluff up the ingredient." Lili demonstrated. "This will ensure that there are no clumps or air pockets."

"Fluff the ingredient." Dom nodded.

Still with that smirk.

"When measuring brown sugar, we want to compress it into the measuring cup." She showed him. "See how I'm pressing down firmly with my fingers while filling the cup?"

Another nod. "Firmly with your fingers."

For some (obvious) reason, certain phrases she would say sounded titillating on the other side of her lips. Especially the ones he repeated. Like *taste* and *knead* and *salty*.

Lili kept ignoring the double entendre, even after the kitchen got a hundred degrees hotter than the oven. The words were burning, but with all the measuring and fluffing and mixing of wet and dry ingredients, there was also a bit of touching that was kinda-sorta driving her crazy.

Her skin on his.

His skin on hers.

Glances that always felt stolen.

The cookies went in the oven, and they moved onto a simple chocolate cake. But once that cake was baking, and they were waiting for it to finish, their work area already cleaned up as it needed to be for now, there was a moment of aching quiet.

Dom used it to brush a bit of flour off Lili's nose. Then her cheek. Finally, her chin as she shuddered and told herself yet again that the constant chills were from all those nonexistent changes in temperature.

The clock ticked extra loud in the quiet kitchen, their flirting having suddenly withered from increasingly physical to silent and awkward.

"Coffee?" she suggested.

"I would drink your coffee at bedtime."

Lili flushed as she made it, then led him into her living room.

She took the loveseat, then Dom went to the couch, apparently to get a firsthand account of its comfiness.

But his butt had barely touched the cushion before he was bouncing back up, making it over to Lili's corner bookshelf in two long strides.

"No way." He pulled her yearbook down from the shelf, already flipping through it on his way back to the couch.

"Are you looking for a picture of me in the beaver costume?"

"No." He shook his head, still looking. "I want to see what I wrote in your yearbook. Maybe get a clue as to why you hate me so much."

"I don't hate you, and you never signed my yearbook."

Dom stopped flipping pages and looked up. "Why not?"

"Because I never asked you to."

A long and awkward moment rolled like a tumbleweed between them.

He started flipping through the pages again, this time pausing at the thing Lili had been afraid of him looking for in the first place.

Dom was laughing as he pointed at the picture of Lili as the Mountain View Beaver, but there wasn't a single note of cruelty in the sound.

"You should embrace the Beaver Girl thing. Sometimes it's easier to be *in* on the joke than the *butt* of the joke."

Maybe it was all the baking they'd done in the kitchen or the warm scents of sugar and butter that kept rolling into the living room and hanging around in a mouthwatering fog, but for some reason, Lili felt compelled to actually look at a picture she always hurried by, thanks to all the ways it gnarled her stomach.

Now she looked at that same photo with a sense of detached curiosity. The pic had captured her mid-jumping jack, the crowd behind her positively bonkers.

"You were the best beaver *ever*." Dom looked up from the yearbook to meet her gaze. "Way better than Zed, and Zed was great before his accident."

Lili shrugged, wondering if she should change the subject to something more comfortable, like maybe her menstrual cycle.

He seemed to sense her discomfort and changed the subject for her. "When did you open High Grounds? *Why* did you open High Grounds?"

"I opened it after my parents died."

"What? Your parents died? I'm sorry ... when did that happen?"

"Two years after graduation. They were together ... in a head-on collision, during Hell Week. Some freshman at MVU bailed on his hazing, but only after drinking enough to die of alcohol poisoning. He survived but killed someone else, going the wrong way on a one-way while headed to his dorm."

"I'm so sorry," he told her again.

"My parents were always there for everything. Losing them felt like it ruined me. I knew they would die one day, eventually, but their passing was *way* ahead of schedule, and so sudden. I had a really hard time. Never felt sadder in my life." Lili sighed as she looked at the evidence of their work. "Baking gave me solace."

"Oh."

"I wasn't in Mountain View at the time."

"Where were you?"

"Living just off campus at Loyola. I quit college and moved back to town. They weren't here anymore, but I felt a little closer to them here."

She pulled the yearbook from his hands and tucked it safely back on the shelf before continuing. "I wanted to start a bakery because there hasn't been one in Mountain View since Sugar Boogie closed. I didn't have enough to buy the full dream, so I'm renting to own with my little coffee shop. Opening Higher Grounds was a nice start, but I've been saving to upgrade the place into a bakery since day one."

"Well, you know my dad died, and my mom figured I wasn't worth the effort of sticking around when she could be mourning with some loser actuary in Florida." He shrugged. "My story's different, but I still understand how painful it can be. And I swear, I couldn't be any sorrier about nabbing your spot in this Upper Crust thing. Eleanor had obviously promised you that chance, and you were clearly planning on those funds for your bakery. What happened wasn't fair."

"It's okay. My dream will come true when it's supposed to come true. At least I love running the place. I get to talk to people all day, every day, and for a lot of them, I'm the person they're happiest to see in the morning. For a few of my customers, I'm also the nicest. Being the reason for that many people smiling feels good."

A little laugh. "Even if it is sort of like I'm peddling a drug—my little junkies are always happy to see me!"

Oops. And *double oops* because the scandal wasn't even his fault.

Now she saw that the story Louise told her had to be true.

Lili was about to apologize for misjudging him, but a ding from the kitchen let them know that their cake was ready and that her moment was over for now.

Dom

D om slipped from one cluster of shadows into another.

He drew several deep breaths, inhaling and exhaling as he waited for another perfect moment to make his next move. Looking back and forth several times to make sure that the coast was clear, he darted across the courtyard to the back door of the gym.

Good thing he was dressed in all black, just in case somebody spotted him.

He rapped his knuckles in a perfect execution of the secret knock he and Titus started using freshman year. Dom hadn't used it since they were seniors.

The door swung open immediately.

Titus stood there, dressed in khakis, an Adidas polo shirt, and his coach's jacket. He eyed Dom up and down, shaking his head as he turned around and walked away from the door, talking to his friend without looking back over his shoulder.

"What the hell is wrong with you? This ain't a secret mission. I'm the coach! I can waltz in and grab the thing whenever I want to."

"But it's a lot more fun if it's a secret mission," Dom replied as he stepped through the locker room doorway behind Titus. "Do you remember the time we filled the hallways with like *hundreds* of cups of water?"

"Total mayhem. No one's feet were dry for the rest of the day."

"How about when Alberto took all that grass from his compost pit, and we put it in Caleb's locker?"

"EPIC!" Titus bobbed his head in enthusiasm. "Punkass got surprised by some nature, and he deserved it." But then his head started to shake. "Alas, poor Micky did not."

"How could we know he was allergic to grass? He played on the stuff every day."

"Who the hell is allergic to grass?" Titus asked like he still couldn't believe it. Apparently, there was a big difference between grass and a grass bomb.

Dom's phone buzzed in his pocket. He took it out and glanced at the screen. "Sorry. I just need a second."

Titus nodded and kept walking toward the locker.

Dom stopped to take the call from his agent. "Hey, Angelica."

"Good news and great news," she said.

"Give me the good news first."

"You've been shortlisted for the commentator position with SportsBar. It's down to you and one other guy."

"That sounds like the great news." Dom could barely believe it. "Unless the great news is that there's something seriously wrong with the other guy."

"There might be. Looks like the other guy might be a little too squeaky clean. Word from my man at the network is that he's more boring than amateur golf. Vanilla, but all base and no extract."

"I get it. They like me for my scandal. Awesome."

"They're eager to hire football's newest bad boy, Dom. Are you telling me that's a bad thing? It's a miracle this little mishap of yours is playing in our favor."

"It would be nice to land the gig based on my merit."

"This business isn't a meritocracy, sweetie. Deals are made when you're hot, who cares what gets the fire going? It's not like you murdered someone."

"I'm glad to know where your line is."

"This is show business. Do you want the gig or not?"

"Of course, I want the gig ... not like I have any other prospects ..."

"Is that my *thank you*?"

"That's what the percentage is for, Angelica. Get me a gig that recognizes me for who I am, and I'll find a new way to thank you above and beyond the plenty you're already making off of me."

Dom hung up and found Titus looking at him.

"All chill in Hollywood?"

"It's not Hollywood," Dom said.

"This that commentating job in Chicago?"

"Yep."

"Sounds like Hollywood to me. So, what's the problem? They only want to hire you because of your little scuffle with the boys in blue?"

"Yep," Dom said again.

"And it don't matter that you'll still be making dump trucks of money and getting all the love?"

"I just want to care about what I'm doing."

"Like I've told you a bunch of times, you could always get a job coaching here."

"And like I've answered you every time, thanks but no thanks. That feels like it would be ... I don't know ..."

"A step backward?" Titus shook his head, smiling because there were no hard feelings here. "That's what you always say, even if you've yet to use the actual words. I hear you, man. I'm just not sure that you're right."

"If I promise to think about thinking about the offer, do you promise to stop bringing it up?"

"I do. If you really promise to consider it."

"I'm promising to think about thinking about it," he clarified.

"I'll take what I can get." Titus nodded to the locker. "You ready for this?"

Dom nodded back at him.

Titus opened the locker, and Dom laughed at the sight of their prize.

The Mountain View beaver suit was more worn than he remembered, it looked like each of the seasons in between his last year in high school and now had aged the suit by half a decade. Its tail flopped down as if pulled low by an invisible anchor, droopy like the deadest of weight. The fur was clumpy, and though none was missing, its body still had the feeling of patchwork.

And yet, the beaver still made him smile. Dom could practically feel all of the memories inside the hollow walls of that body.

This mascot costume was perfect for his plans.

"Does this have to do with Lili?"

"Of course it does. Do you know another Beaver Girl?"

"Is there something going on between you two?"

"Not at all." Dom shook his head, wondering if he wanted there to be. "Liliana Travis does not like the idea of dating a professional football player, or an ex-football player, or whatever I am now."

"Yeah, but she might be interested in dating *you*."

He shook his head again. "We're just having fun."

"Okay." Titus nodded, grinning. "Sure."

"Yes, she's hot and funny, but I'm telling you, Ti, it's a no-go. Besides, even if there was something there, I'm about to move. Chicago, remember?"

Still nodding, still grinning.

"Whatever." Dom shook his head for the third time. "I like the competition. It's for Louise and her bakery."

"Sure." Titus managed to grin even wider. "It's for Louise."

Lili

Re: Re: Re: Re: Re: Re: Column Feedback

Annabelle Lyons <a.lyons@mountainviewuniversity.edu>
To: <submissions@mansplanations.mvdaily.org>

Dear Mansplainer,

This would be more interesting if your side of things held up. Unfortunately, even after all of these exchanges, you've yet to write anything with any value.

Are you as embarrassed as you should be?

Apart from belittling me and my course, you haven't actually given me any scientific evidence on your stance in this argument.

Please tell me … what is your evidence for fate?

Kind Regards,

Annabelle

MOUNTAIN VIEW
UNIVERSITY

ANNABELLE LYONS
Associate Professor of Psychology
MountainViewUniversity.com

Lili swung her Prius onto Main Street and then pulled into a parking spot in front of Higher Grounds, two over from where she usually parked. *What the shit?* — she saw Dom's McLaren sitting in her usual spot and was stricken with a set of questions: *Does that mean he's in the coffee shop instead of the bakery?* And, *Was Lili really bothered ... or happy about it?*

After Summer opened with her keys that first time, Lili realized there was no reason she shouldn't be letting Higher Grounds' newest employee run with the responsibility.

Maybe now she did have a reason, seeing as Summer wasn't even inside and had left the Higher Grounds door unlocked. And definitely no Dom.

The bell jingled, and the door opened again behind her, but it still wasn't her wayward employee. Instead, Annabelle Lyons stomped into the shop, holding a newspaper, practically trembling with barely bridled rage.

"He printed our emails."

"What?" Lili moved into the shop, checking to see that Summer had at least turned on the espresso machine before abandoning her post. Annabelle would *definitely* need her Americano.

"Well, not all of them." She shook her head. "But most of our exchange, which I thought was private, is now out there for all the world to see."

"Is there something you don't want people to see?"

"It's the principle of the thing."

"Did you ask him not to print them?"

"No." Annabelle sank into a chair. "And there's some bullshit disclaimers on every email about any and all communications being potentially printed in the column. I just didn't think for a second that he included ours in that."

Lili went through the motions of preparing her favorite customers' drink, trying to figure out how to tell her *who* was behind the *Mansplanations* column.

"You know." She placed the cup gingerly in front of the still fuming Annabelle. "It sounds more and more like this guy probably isn't a student at all. Like maybe he's more *on your level?*"

"It's way too early for insults Lili." Annabelle cradled her cup, then looked around the coffee shop. "Christ, you're not even open yet, are you."

"I'm always open for a friend."

Annabelle dropped a bill that was almost certainly way too large for the single Americano into the tip jar.

"I'm going to catch this fucker at his own game. He has no idea who he's dealing with." Her eyes flashed. "Wait until he watches my next lecture."

Lili raised her hand for a high five. "Stronger together!"

Well, *not always*, she thought a second later as Summer came in, smiling and laughing up at Higher Grounds' next customer.

Or whatever Dominic Moore's official designation might be.

He was a (former?) NFL star for sure, and right now that baller was regaling Lili's employee with a bit of eager animation, miming some epic play from his glory days that Lili could not have possibly cared less about.

Summer clearly did, twirling a finger into the ends of her long blonde hair while looking up at Dom all doe-eyed.

"That win was sweeter than most because the entire team was *sure* we would lose, Coach included. We weren't just down, I'm telling you, we were *out*."

"Until Dominic Moore got control of the ball!" Summer batted her lashes.

Metaphorically.

Lili had only been in Higher Grounds for ten minutes (the coffee shop that she owned, where she should get to make all the rules and not have to suffer any unexpected and certainly unwanted emotional surprises), and she was already irritated. Not just because Dom was talking to the young and stunning Summer, pretty and blonde and totally the kind of woman the Sports Illustrated cover boy was probably used to being with. Seeing the two of them talking was yet another painful reminder that Mountain View was both the place where he was born and raised, while also being just another pit stop for the little prince who had always been too good for his kingdom.

Dominic Moore had always been about the game. Nothing had changed. While getting to know him might *seem* like a lot fun right now, Lili knew in her heart that it wasn't a good idea.

But then he turned and saw her, stopped talking to Summer mid-sentence, and shined that sunshine of a smile right on her.

Lili was suddenly ice cream in July, melting all over herself, furious at her obliviousness for taking her frozen confection into the unrelenting sun.

"I'll tell you the rest of the story later ... but it involves a beaver and Lili getting full-on tackled," he said to Summer before turning to Lili and calling out from across the coffee shop. "I have your next bet!"

"Oh yeah?" Like she actually cared about whatever nonsense he was about to spout ... or that gorgeous body he kept wrapped like a present in athleisure wear.

"I thought that last bet was to pay me back for your baking lessons."

"Nope." He shook his stupid head, and she ignored the slight dimple in his cheek. "That was just a fringe benefit. Our bets are a whole other thing, and now it's my turn. Unless you're afraid?"

He gave her a shrug. "In that case, we can call it all off … just as long as you're cool with declaring me the winner."

"I'm happy to declare you the winner of some very unfortunate publicity." Lili made a face. "Sorry about that."

"Low blow." And for a blink it seemed like that might have actually hurt him. But then it was gone. "Do you surrender?"

"Only my parking spot," she replied. "What's the bet?"

He grinned. "Follow me."

Dom led Lili outside to his (her) parking spot, then to the passenger seat of his Batmobile. She was already shaking her head before he finished opening the door.

"Nope. Uh-uh. No way." Just in case it wasn't clear: "Not on your life."

"It's your old Mountain View Beaver mascot costume," Dom explained, as if Lili was blind, or unable to smell.

"I know what it is! What makes you think I want to see that thing again?"

"I'm sure you don't. That's why it's a bet."

"I hear you," said Lili with a nod, "but also, you can totally go jump in a lake."

"*Jump in a lake?* My grandma used to say that when I was little."

"Mine too. Where do you think I got it? Oh, the things we can learn from the elder generations. Thanks for the reminiscing, I'm outta—"

But Dom grabbed Lili by the arm and swung her back around before she could scurry back into her shop. He held her gently, only intending to keep her rooted in place. Yet his touch told Lili another unfortunate truth.

She loved the feeling, and wasn't eager to leave it.

"Of course, you don't have to go anywhere near that thing if you don't want to," Dom promised. "I'll drive it right to the gymnasium and hand the costume back over to Titus. *But*, doing this might be good for you. It might finally give you the chance to flip the script on Beaver Girl. Instead of being the joke, you can change the conversation and embrace your past."

"I don't know …" She really didn't.

"Do this right, and it could mean a lot of publicity for Higher Grounds." He shrugged again. "I know it's not exactly winning the Upper Crust Challenge, but it might raise your profile enough that it pushes your little coffee shop that much closer to becoming a bakery."

"Umm … how?"

"You dance. Give out samples. Make it a party in the street." Dom grinned. "Give them something to talk about. No such thing as bad publicity, right?"

Dom had a point, and she wanted to hear him, to believe him, to visualize all the glorious things that might happen if she got over her fears long enough to step inside that stinky suit of furry armor and wage a battle of hilarity with herself like she used to, temporarily forgetting the Liliana Travis inside the costume to fully inhabit that mascot instead. Lili had brought the crowds to roaring life back in high school. Of course, she could do it again now.

But even the best of all that was still in her head. Reality had her paralyzed. She was frozen in front of the car that surely cost at least two times her house, under the unrelenting heat of this quarterback's gaze.

Dom was pillow-soft as he slowly let her go. As he looked into her eyes, he said, "Liliana. I bet you won't put on that beaver suit and parade up and down Main Street while serving this town's best coffee to your fans."

"More like *your* fans. Same as when they all came to see you in the thong."

Lili was suddenly lit up like someone had plugged her into a live socket. Not just at the memory of Dom on exhibition in that little lash of fabric, with Kiss the Cook inscribed across the crotch. She was starting to feel enlivened by this newest bet.

She looked back at the beaver suit, then over to Dom with a sigh. "Are you going to help me get into that thing?"

He grinned again. "I feel like I'm helping a superhero into her costume."

Ten minutes later, Lili's body was entombed in the costume, and she took one last long look in the mirror before donning the mask for the first time since Dom removed it on the football field all those years ago.

With the Mountain View Beaver's head back on her shoulders, the bevy of aromas assaulted her even harder, pounding her with memories, not bad like she had expected, but *much* stronger.

Lili was reminded of the girl she used to be. So naive, believing so desperately in her sense of anticipation that it might as well have been a religion. If she could just get herself to that final victory party, she would have the courage to ask her high school's superstar quarterback out.

Part of her wanted to go back in time and let that stupid girl know how delusional she was. But another part of Lili — and this one was laughing hysterically — wanted to yell at the top of her lungs to that very same girl:

ONE DAY YOU'LL GET TO HAVE SEX WITH THAT GUY!

And not just when he was quarterbacking for a small-town high school, but after he had become famous in the NFL. Sure, it had only been a one-night-stand, but even the only in that sentence was sexy.

Sex was sex.

The beaver suit was the beaver suit.

And if Lili was in the thing, then she might as well embrace it.

"Will this work?" Summer came running into the back room, giggling along with her question. She held the homemade sash aloft, the words *HIGHER GROUNDS* emblazoned across the front in Summer's neat block letters.

"It's perfect." Lili took the sash and draped it over her neck. "Now coffee me."

They went to the bar where Summer loaded her up with the first batch of coffees; the gorgeous mini cinnamon mochas seemed to perfectly match the beaver suit.

Lili tried not to think about how much all that free coffee would be costing her. Then she thought about her supplier and laughed.

Summer opened the front door.

And Lili held her beaver's head high as she walked out onto Main Street.

Dom

D om had put the odds of Lili agreeing to his bet at 50-50 when Titus handed him the costume. And that's where they stayed when she first saw that big heap of beaver piled in his car. He had thought for a moment that she might pass out, given how fast the color had drained from her cheeks. But by the time she walked back into Higher Grounds with the Mountain View Beaver balled up in her arms, Dom was eighty-percent certain she would decide to go through with it.

Yet even that confidence didn't prepare him for the sight of her swaggering out of Higher Grounds like she was born to be a human-sized beaver. He had been leaning against the McLaren while scrolling on his phone. He nearly slid down to the ground and smacked his ass on the concrete as Lili shimmied up the street, wiggling her big beaver butt while waving a tray filled with coffees in the air, somehow managing not to spill a drop of brew.

Dom was delighted that Lili had really gone through with it, and that there was already a noticeable reaction, with people (potential customers) stopping on both sides of the street, pointing and waving, or generally whooping along with all the sudden commotion.

A couple of cars honked as they passed before a third and a fourth pulled over in tandem. Lili had already handed out her first round of coffees and was sashaying back toward Higher Grounds, presumably for reinforcements, when Dom recognized a glaring oversight on his part.

While the Mountain View Beaver was *practically* dancing up and down Main Street, it was hard for her to feel the full rhythm without any music.

He ran across the street and into Queen of Tarts. He fished out the Bluetooth speakers from under the counter that had been put there by Titus when he was helping to set up the bakery, rushing to beat Lili outside.

Dom ran into the back room, where Titus was building shelves for Louise. "Yo, Ti! You got 'Can't Touch This' on your phone?"

Titus shrugged. "I think only the communists don't."

"Follow me!" Dom didn't wait for his buddy to answer, grabbing him by the arm and dragging him outside.

"What the hell?" Titus started to laugh.

Lili had beaten them. She was still almost dancing while lavishly offering coffees to her passerby. This time she was fixed to the spot in front of Higher Grounds. Summer stood beside her, holding stacked trays of reinforcements.

The crowd was multiplying, already doubled at least, surely about to triple or more. The honking had increased as well, now at a swelling echo.

Dom set the Bluetooth speakers on the roof of his car and nodded to Titus. His buddy nodded back at him and then launched an old familiar song.

The opening moments played, and Lili froze in place.

Dom swallowed hard, wondering if maybe he'd gone too far.

The marching band always played this song at half-time. And the Mountain View Beaver — specifically Lili, it had been her innovation after taking over for Zed — had a special dance, the "Beaver Boogie," or so it was called. Once upon a time, the crowd would join her but this random assortment of folks couldn't know about the boogie.

The opening bars to "Can't Touch This" were already over, with Lili still frozen in place. But a few beats later, that big beaver had turned toward Dom, shaking back and forth a few times before Lili finally nodded inside it and stacked her tray in Summer's arms.

She started to dance, deciding it was time for a full-out Beaver Boogie. And just like in high school, the people all around her couldn't help but love the performance, proving their glee with whoops and hollers and all of that clapping along, despite their ignorance of the actual moves.

"I'll be back," Dom told Titus with a grin before darting over to Summer and gently taking the coffees from her hands. "I've got this. You should go inside and help anyone who wants to pay for a drink. A bunch of customers will be coming."

Summer smiled wide and (Dom thought) tried to smell him. "Great idea!"

Lili seemed to nod over at him while executing a perfect moonwalk with a spin, then straight into the sprinkler. Behind that big mask, he had no idea what she might be thinking. Dom knew what he was supposed to do, and did it with gusto, emptying his trays one coffee at a time and directing people into Higher Grounds for a look around:

"Not just the best coffee shop in Mountain View, but my favorite in the world, and I've been all over."

Dom repeated the phrase every time he had a fresh crop of newcomers who hadn't heard it yet. Some stopped to ask for his autograph, but he politely nudged them into Higher Grounds. Soon he ran out of coffees, and Summer was too slammed inside for Dom to expect any more sample cups.

Lili had fulfilled her end of the bet, so the show should be ending soon.

But, Beaver Girl wasn't done.

Her dancing got even wilder as a crowd closed in around her.

Once "Can't Touch This" ended, DJ Titus had #blessed the beaver with back-to-back tracks from Bruno Mars, starting with "Uptown Funk" and ending with "24Karat Magic". The opening notes of "Bad Romance" were now bleating from the Bluetooth, and Beaver Girl was getting her Gaga on.

Dom was no expert on dances, but he thought he recognized the Roger Rabbit and the Running Man, before Lili jumped from the 80s to the aughts with some Stanky Legg, finishing with a sweeping dab and an impressive display of the splits. Dom had no idea how she pulled it all off. It had been a decade since the last time without any practice. She must be dying inside that suit.

Lili rose, laughing loud enough to hear, despite the mask and noise. She bowed to the crowd before offering a curt nod to Dom and retreating inside Higher Grounds to a still swelling round of clapping and cheers.

"That was baller." Titus clapped him on the shoulder as he passed, following the crowd into the coffee shop.

His work done here, at least for now, Dom turned from Higher Grounds with a smile. He retrieved his speakers, then walked across the street and back into Queen of Tarts.

Louise was standing at the window.

"Did you see all that?" he asked.

"Even if I hadn't, I'm sure I would've heard it." Louise laughed, but there were wilted notes in the sound. "They probably heard it on the university campus."

"You saw the dancing?"

"Of course, I saw the dancing," Louise replied.

But Dom didn't understand. She was acting like Lili had been leading a funeral procession instead of giving the world a worthy sequel to Beaver Girl.

He let another long moment of silence settle between them, but after seeing something on her face he'd never seen before, Dom could no longer keep the unsettling questions inside.

"Is everything okay?"

She shook her head and looked at him sadly. "I just got a call from Dr. Morris."

"Oh?" There was nothing else he could say. Dom knew she would want him to listen right now and wait for her to get it all out in her time.

"My blood pressure is worrying him." *Again*, she didn't say. "He says I need to take it easy over the next few weeks."

Dom rushed over to his grandma and wrapped an arm around her. "Are you okay? I mean, of course, you're okay you're always okay, but is there anything I can do?"

"You're doing plenty." She eased out from under her arms. "You know how doctors love to make a big deal about everything and invite you back to their office for another five-minute chat and a three-figure invoice. I'll be fine."

There was a *but* coming, and Dom didn't want to wait for it.

"*But?*"

Louise smiled. "But I can't do the Upper Crust Challenge."

"Of course." Dom nodded, that was disappointing but understandable. "I'll just tell Eleanor that we're out. She'll probably—"

"No." Louise shook her head. "I don't want us to drop out. Not at all." She shook her head again as if needing Dom to know that she double-triple meant what she was about to say. "Even if we don't win, just entering the Challenge is can't miss publicity for Queen of Tarts. Plus, I'd really like to see those kids get their park upgraded. At least the town gets something out of Eleanor being a bitch. So, you know what that means."

"Louise, no … I'm not a baker."

"But you *can* bake. You said you wanted to help me, right? This bakery was your idea, so—"

"And you said I was doing plenty already. Please, isn't there anything else? How about a full-page ad in the Times? I can—"

"You've been baking ever since you were seven years old. Stop being a baby about this. Do it for the kids."

He laughed. "That's not what you told Lili when you made her give me those 'baking lessons' that I 'needed so much.'"

"That poor girl needed a win. And speaking of, now that you're no longer my number two, you'll need a second yourself. I have someone perfect in mind."

She nodded, gesturing across the street at Higher Grounds, now buzzing with customers instead of just passersby.

Lili

Seriously?

Annabelle Lyons <a.lyons@mountainviewuniversity.edu>
To: <submissions@mansplanations.mvdaily.org>

Dear Mansplanations,

I was disappointed to see our emails splashed across your paper. A little warning would have been nice.

Kind Regards,

Annabelle

ANNABELLE LYONS
Associate Professor of Psychology
MountainViewUniversity.com

Lili felt … emboldened?

In truth, she wasn't quite sure how she felt because this feeling was new. It had been a groundbreaking day for her business. Including the cost of all those free samples, Higher Grounds had made more money than it ever had in a single day and even beat out a few of its slower *weeks* by an embarrassing amount.

The best thing about her accomplishment was that even though the totals were hardly a windfall, today's success felt repeatable. Not that exact thing, of course, Lili wasn't going to Beaver Boogie up and down Main Street every day. Plus, the beaver suit would have to go back to the high school, and the past, where it belonged.

But she now felt the courage to think differently. To push her marketing into places she probably wouldn't have pushed it before.

Maybe if she kept reinventing herself or reminding herself of all she used to be instead of sticking to the most comfortably curated parts, maybe she could make her dreams come true more consistently over time, instead of all at once with one sweeping sum like she'd been dreaming about.

"You look happy," Summer said.

And maybe it was due to her elevated mood, but Lili didn't hear or suspect or imagine anything untoward in Summer's observation at all.

"It was a great day!" Lili found herself laughing. "Thank you so much for everything." She handed Summer a $100 bill.

Summer took it with a grin. "Are you kidding me?"

"You totally earned it."

"But you already let me keep all of the tips."

"Fine." Lili held out her hand. "I'll take it back."

"Seriously: *thanks*."

"That's what I thought." Lili smiled. "Now get out of here."

Summer complied and left Lili to herself. She enjoyed the solitude for nearly a minute before the door, — which Summer should have locked on her way out — , swung open, and Dom entered Higher Grounds with a jingle.

He looked sheepish, his eyes on the floor as if tracking bread-crumbs. He probably felt bad, like maybe he'd pushed her too far.

Like right into the best day of her professional life.

"That was the best choreography for 'Bad Romance' that I've ever seen in my life." He whistled in faux admiration. "I hope you're not too mad at me for turning you into Beaver Girl again."

"I'm furry-ous. Get it?"

"Oh, I get it." He smiled. "So you're cool?"

"Like an ice cream sandwich." *Like an ice cream sandwich?* "It was great. Seriously. I'm totally going to get HBO Max now that I can afford it." She laughed. There was something seriously (giddily) wrong with her. "Just kidding. I already have HBO Max."

"Okay. I can't tell if you're laughing like you're watching *The Office*, or you're about to method act as the Joker."

"It was a great day. We made a bunch of money, hence my HBO Max joke—"

"That was a joke?"

"—and I actually got to own Beaver Girl for the first time. Just like you said. So, thanks for that. Did you see the Beaver Girl 2 video that Titus posted?"

"I did." He laughed, seemingly relieved that she had and that she wasn't mad about it. "How many sample cups did you give out?"

"I'm not sure …" Lili replied, embarrassed that she didn't have an answer.

"You have to know that, otherwise you can't know how much the stunt cost you versus how much it made." No response from Lili, so Dom kept going. "Let's assume they cost twenty cents each, the cups I mean, then a quick calculation on your expenditure added to the publicity of the Beaver Girl 2 video …" He appeared to be doing some mental math. "It's hardly precise, especially considering how much you don't know or are keeping secret from me—"

"I'm not—"

"Like your coffee source, for example. I'm guessing that you're still up at least—" another calculation "—$218.37 for today."

"You. Are. A. Nerd."

Dom shrugged.

Lili said, "Do you know how awesome it feels to get some representation as an ass-kicking Mountain View Beaver, instead of the one still lying on her back after getting tackled by some dumb football player?"

"That football player wasn't dumb." Dom shook his head. "But yes, I can imagine."

His whole body seemed to exhale. His smile became more natural. But then he said something that surprised her. "I need a favor."

"Oh? Yeah, sure. Probably ... what is it?"

"It's kind of a big one."

"I'm not posing with one of your Lambos."

"I don't even have a singular Lamborghini. And I don't need you to pose. It's just a regular favor."

"I thought you said it was a big one?" Lili scrunched her nose.

"Big, but not obscene."

"So my posing in front of your Lambo is obscene?"

Dom sighed. "I don't know how to get out of this ..."

"There's no way out!" Lili jabbed her finger in the air and laughed maniacally, — again because something was wrong with her. She even proved it: "*Mwa-ha-ha!*"

"Are you done?"

"I guess. So, even though it's totally my turn to like truth or dare you or do my side of the bet or whatever, you're here to ask me for a favor, like Amerigo Bonasera."

"Who?"

"The Undertaker."

"You're not helping." Dom shook his head.

Lili enjoyed his confusion. "That's the guy who came begging Don Corleone for a favor at the beginning of *The Godfather*. You're like him. Because you're asking me to grant you a favor now."

"It's not your daughter's wedding day."

"You don't know that. So, what do you need, Amerigo?"

"My grandma is sick."

"Oh," Lili said, instantly sobering. "I'm sorry to hear that. How sick is she?"

"It's not dire, but I think she's a lot sicker than she's willing to admit. She's definitely too sick for the Upper Crust Challenge." The rest of his sentence was a forty-one-word pileup: "I know it's a lot to ask since you were already replaced, and that sucked, and now it would suck with even more suction for you to have to represent your competitor, but—"

"I'd be happy to—" *help. And I don't see Louise as my competitor at all. I love Louise! She's my friend, and that's what friends are for!*

That's how Lili would have finished her thought if Dom hadn't kept barreling over her.

"—of course, I'll make it worth your while. Queen of Tarts doesn't need the prize money, just the exposure. So if we win, you could keep the entire pot!"

Then he stood there grinning at her, totally oblivious.

"So." She huffed. "Like I'm your charity case."

"No ..." Dom looked surprised and began to backpedal. "That's not what I meant it all. I just know it's a lot to ask, and didn't want to be unfair. You deserve to have participating in the contest be worth your while — what am I doing wrong here?"

And now he sounded defensive.

"Maybe it would be worth my while *just to participate in the contest*. You don't always have to buy everything, Dom. You act like you're asking me to climb a mountain. It's baking. In a contest. That I entered myself before you shined your light all over it. Because I wanted to. Because I like baking. It's not a lot to ask a *friend* to step in and help. *That's what friends are for.* Sure, it's a lot to ask of a competitor. You're right about that, Dom. So are we competitors, Dom? Or are we friends … Dom?"

"Why do you keep saying my name like that? Of course, we're friends!"

"Because I'm mad at you!"

"What did I do?" Bless his little athletic heart, he looked genuinely perplexed.

And Lili couldn't blame him. She drew a deep breath, then a whole bunch of truth came pouring right out of her. "I've never needed anyone else to give me any handouts, and I'm sure as hell not about to start taking them from some famous guy who thinks he can buy whatever he wants whenever he wants to, just because he—"

"I don't—" he tried.

"—wants it. I know how people like you operate, *Dom*. You think you own everyone. You think you're a god because that's what everyone is always telling you. I know what you really think of us yokels here in Mountain View. I know you think you're better than all the people you grew up with. The people *and* the town they came from. My dream—"

"I'm glad you—"

"—must seem so small to you. Fifty grand, and my biggest ambitions come true. I bet you have at least one *gadget* that cost more than that."

Lili could tell by his face that it was true. "I must seem *so tiny to you*." She turned her voice into a squeak. "It must be nice to just bestow whatever you want upon others. Well, I sure doth appreciate it, *Dom*."

She made her voice inexplicably British. "Excuse me, sir. Can I please save you from your drug problems or perhaps interest you in a bakery? And no—" she laughed like an Englishman "—I won't be needing to see you as a real person with real problems or agency in your life."

"Are you done?"

"No." But she was for now, and he knew it.

"I do see them as real people. I see everyone as a real person. The problem is that respect only goes one way! You know what the biggest problem in my life is?"

"Your scandal?"

"*Exactly*. But not the way you think. Even when the content is positive, it only covers me as a concept. A commodity. An idea. But never me as the real person you accuse me of not seeing in anyone else."

He shook his head almost violently. "It's not fair. And just because I'm famous, everyone thinks they own the details of my life. Even you don't see me as Dom, not like I want to be seen. You're always seeing the quarterback — the piece that's becoming a smaller and smaller part of me. I'm so sick of you throwing it in my face all the time. No matter what I do or how hard I try. Did it ever occur to you that I'm going through a major change in my life? That maybe I have *no idea* what to do, because the only thing I've ever done is football, or at least that's the only thing anyone ever slapped me on the back for or gave more than an ounce of shit about?"

He stopped, panting hard as he stared at her.

Lili stared back at him, her mouth hanging open, either because she wanted to spit one of a dozen furious retorts at him or because she suddenly desperately wanted him to close it with his lips.

"Maybe if you drop the magnanimous rich dude act, then people might—"

And suddenly, his mouth was on hers just like she wanted, surely because he knew she couldn't possibly mean all those terrible things she'd started to say.

Or already said.

Right now, she wanted to forget about all of it. Right now, his breath mingling with hers was like frosting on a perfect piece of cake.

Right now, she craved him with a righteous hunger.

His mouth was all over hers until she pulled her lips away to brush them all over his body, stopping only when he took her hand, leading Lili to the table, draped in a cloth covered with little yellow ducklings.

Her ass hit the top as she looked up into his eyes. "The door isn't locked."

"Do you want me to lock it?"

She shook her head. "I don't want you to leave me."

He had a condom out of his wallet, unpacked, and positioned in seconds. Lili ignored the stab of hurt that came with knowing he'd done this so many times before.

Right now, she reminded herself.

Lili stayed in the next several fast and glorious moments, basking in the aggression and passion, sweating out the anger and frustration and sexual tension that had been building steadily between them.

The climax was clearly cathartic for them both.

When they were done, Lili slid off the table, suddenly so aware that they were practically naked in her cafe on Main Street. She walked over and locked the door. "Sorry."

"Don't apologize. It's smart to lock your door after—"

"I wasn't apologizing for that." She smiled back at him. Awkwardly pulling her clothes back in place. "I'm sorry for snapping at you. Of course, I'll help with the Challenge. But I want to do it because Louise is my friend. You and me—" Lili gestured from herself to him. "We're just a ... two-night stand, I suppose. This was great. Really. Both times. But we won't be doing this again."

"Oh. Okay. Of course not." He shrugged. There was something on his face that Lili couldn't read. "I'm too rich and famous to date a townie after all."

"Whatever ... townies always win. And now that you finally have one on your side, you might find that you aren't losing for once."

She was still trying to read his face, wondering what he was thinking and wishing she was more fluent in Dom.

With the Upper Crust Challenge looming in front of them, it looked like Lili would have plenty of time to learn his personal language.

Dom

Dom was sipping coffee in the Queen of Tarts' back room.

Good coffee. Maybe even great, thanks to Lili and her vat. Plain old drip, and truly delicious. Now that they were working together, maybe—

"I'm not giving you the name of my supplier!"

"That's not what I was thinking." He laughed.

How did she know?

Lili set the two sacks of flour she had been carrying onto the counter in front of them, looking back at him with a knowing smile.

Dom would have wondered how she had been reading his mind. But the truth was obvious: Lili was one of *those* women. Like Louise, someone who was so tuned into everything all that time, few people could ever get anything past them.

The similarities between Lili and Louise made him unreasonably uncomfortable, and for a reason, Dom couldn't quite articulate to himself. Maybe it was because the two powerful women together were clearly going to run rings around him. Maybe it was because someone who could see right through him, who seemed to get him on a level that nobody else had in a long time (or maybe even ever), didn't seem to want him to stick around.

The one person in Mountain View who didn't get all starry-eyed over his success didn't even think he belonged here, in his hometown. And maybe she was right.

"It's totally what you were thinking," Lili finally replied. "You were goggling at the coffee vat. Now, let's get to it. I left Runa running the shop with Summer, so there's a pretty good chance that Higher Grounds is looking more like a singles club than a coffee shop by now."

"Is that a bad thing?"

"A lot of people coming in and taking up space without buying any coffee? It's not my favorite thing."

"If Runa's working, then Titus will be haunting the place. Not only will he happily pay for his coffee, but he'll also sweep the shop for anyone coming in just to talk to Runa."

"Except for himself." Lili looked to the whiteboard she and Louise had set up with The List, including all of the baking competition's possible categories. The Upper Crust Challenge was a two-day, two-dessert event, but random assignments turned it into a roll of the dice every time.

Possible Baking Categories in the Upper Crust Challenge

- Cakes (layer cakes, cupcakes, snack cakes, roulades ... even cheesecakes?)
- Candy (caramels, chocolates, gummies, misc. confections)
- Cookies
- Pastry (shortcrust, filo, choux, flaky, and puff)
- Custard
- Frozen and combined desserts

Lili had apparently copied The List word for word from Louise. Dom had made some calculations of his own, neatly lettered on the other side of the whiteboard.

"Louise said that baking is *always* a part of the contest. She thinks that between what I already know and what I was able to teach you, we definitely have that part down."

"That's great to hear," Dom replied with a smirk.

Lili ignored his bravado and continued. "The competition is tomorrow. So that means we only have today left for practice. We should decide on how to spend that time. Any thoughts?"

"Oh yeah. Plenty."

Dom walked to the whiteboard, flipped it over to the opposite side, and proudly showed Lili what he had been working on.

"That looks complicated," she said.

"Oh. Sorry. You must not be the Liliana Travis I used to know in Stats." He shrugged. "I guess I'll just have to explain it."

He pointed at the (simple) graph. "This shows the number of times that different categories have been chosen in the past. I've been digging through a bunch of the data from prior years and competitions."

"What's the difference?"

"You're not impressed." He shrugged again.

"Did you watch game tapes too?" Lili laughed.

But to Dom, it wasn't a joke. "Of course. Haven't you?"

Lili thought about it, and was surprised to realize that, yes, she had in a way. "I watch the Challenge every year, and a couple of times, I watched the recording more than once. And the one with the sugar butterflies, I think I watched about ten times." Lili laughed at how silly that sounded out loud.

He laughed back, hoping that it sounded like he was laughing *with* rather than *at* her. Dom was also wondering how much longer this weirdness between them was going to last, now that they'd had sex not just once but twice, with that second time like lighter fuel poured onto a fire.

At least the teasing seemed to help.

"Nerd." Dom shook his head in mock sympathy.

"Said the dude with the graph."

But his graph was great, and she knew it. Dom had mapped the most recent events, along with established patterns charted across the Upper Crust's entire history.

"Okay, that is pretty cool, once you explained it all," she conceded. "But you should know that your graphing skills are a little too ... *neat*."

"What's that supposed to mean? There isn't such a thing as *too neat*." He pointed at the graph. "I didn't even use a ruler."

"Exactly. Anyone who can make lines that straight without a ruler ..." She shrugged. "I'm just saying, you were probably the kind of kid who never ever made poopie in his diaper."

"What?"

"I'm calling you anal-retentive, quarterback. I guess they don't make footballers read Freud?"

He sighed dramatically. "Here Ego again."

Lili meant to laugh but snorted instead. "That was fast."

"I get that from playing football. So—" Dom redirected their attention to the graph. "It looks like we're most likely to get either pastry or chocolate confection."

"Either one of 'em give you the sweats?" Louise asked Lili as she entered the room.

Lili almost looked scared. "I've never worked with chocolate before, but choux pastry is—"

"The bane of your existence," nodded Louise. "I remember you telling me when you helped with my meringue. The shells crack and make 'em hard to work with. Maybe we start there since that's always been hard for you?"

"I don't know …" Dom didn't want to disagree, but Louise's reasoning felt off to him. "I think we can handle the choux pastry if it comes up, but neither of us has *any* experience with chocolate."

"You're the choux master now?" Lili laughed. "Louise is right. I'll have a panic attack if we get choux pastry. So—"

"Do you really want to work with one of the most infamously difficult ingredients for the first time on a televised competition? And why *haven't* you worked with chocolate?"

Lili shrugged. "I guess because it's not really baking. I always envisioned selling cakes and scones and pastries. I can't imagine having chocolate truffles in my display case. But I've worked with modeling chocolate a bunch. Did you see those dinosaurs on Harvey's cake?"

"Can I change my mind?" Louise said to Lili, her voice apologetic. "Cracks in choux are nowhere near as problematic as what can go wrong with chocolate if you don't know what you're doing. And we have enough time to cover the basics if we start there. I'm sure the two of you can handle pastry together. So let's do chocolate."

"Are you sure?" Lili asked them both, seeming uncertain herself as she looked from Dom to his grandma.

"Yes," they answered in tandem.

"Well, okay." She tried to sound bright. "It looks like we're working with chocolate!"

Louise grinned, glad about the outcome, then taught Lili and Dom about chocolate for real. "You might never work with anything more delicious, but chocolate is intimidating. Even a single drop of water on your work surface can ruin the batch. Sometimes it clumps up, sometimes it burns, and it's definitely a bitch and her sister to master. But I'm positive that you two can do it."

Despite Dom's experience in the kitchen, most of what Louise shared was new to him. Some of it he could have figured out like that chocolate shouldn't be stored in the fridge or that you should always use a serrated knife when chopping bars unless you wanted a throbbing hand to go with your pieces of chocolate. But she also delivered plenty of tidbits that he'd never heard before, like:

Chocolate should be melted in a double boiler or in the microwave, never over direct heat.

Chocolate chips shouldn't be used as melting chocolate because many are designed not to melt.

Melted chocolate shouldn't be stirred with a metal spoon because cold can shock the chocolate.

A bit of vegetable oil added to chocolate works well for a thinner dipping coat.

And chocolate placed on plastic wrap to set will get a shiny finish. Perfect for fancy garnishes or the chocolate bark they were working on now.

"But with a *twist*. Instead of using a traditional sweet ingredient, we'll be making our chocolate bark with potato chips and cranberries." Louise smacked her lips. "Sweet and salty is one of the most satisfying experiences for the mouth."

"True story." Dom nodded. "I thought burgers with sundae toppings tasted crazy amazing after I ate two of them on a dare. I never would have believed it."

Lili snorted a laugh. They both fell silent as Louise delivered her instructions, mostly just watching her work and asking questions to fill in the blanks, but once the chocolate bark was well underway, she opted to leave Lili and Dom on their own.

"I've got to get back to the shop, but remember, your bark can't just be bits of chocolate. You'll need to do something with it." She smiled at them both. "I trust the two of you have it from here?"

"Your trust shall be rewarded," Lili promised with a laugh.

Suddenly, it felt like they were too alone. Were things still awkward? Dom was waiting for Lili to somehow let him know.

She broke the weirdness with a joke. "Maybe we should recreate all the sex toys from the key party. Call it A Peek into the Pleasure Box of a Mountain View Swingers Club."

"Or Selected Items From the Analtech Trade Show."

"They sell chromatography plates," Lili reminded him. "To more than forty countries on six continents."

"Oh yeah." Dom laughed, and just like that, it wasn't awkward at all.

"So, what do you want to make besides sex toys?" Lili asked.

"A bust of Eleanor Boothman. Is she a judge?"

Lili pinched her voice into an impressively accurate Eleanor Boothman: "I came here to deliver what I saw as excellent news. I'm sorry to hear that you all don't feel the same way. I guess we'll all just have to live with that."

Dom started laughing even harder than last time.

They batted around another few ideas, then settled on shaping their cake into the Queen of Tarts logo, using a style of craftsmanship called Kintsugi, or the "art of putting things back together."

The ancient technique was originally used to repair ceramics and pottery. But rather than trying to make the old work new, that fresh repair was done in a shiny gold resin that became part of the item, transforming something broken into an original prize with an inherent beauty of its own. A piece of ceramic threaded with beautiful gold lines.

Instead of using lacquer and gold-colored resin to repair a bowl or plate, Dom and Lili used a dyed melted sugar mix to assemble the larger pieces of bark with gold sugar inlays. After adding a sugar flourish on top, their piece would stand out for sure.

Sugar flourishes were one of Lili's favorite things to make. Plus, she and Dom were already joking about how the judges would be easy to bullshit if they were to present their reconstructed logo as a representation of "Dominic Moore's life in the aftermath of his scandal."

"Are you trying to capitalize on my misfortune?" he asked when Lili made her suggestion.

"I'm trying to win," she had replied with a grin he was starting to love.

In a weird way, it felt like Dom had already won, regardless of what actually happened in the challenge. That feeling sat in his stomach, same as it had during all of those times when a game ended with the score in his favor.

Together they worked on their practice bark Kintsugi logo, creating something not just tasty but beautiful. Awkwardness from before had surrendered to a fluidity of motion. They worked as one like they'd been doing so their whole lives. Passing ingredients without request, moving gracefully around each other in the tight space, with gentle touches throughout, soft looks, and grazing fingers.

What would have stoked a fire of sexual tension before felt natural, comfortable even. A connection that seemed to have become a deeper, steadier flame than the hot sparks from earlier. And while Dom loved every touch and look, the unsettled feeling grew as the morning gave way to afternoon. Because that steady flame would surely be snuffed out when he moved to Chicago, and he could already feel the windy chill of its absence.

"I've gotta go," Lili said as they stood admiring their finally completely chocolate creation. "I promised Runa she wouldn't be late for her date if she covered for me."

"I don't know how she does it. A different dude every day."

"Usually with a smile. The university gives her a fresh crop every year."

"Isn't she worried about aging out of that?"

"Not yet. And tonight her date is awfully young. Just three years old." Another little laugh. They had been falling effortlessly out of her lips for a while now. "It's Harvey. Plus Alicia, Jeremy, and me. Thanks for today. It was fun."

Then just like that, Lili was gone.

Louise didn't waste even a minute before coming into the room and interrupting his thoughts with a sly little smile. "You could do a lot worse, you know."

"She's made it crystal clear she's not interested. I'm sure I don't need to remind you that I won't be sticking around Mountain View for long."

"Maybe you should."

"Right." He nodded. "Because this town is sick with opportunities for ex-NFL players like me."

"This town is sick with opportunities for *people* like you." And then, in case her grandson didn't get it, she added, "*Specifically.*"

Lili

✉ ☆ ↩ ☑ ⋮

Sorry

Submissions <submissions@mansplanations.mvdaily.org>
To: Annabelle Lyons <a.lyons@mountainviewuniversity.edu>

Dear Annabelle,

I apologize for posting your emails without consulting you first. I actually thought you'd raised some interesting points that my readers would enjoy seeing for themselves. They love discourse on this topic, and frankly, two opposing voices can be far more interesting than one.

Please accept my humble apology.

Best,

Mansplanations

"Are you *sure* this is meatloaf?" Lili asked Jeremy.

"Do you think if you keep asking me the same thing over and over and over again that I'll eventually answer differently?"

"That's what Titus keeps trying with Runa."

Runa laughed.

Lili said, "It's just that it's more spongecake than meatloaf."

"But not sweet," added Alicia.

"Or flavorful," Runa chirped.

"It has flavor ..." Alicia started but didn't know how to finish.

"It's Harvey's fault," Jeremy explained blaming the culinary disaster on an innocent child. "Our son has a very particular palate."

Alicia rolled her eyes but didn't disagree with her man out loud.

Harvey picked up a handful of "meatloaf" and hurled it onto the floor. Lili was almost surprised that the food didn't bounce. Jeremy got out of his seat, shaking his head on the way over to the mess, primly picking it up off the floor with pinched fingers as he looked up at his son.

"We need to keep our food on our plates, sweetie," Jeremy said.

"So, tell me more about your day at Higher Grounds," Lili said, changing the subject before Alicia could make fun of her husband.

Runa started to giggle. It was always the sweetest little sound once the pixie got it going. "I haven't had that much fun in years."

"If you enjoy serving people who barely know how to appreciate you, you're welcome to a shift here at Casa de Toddler," Alicia told her.

Lili smirked. "Runa isn't into the serving. I'm sure she just loved all of the gossip."

"Oh, my God!" Runa giggled again. "*So much gossip!* It's like TMZ in there."

"Welcome to my life." Lili nodded. "What was the tea all about today? Last week half of the customers were bitching about the color Carson Gruntish was painting his fence. I've not seen the results, but apparently, Carson didn't finish what he started. The fence is only half-finished and—"

"What do you *think* they're gossiping about?" Runa exclaimed, apparently shocked by Lili's ignorance and having zero interest in Carson's fence.

"I don't know!" Lili snapped. "The price of tea in China?"

"They're gossiping about *you*, dear."

"What could they possibly be gossiping about?"

"You and Dom," Runa replied, her expression adding, *Duh*.

"You have to be kidding me." Lili was mortified. "I spent the entire day with his grandmother. That's not exactly fodder for gossip."

"The *whole* day?" Alicia pressed.

"Well, not exactly the *whole* day, but it was probably most of it."

"*Probably most of it*," Runa repeated with a laugh.

"We were just cooking," Lili insisted. "For the Upper Crust Challenge."

Jeremy looked up from the floor. "All the guys are talking about it, too."

"Talking about WHAT?" Lili threw her hands in the air, exasperated.

Jeremy gave her the same *Duh* expression as Runa. "Everyone is wondering when the two of you are actually going to get together."

Lili rolled her eyes. "It's hard to get with someone who isn't sticking around town for long."

"All the guys think that Dom is like totally smitten," Jeremy added.

"Is that, like, what they all totally think?" Alicia asked him.

"*Smitten*," Runa giggled, "He sounds like an old English lady."

"I do not!" Jeremy tried to defend himself.

But his son was a Benedict Arnold, yelling "Do too!" as he threw another handful of meatsponge onto his father.

"That's not nice," Jeremy said as he stood, the tone of his voice like he was offering Harvey a handful of candy. "We don't throw things in this—"

Another handful of squishy meat hit Jeremy in his chest before making a molasses-slow slide down the front of his shirt.

Harvey picked up another fist full of his unwanted dinner, squeezing it between his tiny fingers as he got ready to hurl it.

"Harvey ... NO!" Alicia barely raised her voice, but the entire table heard the steel underneath it.

The toddler stopped immediately, dropping his meat into a pile on his tray.

Jeremy turned to Alicia, but he didn't seem grateful for her intervention. "You know how I feel about the word *no*."

"And you know how I feel about growing babies inside my body. But guess what, Jeremy? Sometimes someone needs to do what has to be done." Alicia turned to Lili. "It really doesn't matter what anyone else has to say on the matter. You need to do what *you* want. You got me?"

She looked at Lili with her most penetrating gaze, but Lili could barely blink, let alone conjure an appropriate response. Pulled in by the tractor beam of a friend who could inspire an honest answer from anyone.

"I don't know," Lili finally replied.

Alicia shook her head. "Bullshit."

"Please ... language." Jeremy tried to remind her.

"*Bullshit*," she repeated with emphasis. "With your two best friends in the world as witness, how do you feel about Dominic Moore?"

Lili squirmed in her seat, but she wasn't getting away with this. "I like spending time with him."

Alicia glared at her: *And ...*

Jeremy and Runa both watched. Even Harvey seemed heavily invested in whatever happened next.

"He could have anybody ... aren't we like, in different leagues or something?"

"That's crap, and you know it!" Alicia still hadn't blinked.

"*Please*. Language."

Runa was trying not to smile at Jeremy's futile attempts to corral Alicia.

But when Lili still didn't respond, she continued, still using her eyes as a chisel chipping away at the truth. "Everything you just said is proof that you're still waiting on life to happen instead of making it happen for yourself."

"That's not true! Or fair." Lili had to defend herself. "I'm hardly waiting. I danced in a beaver costume! In the street."

"Because of Dom," Runa pointed out.

"Why does that even matter? I still did something, and Higher Grounds is doing better because of it. I've even been learning a few new skills in the kitchen, including today while I was at Queen of Tarts with Dom and Louise, not knowing that the entire town was gossiping about me!"

"The gossip was just in your coffee shop," Runa clarified.

"And—"

But that's all Jeremy could manage before Lili snapped at the room: "I think it's a fair ask that everyone get all the way off of my back about this already!"

Anxiety was rising inside her like a tide. Alicia knew what she was doing, stirring her up like this. Jeremy, Runa, and Harvey all watched. They may as well have had buckets of popcorn instead of meatloaf in front of them.

Lili opened her mouth and let it all pour out. She was genuinely unsure of how she felt about Dominic Moore ... but she didn't want to let herself get all excited, only to be let down again ... like she had been in high school.

And this situation was different, both better and worse. Lili had never entered any sort of competition like the Upper Crust Challenge. Nothing even remotely close to this big. Or important. Two fairs and a jubilee at the Mountain View Community Center. She was an amateur baker, at best. Even before Dom was part of the picture, entering the contest was a perfect example of Lili getting in over her head.

She was going on TV with an amateur by her side, and *she* was supposed to be the one in charge.

Louise might be the nicest lady Lili had ever met, and the last thing in the world she wanted to do was let her down. Same for her grandson.

The famous footballer that she had a hard (impossible) time not thinking about. Probably because she had slept with him. *Twice now.*

"Wait." Runa shook her head in surprise after Lili finished her confession. "You've had sex with him twice? When was the second time?"

"You won't get any friendship demerits for keeping this a secret if you tell us everything now." Alicia turned to Jeremy. "You should definitely leave and take Harvey unless you want him to hear all of the filth that's about to come out of Lili's mouth."

"There will be no filth leaving my mouth," Lili protested, suddenly finding it suddenly harder to swallow.

"When was the second time?" Runa repeated.

"And where?" Alicia added.

"It was in Higher Grounds," she admitted.

"I thought I could smell something." Runa laughed.

"You could not!" Lili was horrified, even though she knew that Runa was only trying to trigger that exact reaction.

Alicia grinned.

Jeremy whistled.

Runa started a slow clap.

All while, Lili began to hyperventilate.

Alicia reached out and put a hand on her friend's shoulder. "See. You *have* been living more lately, and living is a lot scarier than staying safe. But tell yourself the truth, Lil, hasn't it all been worth it?"

The room seemed to be holding its breath, awaiting her answer.

But Harvey broke the moment by hurling another fistful of meat-sponge at his father's face.

"Bullshit!" Harvey exclaimed.

"No, it's meatloaf," Lili corrected him.

Dom

D om pulled up in front of the White Dove Hotel and killed the engine.

He looked over at Lili but still couldn't read her expression, same as he'd been unable to decipher what she might be thinking throughout the entirety of their three-hour drive into the city from Mountain View.

He felt self-conscious, like Lili must be judging him for stopping at the valet instead of driving his fancy-ass McLaren to the parking lot like any other regular Joe.

"We're here," he said.

"Sure looks that way," Lili agreed, with a ghost of a smile.

Dom opened his door and stepped out onto the ground, still uncertain. Lili should be excited. Entering the Upper Crust Challenge had been her idea long before he'd ever heard about it. She watched the show every year and seemed to know everything already. But Dom would never think she was in an elevated state, judging by her face right now.

Why was she so quiet? And why had she stayed so silent during their long drive, when it was just the two of them with no escapes or excuses, listening to the radio instead of each other.

"Thanks." Dom nodded to the valet, whose eyes were as big as saucers looking at the beautiful car he was about to park. "Fob's in the console."

He thought about warning the guy not to pull a Ferris Bueller with a joy ride, but in truth, Dom would love for his McLaren to get stolen so he could get that matte black Range Rover he actually wanted.

He followed Lili into the hotel lobby, telling himself yet again that it was only the nerves. She had a lot riding on this. Though she'd barked at his offering her the prize money, he still wanted Lili to take it. That would give her enough to start her new life, even if she didn't want him to be a part of it.

They stood in line, waiting for an available clerk to check them in. Their bets had always paved the way for banter, maybe that was his ticket in now. Maybe he could think up the right wager to loosen her up.

Unless the game was over, and Lili didn't want to be loosened.

Her silence made guessing impossible, and the draining of Dom's confidence inevitable.

This situation was surprising, how much he cared about her opinion in the first place. He wanted to ignore the realization, leave the knowledge behind him like lights he forgot to turn off. But even with his back turned, he couldn't ignore the illumination entirely.

He was desperate for Lili to think the best of him and sad to imagine that she might still just see him as a dumb jock who had yet to grow up, even after all that time he'd spent doing his damndest to prove the opposite.

"Next." The hotel clerk waved them over.

Dom nodded, then took Lili's bag in an effort to be a gentleman. She looked at him in surprise and surrendered it.

He approached the desk with a bit more spring in his step. Dom smiled, but the clerk — a man with piercing blue eyes and hair slicked back so tightly that it looked like lacquer on his head — did not return the gesture.

"Name," said the man in a monotone, eyeing Lili and Dom with suspicion.

"We have two reservations: Dominic Moore and Liliana Travis," said Dom.

The clerk looked down without a reply and started typing. He glanced back up a few seconds later, bad news leaving his mouth without a matching apology on his face. "I only have a reservation for Mr. Moore."

Lili took a step toward the counter. The clerk didn't return her smile either. "I made my reservation months ago. Could you please check on it for me?"

"I just checked. Like I said, you don't have a reservation."

"Can you check to see if I ever *had* a reservation?" Lili sounded tentative like she didn't know what else to ask.

The clerk clacked at the keys and then looked up again. "It seems that your reservation was canceled."

"Canceled by *who*? Because it definitely wasn't me!"

More clacking. "It appears that your reservation was canceled by an Eleanor Boothman."

Lili drew a deep breath, then exhaled through her nose. "That room was canceled without my permission. I need to reclaim it. Please."

"We have no available rooms." And not even an *I'm sorry* to go with it.

"You must have *something*." Lili now sounded closer to begging.

"Like I said—"

"Do you know who I am?"

Of course, Dom hated himself a little as the words left his mouth — this was something he never did — but Lili needed help, and the snooty clerk had left him with no other choice.

"Your name is right here on the screen, Mr. Moore." His voice was terse, even sharper than before. "But unfortunately, celebrity does not entitle one to rooms that simply do not exist. If there was anything else to do here, you can rest assured it would be done."

"Something can always be done." Dom tried again, but he could feel the weight of Lili rolling her eyes right beside him.

"I'm sorry, Mr. Moore. I suggest trying one of the other local hotels." He offered Dom a smile, thin enough to see through. "Perhaps you might find the Drury Inn over on Madison Road more accommodating."

Dom pictured himself in full gear, tackling this asshat of a hotel clerk, but he simply smiled as best he could and thanked him before turning back to a still flustered Lili.

"We've got this," he tried to assure her.

Apparently, those were just more empty words out of a (former?) celebrity's mouth. He took charge, calling around to several hotels and even dropping his name another couple of times, as embarrassing as that was for him. When the hotels failed to pan out, he got started on the motels.

But Dom didn't fare any better. "Seems like the entire town is booked up for the competition," he reported with a frown.

"Of course they are! The challenge has a live audience, and people come from all over to see it, not even including all the contestants and groups of fans who travel from competition to competition."

"Like the Grateful Dead? That's crazy ... I had no idea that the Upper Crust Challenge was so big or that the fans were so rabid."

"They're almost as fanatical as sports fans." Her laugh sounded hollow, born from a need to make herself feel better.

Dom was loathe to make his suggestion, afraid of what Lili might think of his intentions or how she might respond.

"We could share my room," he finally offered with a shrug, looking over at Lili as his heart started pounding out of nowhere.

Her expression instantly shifted, flashing with panic before it resolved into something like extreme trepidation. The compounded effect of seeing one followed right by the other was like the tip of a knife sliding into his emotions.

"I'm not trying anything here," he worked to assure her. "There are two beds. It's not like I was going to *share a bed* with my grandmother, right? I wanted a suite — and you'd better not judge me for that — but we had a hard time getting *any* room. Eleanor assured me that ours was the final one."

"That's because I'm sure she gave you *my* room," Lili grumbled.

"And I'm sure you're right, but now that we have this problem, I just want a solution. So that we can win this thing. Together."

"*Together*," she repeated with a nod.

They returned to the front desk, waited in line again, and ended up with the same snooty clerk, who apparently saw their return as a victory.

"Will you be sharing a room then?" he asked while checking them in, giving the guests a smug little grin that Dom imagined tackling off of his face yet again.

"Yes," Lili told him, her body language as aggressive as her voice, "and we're going to do *all the things*. So thanks for that."

Dom wasn't even sure what point she was trying to prove with that last little exchange, but he sure appreciated her effort. They finished checking in with the receipt of two keys, then left the counter and made it halfway to the elevator before Eleanor jumped out in front of them, seemingly from nowhere.

Lili was furious on sight, stepping in front of Dom to snap at Eleanor before he could get a word in. No greeting or preamble, just an accusatory sentence vented with restrained fury.

"Why would you cancel my room without permission?"

Eleanor insulted Lili with a careless laugh. "Your room wasn't exactly going to be needed if you were no longer in the Upper Crust Challenge."

"Even if I wasn't *in* the contest, I still might have wanted to come. That was my room! You had no right."

Lili really seemed like she wanted to yell.

But Eleanor wasn't even listening. She had her eyes all over Dom.

"I just *know* you're going to do *so well*." She clapped, looking around the lobby as she crowed. "You're going to make Mountain View so proud!"

"I wouldn't be making anyone proud if it wasn't for Lili. I'm only here because of her. So it's really *Lili* you should be thanking, Eleanor. Without her, Mountain View probably wouldn't have an entry at all."

Eleanor didn't just look like she was being forced to swallow a particularly bitter pill. It was like she had been handed an entire bottle of them.

"Thank you, Lili." The corners of Eleanor's mouth twitched in an uncomfortable smile.

"My pleasure!" Lili replied, really turning it on.

The ghastly smile faded from Eleanor's face. When neither Dom nor Lili had anything else to add, she took her cue, making an about-face before trudging back toward the hotel entrance.

Lili flipped her retreating back the bird and said, "So, shall we?"

They took the elevator to their floor and walked the hallway to their room. Inside, Lili reminded Dom of the score.

"Thank God!" she declared, pointing at the pair of beds, seeming surprised even though Dom had already told her that he wasn't planning to sleep with his grandma. "I thought we'd get here, and there would only be one bed. Like we were actually trapped in some stupid rom-com or something."

"That would have sucked." Dom said the opposite of what he meant.

Dom had been silently nursing the hope that Lili might change her mind on this trip, but she kept making it clear that their feelings weren't aligned.

He decided to try one final time. "Do you want to get some dinner?"

"No." Lili shook her head without giving his offer even a blink of consideration. "I'll figure something out on my own."

"Cool." But it wasn't. "I guess I'll see you later then."

"Later," Lili agreed with a nod.

He left the room to give her the space she so clearly wanted, feeling dejected but still working not to show it.

The elevator doors dinged open to a packed lobby.

Dom spied an entire gang of people from the Mountain View town hall, fronted by their fearless leader, Eleanor Boothman.

He slipped out of a side exit, wanting to steer clear of anyone who might know his name.

He inhaled the fresh air, relieved to take a long walk now that he was finally back outside and alone with his thoughts.

Because Dominic Moore sure as hell had an awful lot to think about.

Lili

Lili woke up with a smile.

It was the day of the Upper Crust Challenge, and she couldn't remember the last time she had felt so vibrantly alive. Not only was Lili a born competitor (not too different from her partner in the contest, now that she thought about it), this would be the biggest challenge she had ever taken on — really, the biggest thing Lili had ever done, *period* — and she couldn't wait to see how she performed now that her chance to compete where it really counted was finally here.

Lili didn't need this win for herself, and somehow that made her that much more determined to take the prize. She was eager to show the entire world what she could do.

That meant the live audience and all those viewers at home, of course, but most of all it meant Dom, Louise, and all of her friends.

Everyone she knew agreed that Lili was an excellent baker, but her skills had never been tested like this. She had been plagued by a cornucopia of relentless uncertainties yesterday, not just about her own abilities but all the feelings about her partner in all of this that she had been forced to wrestle with during what felt like such a long and awkward car ride.

It had been brewing since all those pointed questions from her friends the night before, and as she had slid into the Batmobile for their three-hour trip, it had hit Lili like a lightning bolt that she was far too excited to see him and not in the way a friend should be.

He flashed her a smile as she tried squeezing her bag into the tiny cabin, and it hadn't infuriated her in the least, instead of sending butterflies through her system and making her want to giggle.

She couldn't — *absolutely could not* — have real feelings for Dom. Not only because he was famous, a football player, and uber-rich, but because he wasn't in any way, shape, or form, part of the plan. Lili was waiting to find the nerdy guy who would get all of her weird jokes and support her dreams. She was supposed to meet him *after* her bakery was up and running, all by herself.

But it was almost like all those residual feelings from high school had been enflamed instead of settled by their one (TWO!) night stand.

So she sat quietly in the car, determined *not* to encourage her own treacherous feelings by engaging in any lovable banter with Dom. She'd almost lost her inner cool while they were trying to wrangle a second room, and she would have lost her shit for sure if she had to sleep in the same bed as Dom while pretending she wasn't totally into him.

Lili only relaxed after they got inside the room, and she saw the solace of matching beds. He left right after that.

Her inner world felt soothed by the sunrise. Thinking about everything in the earliest morning light, it really did seem like Dom had been doing his best ever since yesterday. Not just during that awkward car ride, or when he tried to get her a room by battling Mr. McSnooty at the front desk with his sword of celebrity, or even when they arrived in their room.

He was so matter-of-fact and friendly about everything. Dom didn't make a single joke or untoward suggestion in regards to their sharing a bed. If anything, it seemed to Lili that he was looking for the opposite.

His lack of interest made it easier to stuff all of those feelings down and focus on the day ahead.

Errant emotions needed to stay put so Lili could focus on the Upper Crust Challenge. Today was cake day, so she would be spending most of her hours in the happiest of places. It didn't even matter that Stan was left behind in her kitchen. Everyone from Alicia and Runa to Dom and Louise kept insisting that the Upper Crust's mixers would be state of the art and that bringing Stan with her was silly. She finally relented, but a part of Lili wished she had stood her ground. Then she would be mixing ingredients with an old friend, instead of the single-serving instrument, she'd be working with this morning. But despite the lack of Stan, Lili was glad she wasn't going into this challenge alone.

Her thoughts were already warm when she looked across the way from her bed to Dom's. She reminded herself of all the things that didn't matter. Like how kind he had been to her, how handsome he was, or how sweet it sounded within the room with him softly snoring just two feet away.

She could almost reach out and touch his face. And, of course, she wanted to. But instead, she stared at him, thinking about how sweet and innocent he seemed while sleeping.

An awful lot like the boy Lili once considered herself in love with.

She reached out to touch him ... just a brush across his nose—

Dom opened his eyes, and Lili instantly flinched her hand back.

His expression was already bright, his smile surprisingly wide. That dimple reappearing. The enthusiasm was clear in his words.

"Ready to kick some ass, Beaver Girl?"

Her serenity disappeared. The calm Lili had been telling herself was inside her vanished like morning mist in the rising sun.

His shine felt almost too bright on her.

And why? Because the wall she'd been carefully constructing around her heart since getting in his car yesterday — or since he had pulled that beaver head off of her in the final game of senior year — came crashing down.

Lili could no longer deny it or pretend her feelings weren't real. She was totally into this guy, regardless of the lies she had been telling herself.

Maybe she wasn't "in love with him," but she was definitely "in like." Or something.

It wasn't just his smile or his abs or his way around a joke — Dominic Moore was more than an idealized idea. Lili found herself in a head-on collision with the reality that she actually liked him as a person, despite his unrelenting sense of entitlement.

The harder dawning — this one was more like a lump in her throat — was knowing how much she was going to miss him once he was gone. It would be hell getting over his leaving. Again.

"Never been readier!" Her words sounded chirpy, and she tried to find a smile, but she probably got it wrong, judging by his crooked expression.

He got out of bed and grabbed his overnight bag off of the floor, then reminded her of his entitlement. "Dibs on the first shower."

But then, like a gentleman (because he was totally great at pretending like anyone else rich and famous, who lived with having cameras on them all the time), he turned back at the door.

"Unless you want it first?"

"Knock yourself out." Lili (kind of) smiled again, hugging her pillow as he closed the door, then turning around to stare out the window, looking at people milling about in the street because that was better than imagining Dom in the shower ...

Twenty minutes later, Lili was making the mistake of wondering if Dom was picturing her naked, now that it was her turn in the shower. Probably not. *Of course not.*

And then Lili was back to feeling bad instead of topped off with fuel to win like she had been upon waking.

Breakfast was better. Her emotions had mostly returned to normal by the time Dom was telling her all about the Upper Crust Challenge like he was the one who had been following the contest for years.

"I've been doing some research," he laughed when she chastised his knowledge. "It helps to know the odds that bookies are giving on the Challenge."

"Wait." Lili shook her head, unsure of whether Dom was messing with her.

"You can bet on just about anything. Including whether or not a shopkeeper will dance up and down the street in a beaver costume."

"So you've been running the numbers ... same as you would in a game?"

"Exactly. You can totally go ahead and make fun of my love affair with numbers if you want to, but yes, the numbers are half of it."

"And the other half?" Lili asked, declining to make fun of his love affair.

"Knowing your competition." He tipped his chin to a couple sitting two tables away from them. "See."

Lili looked over and tried not to laugh at the sight. Their outfits weren't matching, so much as codependent. He was dressed in jeans and a T-shirt full of ingredients, while her tee boasted the finished cake. Lili would have found their ensembles garish if they hadn't been so (unintentionally?) hilarious.

"So," she whispered, "do you consider them stiff competition because they're so devoted, or a non-threat on account of ... you know ... the crazy."

"I have a healthy respect for lunacy. Disregarding it can get you in trouble. I would classify that couple as a definite wild card."

"Do you think maybe we should have worn matching outfits?" Lili asked.

"Maybe thongs? We'd still have our aprons, of course."

Lili laughed, and everything felt like it was suddenly back to normal.

The dining room filled. More competitors made their conversation easy.

A mother and daughter team marched in like they owned the place. Mom had apparently worked not one but *two* events at the White House, and she needed everyone within earshot (or not) to know it.

She started talking loudly about Bush, and that sent Lili into hysterics.

Dom kept stoking her laughter, starting with jokes about how the woman's Bush was completely out of control and concluding his color commentary with a simple observation. "Maybe we should rescue the daughter. She's being held against her will."

"I know her." Lili nodded to another girl sitting a few tables over.

"Oh yeah?"

"Well, I don't *know* her. But we did meet a few years ago at a Frosting Intensive. I think her name is Bria."

"A FROSTING INTENSIVE?" Dom laughed even louder than he'd exclaimed. A few people looked over. He lowered his voice. "Please tell me more about this event. It sounds like an *SNL* skit."

"It was *very* informative." Lili hated that her voice sounded almost professorial. "It's where I learned how to really measure my buttercream."

"You keep saying things that sound like sex acts."

She shrugged. "If that's where your mind is."

"There is literally a sex act called 'frosting.' Am I supposed to pretend I don't know that?"

"I'd be disappointed if you didn't." Another shrug. Then Lili looked over at Bria again. But this time, Bria was looking back, her expression clear: *You go, girl!*

Lili loved the acknowledgment, even if it wasn't deserved.

Like she and Dom were actually together. Like they ever really could be.

"They seem nice." Lili nodded at another pair of competitors. Two Indian girls that looked enough alike that they almost *had* to be sisters.

"Ooh." Dom made a face, shaking his head. "I would peg them as the 'ones to watch.'"

"They haven't stopped smiling. And watch how their server acts whenever she stops at their table. She's smiling too."

"That's her job."

"Nope." Lili shook her head. "She definitely smiles more at their table. I bet they're both being super nice to her."

"So they're nice ..." He shrugged. "That doesn't mean they don't know how to bake their faces off."

"I'm not sure that baking their faces off could help them win." Lili smiled. "But if you say they're the ones to watch, consider my eyes all over them."

For a fleeting second his eyes were all over her.

But then the producers (a tall man who wore his hat like a wig, and a brunette woman who started eye screwing Dom the second she saw him) entered the dining area to sour their moment, announcing that it was time for hair and makeup.

The room hummed with excitement.

Except for Dom, who didn't seem excited at all.

People were out of their seats and headed for the door. Dom stood in what seemed like defeat.

"What is it?" Lili asked.

"It's nothing. Really."

"Please? We're about to—"

"It's stupid." He shook his head. "Of course, there was going to be hair and makeup ... I just didn't think about it."

"Don't you do this for like, *every interview?*"

"Sure, but I'm expecting it then." A weak argument, so he added to his inner debate with a shrug. "PTSD, I guess."

He offered Lili a smile and followed her to the line.

"The White House took me to Bloomingdales to get all done up," said Bush Lady. "You know, before meeting the President."

Lili and Dom were second to last in line. He whispered, "*Did you know that the Bush likes her pie?*"

Lili laughed quietly as the sisters he said to watch out for fell into line behind them. "Hi there," said the one who might have been half an inch taller, "My name is Dipti Kumari. This is my sister Rati."

"Hi." Lili smiled at them both — the sisters were both beautiful, and a little intimidating, especially because Dipti instantly seemed *so nice*. "I'm Lili and this is my partner, Dominic. For baking, I mean. We're in the contest together. I know his grandma."

Lili's smile was hurting her face.

"The buzz is all about your team," Rati told her.

"Oh yeah?" *Great. Captain Quarterback strikes again.*

"Oh yeah." Dipti nodded. "You guys are total wild cards because no one has ever seen either of you bake anything before."

"Oh." Lili smiled again. This one felt better.

"We can't wait to see what you do!" Rati chirped.

Dom had brightened at the mention of their names. "I read about the sugar phoenix you guys made at the *Just Desserts Bakeoff*. That was *epic*."

"Thanks!" said the sisters together.

Once they had filed through the exit and found themselves in the hallway again, Dom turned and whispered to Lili again. "This is great! I *love* being the wildcard. It's always the best position because no one sees you coming."

But Lili thought the word *wildcard* was an awfully nice way of saying the truth. In reality, they were amateurs.

And neither Lili nor Dom had any business being here.

Dom

L ili was doing ... poorly.

Dom didn't know what to say. He felt helpless next to her, unable to help or even speak without it seeming like she might have a meltdown. Maybe it was all the cameras, and of course, given their history, it could have been him, but everything Lili was doing seemed almost perfectly out of sync.

The host, Phoebe Brooke (the morning show personality that had made it her business to get uncomfortably close to him), kept trying to make light banter to encourage Team Mountain View, but they were already one hour into their six-hour window. While that was plenty of time to bake several cakes, the competitors were tasked with making a "cake creation" that measured at least three feet high.

That was a lot of cakes to bake and stack and sculpt and decorate and—

What is she doing? Dom sighed again instead of saying anything out loud, looking around at the cameras, wishing they weren't like ants on his skin as Lili grabbed the milk from his hands.

She had put together the dry ingredients without sifting the flour, but now she was taking over the wet ingredients when she should have been prepping the decorations and leaving the simple cake baking to him. He would say that things were quickly falling apart, but it had unfortunately taken them an hour to get here, so it was more of a slow and steady procession toward their inevitable failure.

"What can I do?" Dom asked her in a low voice. "I'm just standing here."

"Let me just catch up. Then I can gather my thoughts."

It wasn't an answer, and still, he was stuck doing nothing while Lili was crumbling like cake without gluten. If he didn't act soon, then Dom could only blame the resulting disaster on himself.

They had started this morning with a plan, with both of them knowing what needed to be done. None of this was a surprise. They had carefully architected the cake they would make if given something large. But now it was game time, and their team was already losing.

She had lost the ability to manage her time. Her confidence was a mountain of sugar left in the rain. And the way she was collaborating, refusing to let Dom do a single thing on *their* list, Lili might as well have been a saboteur intent on taking them down.

The clock was ticking. An hour down with only a single cake in the oven. Her face was cherries jubilee, long strands of hair hovering around her round cheeks in wisps.

Lili looked lost, and Dom was failing his teammate.

He could run with his usual and goad her into action. But Lili was several raw nerves passed already stressed, and nudging her now would almost certainly backfire. What usually inspired her confidence might instead trigger Lili into a fit and send her screaming from the room.

His second option was so much better.

"I'll be back," he said.

No need to wait for an answer. Lili didn't have one.

One of the two producers stopped him a hundred yards from the hotel exit. "Do you have just a minute?"

She tucked a long strand of silky hair behind her ear and beamed at him.

"I just needed to take care of something real quick. I'll—"

"I was hoping we could talk about your sit-down interview ... for the televised part of the Upper Crust Challenge."

"Diana? Is it Diana?"

"It is." She beamed even brighter. "Thank you."

"Sure thing, Diana. I would be happy to have that conversation, but right now, I've gotta focus on the contest and—"

"But it looks like you're about to go outside. "

"I need to—"

"Plus, it's just the two of us right now." Her cheeks began to redden.

"Sorry, Diana. I gotta go."

Then Dom was outside, talking the valet into escorting him to the McLaren, where he opened the door to dig out his prize. The shining red mixer that Lili inexplicably loved so much.

It had been hard work convincing Alicia, but Dom finally managed to remind her that Stan was a totem to Lili, representing her confidence in the kitchen. Alicia had argued that Stan was a crutch and Lili could "bake the Cake Boss into embarrassment" without it but ultimately relented in the light of his smile and a promise to reveal the mixer only in an emergency.

Alicia had snuck the mixer into his car just moments before Lili showed up for the trip. It was a big risk, bringing him in now, but this was definitely a baking emergency and a chance he was willing to take. Lili would either freak the hell out that her precious Stan had been touched, or she would be two stars over the moon that someone had known how to save her.

Dom exhaled with relief, seeing that Lili was emphatically both.

"Oh my God!" she squealed at the sight of him, the notes in her voice sounding half-manic, though Dom couldn't tell which side of insanity her exclamation had landed on. "Is he okay?"

She took Stan from his arms, apparently fretting at first that her old friend might have been somehow damaged in transit. But once she saw that Dom had delivered him unharmed and had Stan plugged into an outlet proudly purring with a whir that instantly grounded her, Lili turned to her partner with a more easily definable squeal and threw her arms around him.

"THANK YOU!"

Lili was instantly in flow, moving with graceful intent like the born baker she was. She started by tossing the mealy batter she had been working on. "Stan and I are going to rock a batch of my world-famous — in Mountain View — buttercream like a drum of corundum."

"What?" Dom wondered if he heard her wrong. "What's … *corundum?*"

"The second hardest mineral known to man. Diamonds are the first, but saying I would rock a batch like a sack of diamonds sounded so pretentious."

"You're right." He nodded. "Always better to go with nerdy."

"Can you start on the cakes on one of *those* mixers while I beat this buttercream like smallpox?"

"Stay nerdy, but don't forget that you're talking about food. Smallpox and corundum are probably not the words you want anyone to use to describe your world-famous-in-mountain-view buttercream."

Dom got started on their cakes with a smile.

Lili stayed in the zone, throwing her butter and powdered sugar into Stan and then blending her mixture while grinning with the feeling of a winner in waiting. She carefully added her heavy cream one tablespoon at a time and shouted at Dom: "Bring me some cocoa powder and cayenne!"

He was happy to serve, even though this was different than what they had talked about making. The new direction might have even been making it easier. Her flow was obvious, like sending a football sailing through the air without a thought and still knowing exactly where the pigskin would land.

Who cared if they had planned on making a chocolate buttercream with a dash of pistachio, just enough to upend expectations. Dom didn't know what Lili was doing, but whatever the new plan turned out to be, she was clearly doing it well. He followed her every instruction, admiring the command in her voice as they left her.

He kept bringing Lili ingredients while working on his cakes, pulling them out of the oven, cooling, and stacking them. He used twice the number of dowels that he'd planned on, but the structure was sturdy as he carved into it.

Lili worked on the opposite side, embossing the cake with modeling chocolate, creating characters and textures that brought their creation to life.

A beaver, a football, and a goal, a little figure with its arm outstretched.

And the biggest prop on their cake: *a trophy.*

Which is exactly what they planned to leave this Challenge with.

Dom reached for the buttercream to start covering the cakes, dipping his finger in for a taste before he got going. His eyes widened, at first with surprise and then from the pleasure on his tongue.

"Chili spiced frosting ..." he moaned in appreciation while dipping his finger into the buttercream again. "Just the right kick."

"It elevates the chocolate and brings the sweetness down—"

"To exactly where it needs to be," he finished her thought with a wink. "Ingenious tweak. I love it."

The rest of their cake felt like it almost assembled itself, the way Dom's hands kept dancing across it with Lili's. They carefully layered frosting over every inch of their creation meant for eating, then delicately laid fondant over the mountain part like a Persian carpet.

They only added the figures once a countdown to their final five minutes was underway, and their creation officially became The Climb to the Top.

It had been Lili's idea to play on Dom's celebrity. He didn't love it and had even objected at first, but his partner made a strong argument, and he'd been willing to please her. This contest was for Lili (and Louise), after all. But now, seeing her idea fully realized, it was obvious that she had been right.

She turned their creation into a story. As someone who had both benefited and suffered in front of the media, Dom had an intimate understanding of the power of even the simplest narrative.

Lili got it too. It wasn't hard to convince her to run with his idea of adding the beaver. He loved that she did. Now it was *their* story instead of just *his*.

Of course, if it was truly theirs, then The Climb to the Top would also have a bakery sitting on its zenith instead of just a trophy.

And that trophy should probably be a microphone ... if he managed to land that SportsBar commentating job.

Time was called, and Lili suddenly hugged him. No squeal this time, but she was still just as joyous.

"How long do they take to judge?" he asked her.

"I don't know." She shrugged with a laugh. "It's usually one commercial break."

"Oh yeah." No matter how long it took, the wait would feel like forever.

They shortened it by admiring the competition.

The Kumari sisters made a wedding cake. Six tiers, with elaborate scallops and intricate spires that should have been impossible given their time.

The couple with the matching outfits made a stack of presents. The execution was outstanding, but the design itself was less than inspiring. Accents of tassels and ribbons were almost as simple as the boxes they were garnished upon.

Bush Lady and her daughter recreated a White House, several unfortunate inches shorter than it needed to be.

Bria and her mother, Rebecca, made a skyscraper. Their monument to mankind's dominance was impressive as the contest ended, less so as it started to lean, and eventually a total catastrophe when it collapsed entirely.

Perky producer Diana started raging because the cameras hadn't been rolling. Bria and Rebecca worked furiously to prop it back up before eventually surrendering.

"*It's happening*," Lili whispered to Dom as the doors opened again and the judges entered, presumably with the results.

"Our odds are excellent." Dom nodded at the toppled building, then at the miniature capital while stating the obvious. "Two teams being disqualified gives us a sixty-six percent chance of making it. I'd take those odds every day ending in Y."

Dom didn't say it out loud, but he had zero doubt that this was between The Climb to the Top and the Kumaris' Love Story.

Tweedle-Dee and Tweedle-Dum's stack of gifts just wasn't good enough.

Lili knew it too. He was sure of it.

But she screamed with delighted surprise when the judges announced the first day's results, anyway.

Lili and Dom had made it into the finale.

Lili

Are we still talking?

Submissions <submissions@mansplanations.mvdaily.org>
To: Annabelle Lyons <a.lyons@mountainviewuniversity.edu>

To answer your previous question about fate (before I so rudely ruined the conversation by publishing it), I say this:

(for A)

What sound was that?

I turn away, into the shaking room.

What was that sound that came in on the dark?

What is this maze of light it leaves us in?

What is this stance we take,

To turn away and then turn back?

What did we hear?

It was the breath we took when we first met.

Listen. It is here.

~ Harold Pinter

P.S. Have you ever heard of The Planck scale?

"How amazing do you think this dinner is going to be?" Lili asked.

Dom was a lot less excited about whatever they were about to be served than Lili was expecting. He shrugged, and even his show of indifference seemed like feigned enthusiasm. "It'll be okay."

"How can it not be good?" she demanded. "This is the Upper Crust Challenge?"

"So, because it's a baking convention, the food will be good?" He raised his eyebrows. "That's your logic?"

Lili nodded.

Dom shook his head. "The competition is put on by the Upper Crust Challenge. Our food will be prepared by the good folks at the White Dove."

"But the people who run the Upper Crust Challenge would know what to ask for. And the White Dove is a nice hotel. Nice-ish anyway. Are you being a snob right now?"

"Not at all." He shook his head, then considered. "Okay, a little bit, but not in the way you're thinking. It's not just that most hotel food can never touch the dishes you could get in a dedicated restaurant, including — or maybe even *especially* — some hole-in-the-wall mini bistro or a mom-and-pop dive. The food they serve at conventions ..." Dom made a face. "Ask me how much experience I have in that area. Maybe not as much as football, but it's close. Trust me, even a best-case scenario here will be good bordering *meh*."

"You're being a snob."

Another shrug. "We'll see."

Not that she needed to. Lili realized Dom was right when the bread baskets on the table turned out to be filled with dried-out husks of sourdough. She was just playing with him because calling Dom a snob was fun. And he was more of a snoot than he realized, though admittedly less obnoxious about it than Lili had perhaps imagined he would be.

Maybe she was still just blissed out from such an impossibly wonderful day. It wasn't just that they were moving on in the contest, it was how they had got here. She and Dom had totally pulled it off together.

Or, *Lili* had pulled herself together, after Dom had helped her. He'd been doing just fine, both before and after her semi-meltdown.

He brought her Stan. Even now, Lili could barely believe it. Her lava had been about to boil over when he suddenly left her an hour into the contest without any explanation or farewell beyond, *I'll be back.*

What the hell was that supposed to mean? Lili was about to go nuclear over her partner disappearing when he suddenly reappeared with a metaphorical S on his chest and a red cape flapping behind him, holding her beloved Stan in his arms.

From that moment on it was like someone had written Lili and Dom a concerto to play. Assuming they each knew how to play an instrument, which they probably didn't. Lili said she knew how to play the recorder and liked to believe it, but doubted she could perform if actually challenged. Middle school was an awfully long time ago, and while Lili would bet good money that Dominic Moore owned two or more guitars, with at least one of them signed by someone who snorted their weight in cocaine through the 80s, he was probably a poser who couldn't play more than a couple of chords and thus hung his guitars on the wall.

So maybe it was more like someone had written them a recipe to follow.

Tomorrow would be scary for sure, with only one team to go up against, and the best team at that. Lili still couldn't get over seeing how amazing the Kumari sisters were and how they had managed to make such a glorious-looking wedding cake in only six hours. With just the two of them.

If they could do it, then so could Lili and Dom.

They simply needed to start out stronger than they had this morning, only getting themselves into gear after losing nearly an hour and a half to Lili's ineptitude. If their team could manage that, then Lili and Dom had a (better than) decent shot at winning.

Plus, Lili was in love with their idea for the chocolate confection they would likely be creating. Their Kintsugi logo was an epic idea. Plus, it brought to mind the two of them baking in Queen of Tarts … the morning after she and Dom were together in Higher Grounds. *On the table*. No matter how delicious the dessert, baking for Lili had never been better than that.

Dom was right. Dinner was a disappointment. And not so much a meal as a steady procession of lackluster appetizers. None of those starters without finishers was especially good, but at least Lili understood their purpose once served. The producers were using food as a way to kill time in between calling contestants in for their interviews. Dom took one look at the fried mozzarella and declared that he was "full for now."

He joked that he wanted to "know his enemy" then got right to schmoozing with everyone. He was so confident and such a natural. Lili felt grateful that they'd had the chance to perform in the Upper Crust Challenge together. She had learned something about herself today.

Even if they lost the contest, this was still a big win.

Dipti approached Lili without her sister but wearing a smile wide enough to more than make up for the absence. "Your chili-chocolate buttercream—" Dipti shook her head while licking her lips. "*The best* taste in my mouth today! Would it be totally inappropriate if I asked you for the recipe?"

"Oh my—" Lili touched her chest, buying a moment to think. "That's so kind of you. Of course, it's not inappropriate! I don't mind you asking at all," she shook her head to show it, "but I hope you won't hate me if I said that even as flattered as I am that you love it so much, and I really, *really* mean that, it took me years of practice to develop that buttercream, and it's still a little too much like a baby to me, you know, since I've not had any babies of my own. Yet. I mean, someday ... a long time from now ... if, or I guess *when* things work out."

OMG. Lili laughed to cover how annoying she was being.

"I knew it was a long shot." Dipti kept smiling. "Honestly, I'd keep that recipe to myself too! But it never hurts to ask. Ask me how I got the recipe for my no-bake tiramisu ..."

They laughed together. Lili stopped, then kept going on and on with a six-course meal of compliments about the Kumari's incredible creation, citing Love Story as not just the best cake in this round, better than their mountain, Lili had to admit, but also one of her all-time faves.

"Thank you. Really. That means so much." Did this girl ever stop smiling?

Not really. Not even when she was talking about their morning's most disastrous moment.

"We left our butter a little too close to the stove, and the fat separated," Dipti admitted.

Compelled to reciprocate, Lili started talking about her earlier freakout but felt safer confessing a couple of her historical disasters, like the time she tried to melt chocolate and thought it "needed a little something" just before pouring a full cup of milk into it.

The smile finally fell from Dipti's face. "The chocolate seized?"

"Big time. Cold milk." Lili shrugged. "I haven't worked with chocolate since. Well, not until prepping for this challenge, but it was fine. That's when I learned that baking was more science than art."

And saying that simple sentence out loud, Lili felt like more of a professional than an amateur for once.

Rati joined the conversation, and Lili fell deeper in awe, not just with the sisters but with this entire situation. She was talking shop with two of the top bakers in her region, and keeping up with her part of the conversation.

No, Lili wasn't an amateur anymore. Alicia was right. She really needed to stop seeing herself that way. Participating in this competition, testing her skills, and connecting with fellow bakers, the totality of it all had proven that *this* is what Lili should be doing with her life.

The realization was like smelling freshly baked cookies from inside a musty room. She looked over at Dom, seeing him surrounded by Bria, Rebecca, and that producer lady, Diana … who seemed to be around Dom a lot more than she needed to be … or was around anyone else.

Diana was also looking at him more than she should have been. Probably imagining his abs like a harlot. Thinking about ways to get him naked.

Dom saw Lili looking and waved at her. Absorbed by the horde, he was probably looking to her for an exit.

"I'll be right back" Lili told the Kumaris, as soon as she felt certain it wouldn't sound rude.

"It's something she added to the milk, I think," Dom was finishing a thought as Lili approached the conversation. "It's like crack. Not only can I not get enough of the stuff, I've seen half of Mountain View lining up outside her little coffee shop begging the person in front of them for a spot because everyone is so desperate to get inside before she runs out for the day."

He spied Lili approaching, then turned back to the women. "I guess it's time for our interview." Dom shook his head in feigned disappointment. "Sorry, ladies, but it looks like duty calls."

He grabbed Lili and steered her out of the dining area, then into the hallway outside the interview room. "Thanks. I had to get out of there."

"Were you talking about me?"

"I sure was." He grinned.

"Weren't you laying it on a little thick? Half of Mountain View?" Lili laughed, because really, this was sweeter than their cake today. "The only thing anyone has ever begged me for at Higher Grounds is a discount."

"They don't know that. It's called advertising."

"It's lying." She laughed again.

"Marketing then."

"Potato, Po-tato."

"Fair," He shrugged, "but it's still worth talking Higher Grounds up as much as we can while we're here. We can only mention one business on the actual show, but most of the people I've been talking to are relatively local. And a lot of them consider themselves mavens and really like to talk. Maybe they'll go back and talk about you."

He grinned again.

"Thanks." She didn't know what else to say. "Seriously ... this is ..."

It was stupid, that's what it was. All these dumb feelings coming out of nowhere, making her heart melt like butter left too close to the stove on account of his wanting to look out for her.

"This is ..." Dom prompted, wanting Lili to finish her sentence.

She looked at him, telling herself how easy it would be to just say what was on her mind. Let him know how she had been feeling.

He obviously wanted to know.

She drew a breath, ready to speak, but a door opened right next to Lili just as she opened her mouth. A producer — not the one who was clearly trying to have Dom's baby, but the tall guy, Jamal, who seemed perfectly nice — came bustling out of the interview room.

"Oh, there you are! Perfect. I was just coming to get you."

The interview was short, and it went well at the start, despite Dom having to redirect the exchange a few different times after their interviewer seemed more interest in subjects like football and (insultingly) a trip to the Playboy Mansion than the Upper Crust Challenge, or why either Lili or Dom had decided to enter the contest.

"The Queen of Tarts is a really special place." Dom smiled for the interviewer, but really it was for the camera, his grandma, and even the partner sitting right next to him. "So is Louise, the amazing lady who owns the place. She's my grandma, and I wouldn't be who I am today if not for the lovely woman who raised me. Unfortunately, Louise wasn't able to make it. But I think we were all big winners anyway: Mountain View, me, and everyone watching the Challenge either here or at home. Thanks to her absence, our local baking legend, Liliana Travis, was able to represent the town."

"And how did you two meet?" The interviewer pushed a pair of Buddy Holly glasses higher on his nose and waited for Lili to answer.

"It was in high school. We had Stats together."

The interviewer sighed, and Lili knew what he was about to say. The same thing he'd already corrected her on a couple of times (and Dom not at all) already.

"Please remember to rephrase the questions in your responses and speak in the present tense about each moment. We need your interview to—"

"I understand. Sorry. I'll do it again."

Then she did. TV was so weird. The interviewer had her rehash the day, rephrasing his questions and answering in present tense about those events, of course, until the queries suddenly ended, and she found herself bumping shoulders with Dom.

"You did great! Seriously. You should be a celebrity baker or something."

"No way." Lili shook her head. "Not for me. Once upon a never in hell."

"I hope that one day you can see all the things I see in you." He touched her arm, and it didn't even seem like a line.

"Okay, Hallmark." Though Lili melted like butter again as she followed him out into the hall.

Jamal was there again. He flinched when he saw them, quickly regaining his composure and appearing to reassure Dom with a friendly pat on his shoulder. "Don't worry. It happens to the best of us."

Lili had no idea what he was referring to. By the look on Dom's face, neither did he.

Oblivious or not, the producer continued. "I mean, not me ... but, you know. All big celebrities have a sex tape at some point. It's like a right of passage."

Lili's heart scraped the floor as Dom whipped out his phone. She watched his eyes widen in horror as he found the clip.

The phone trembled in his hand as she peeked at the screen. He gasped, nearly dropping it. Lili tried to decipher what she was seeing.

She didn't care who it was with nearly as much as when the interlude might have taken place. Was Dom sleeping with someone else while sleeping with her? Well, no, their encounter was just a two-night-stand. She had no claim on him.

But now that Lili had finally come to terms with her true feelings for him, the idea of him sleeping with another girl was agony. That didn't stop her from pulling his arm closer, so she could get a better look at the screen.

The first clue hit her with a slap of familiarity as Lili recognized the duck-covered tablecloth and realized that the footage was from Higher Grounds.

And the reality was so much worse than him sleeping with someone else.

She screamed loud enough for half of the White Dove to hear her as the realization struck her like lightning: the girl in Dominic Moore's scandalous sex tape was one Liliana Travis.

Dom

Dom had never seen Lili run so fast.

At first, he gave chase, leaving the prattling Jamal behind him, catching up easily, then backing off after Lili reeled around on him and yelled, "STAY AWAY FROM ME!"

Then she turned back around and somehow managed to run even faster.

Dom let the doors close on her elevator and took the stairs, making it onto the hallway carpet as Lili was halfway to the room.

She almost slammed the door, but he caught it with his foot, then slipped inside, where Lili was already freaking out.

"It's going to be okay." Dom made a promise he couldn't keep because he didn't know what else to do. It wasn't safe to approach her, and a punch to the gut watching her wear down the carpet with angry pacing heels, barely controlling her breath and trying not to hyperventilate.

"It's really not even that big a deal." He tried to calm her. "No one will be able to tell it's you. The clip is less than thirty seconds, and you can't see the name Higher Grounds, or who—"

"THEY WILL KNOW!"

Dom couldn't help but fall back in surprise.

He swallowed, not just realizing how big of a deal this actually was, but how big of a deal it was to *Lili*. Wanted or not, he was used to the spotlight, even if it made him uncomfortable, he knew how to handle it.

Lili had never had this sort of exposure, especially with so many circumstances beyond her control. Except for that time she was captured on a video that still made Titus a C-note each month. And she had only just started to forgive them both for that, much tamer, incident.

Lili recovered her breath and made her argument stronger. "The town will know, Dominic. I'm so not into any of this. I just wanted to bake and maybe get some attention for the bakery I might one day possibly open if I could ever get enough money or courage or a heart or ruby red slippers or whatever it is that's keeping me from being brave like I know I should be."

A deep, heaving breath, and for a moment, Dom didn't know whether Lili would continue.

But then: "Now there are cameras everywhere, and interviewers telling me that I can only talk about my day in present tense like my life is a YA novel, or producers constantly pawing you to—"

"Only one of them is doing that."

"I mean, the women, Dom. It's unrelenting. I mean, fine, whatever, I get it, really I do, but it's not just the harem that follows you *everywhere*. It's that now there are FUCKING SEX TAPES!"

Lili flopped back on the nearest bed and started to sob. Full-on rage tears as she muttered a flow of upset and indecision.

"*I just can't do this anymore,*" was the only thing Dom could decipher.

He lay on the bed next to Lili and squeezed her hand. He waited through a long moment, wanting to make sure that she knew he wasn't trying to rush her into getting over it in a hurry. Even tried to make it, so two sets of breath eventually eased into a similar track.

Then he said, "I promise, it does get easier over time."

Lili had stopped crying, and for the first time since fleeing to the room, her voice sounded clear. "It's all a disaster now, but it wasn't before you came back. Really, for so long, it wasn't. You were finally gone, and my life was simple. Now I'm in over my head."

"You're not over your head, Liliana. We both know you were doing what you were born to do today."

"You don't know what you're talking about." She shook her head.

"Then tell me." He squeezed her hand harder. "It sucks to have a sex tape, but you're not alone in this. We're—"

"I think I might be in love with you!" Lili blurted, and then as if guest-starring in a comic strip, she slapped a surprised hand over her O of a mouth.

Dom felt frozen. His heart was beating too hard, yet somehow expanding. Previously buried emotions were already swarming up to war inside him.

Of course, it was an out-of-this-world revelation to discover that Liliana Travis might actually love him. *Dom.* Not the footballer, Dominic Moore, but the kid who sat a few seats away from her in Stats, and the man he grew to become.

But Dom couldn't be the person Lili needed or deserved, especially seeing as he was on his way out of Mountain View; the second opportunity sent him a ticket. If not sooner.

He needed to end this.

"I should never have just said that!" Lili covered her face.

"You should always say what you mean." He turned and pulled her around, so they were facing each other on the bed.

He gently moved Lili's hands away from her face so he could see her.

Even tear-streaked and a total mess, she was beautiful like always.

Her eyes were big and shining bright ... and the way she was staring into his ... there was only one thing to do. The one thing he really shouldn't do.

But he did it anyway, leaning forward to kiss her.

She kissed him back, harder and hungrier than he'd been expecting.

There was something more than their mouths in that kiss, but Dom told himself to ignore it. He needed Lili as much as Lili needed him.

They only broke their connection for the time it took to wrangle a condom, then they were connected like never before.

Dom was alive inside her, moving in and out of both her body and time. Feeling not only the fever of passion but the overpowering need for Lili to know at this moment that he was breathing only for her.

In and out, slow and then faster, meeting each other with twin stares as a bridge to each other until they finally finished.

And soon, she was asleep in his arms.

But slumber proved impossible for Dom. He stayed in bed, staring up at the ceiling, wrestling with a withering guilt, admonishing himself for his wrongs, using Lili to fill the need in himself.

Yes, their connection was deeper than it had ever been. But this was still a mistake. With Lili using words like love. Unless he was planning to stay in Mountain View, he was only leading her on.

But … could he stay in his hometown?

Thinking back to his recent time with Lili, it was easy to imagine a nice life in Mountain View. He didn't need to work and could pay for Lili to open her bakery, not that she would want that.

If Louise couldn't keep up with Queen of Tarts because of her blood pressure, Lili might even be willing to take it over.

Maybe they could run the place as a team, working together like they had been doing so well … more often than not.

It almost hurt to imagine a life with Lili in Mountain View. Like too much sugar in his system. Dom had never felt like this about anyone, so of course, he smelled a trap.

But what if it wasn't?

What if this was exactly what love was supposed to feel like?

The thought was inescapable, no matter how hard Dom kept trying to sleep. It came circling back every time. He was grateful when he saw his phone flashing on the nightstand with a call.

He leaned over and grabbed it. He looked at the screen, saw the call was from Angelica, and swung his feet onto the floor, creeping into the bathroom to take the call.

Dom redialed, having missed his agent by the time he closed the door.

"What's up?" he whispered.

"I guess you have company."

"What makes you ask that?"

"You're whispering, and there's an echo. Are you in a bathroom?"

"What's up, Angelica?"

"Sound more excited. I am. You got the gig! This isn't an almost-thing or pending audition. Business Affairs just sent over the contract."

"That's great!" His exclamation felt like a farce.

"This is *such* a big win for us, Dom. I didn't think we were going to make it out of the scandal at all, let alone turn your biggest loss into a win."

"Well, I guess I appreciate you lying to me then."

"Necessary. I called in a lot of favors to get you considered. Great job landing it. Now don't mess this up. Altruence Brown is apparently thrilled with the decision. He says that he can't wait to work with you."

"I don't have the words." Really, he didn't.

"You need to be in Chicago tomorrow."

"*Tomorrow*? Are you serious?"

"Yes, tomorrow, Dom. Do you think Business Affairs would be in touch today if you weren't expected in Chicago tomorrow?"

"How would I know that?"

"Trust me," Angelica said.

"I can't be in Chicago tomorrow. I need at least one more day."

"You might as well ask for a month. Some exec is flying in from New York. They have a whole thing planned. You need to be there, and I promised you could be. That you *would be*, Dom. I did that. For you."

"And here I was, thinking you did it for a percentage."

"Tomorrow. Chicago."

"Tomorrow is the final day for the Upper Crust Challenge."

"I don't know what that is, but I bet it doesn't pay you seven figures a year after a scandalous ejection from the NFL. Are you in or out, Dom?"

"You have to buy me one more day. This isn't on me, Angelica. It's not like I agreed and am suddenly pulling the rug out from under you. It's either one more day or my answer has to be no."

"Fine. Hold on." There was a long pause wherein Angelica might have been texting. Dom reminded himself to keep breathing, but he felt like his future hung in the balance, and he wasn't at all sure which way he wanted it to go. Finally, his agent came back on the line, sounding more annoyed than pleased. "They need to see you the day after tomorrow. I hate you for making us start off on the wrong foot with—"

"But you love the juicy percentage that makes it all worth it."

"You're welcome."

"Thanks." Dom ended the call with another word he didn't feel.

Looking into the mirror, the only emotion percolating to the surface was guilt. He felt sick to his stomach, thinking about his selfish mistake.

What am I going to tell Lili?

Lili

L ili woke up feeling like she was glowing, and the sensation had yet to pass despite her being well into her morning. They were prepping for the day, but her thoughts were scattered all over the place.

Mostly on the past, present, and future.

As impossible as it was to believe, Lili was kinda, sorta in a relationship with Dominic Moore. The guy she had been crushing on ever since she knew about a thing called crushing. They were also a team, and they were about to kill it on their second day in the Challenge.

The Kamaris had nothing on them.

It was easy to smile at all the other contestants from her spot on top of the world. She waved across the breakfast room at the couple with their crazy matching outfits — today they had left baking behind, she was in cats, and he was wearing dogs — and over to Bria and Rebecca.

She saved her widest smile and her heartiest wave for Dipti and Rati. Even if they wiped the floor with her today, Lili had already won more than she could have ever imagined.

"You've got this," Dom assured her.

"I'm not worried." Lili laughed because really she wasn't.

"You look like you're thinking hard enough to give me a headache."

"That's not how headaches work, but yes, I've been going over and over the plan in my head. Thinking through my steps." She told him one of the things she'd been considering. "I was wondering if we should use blue dye in the sugar?"

"That is the color scheme."

"But we were planning on going with gold. Should we stick with that?"

"Maybe we could—"

"Maybe we can make it extra vibrant by mixing a bit of edible gold paint into the mixture. To get just the right sparkle for our Kintsugi effect."

"Pretty much what I was going to say." He grinned. "Let's make time for a mold. We can make the producers love us more than they already do by breaking our creation before putting it back together with the—"

"Why will that make the producers love us?"

"Because the producers love whatever the cameras love, and smashing the shit out of our glorious work will make for quite the moment."

"I love your thinking," she replied with a flush.

Should she have said *like* instead?

Lili dismissed her nonsense, but it was harder to ignore all the cameras.

"You'll get used to it," Dom said as if reading her thoughts.

"I'm not sure I ever will. That guy over there is recording everything."

"That's the local news. They do seem to love the minutia."

"Do they always have to record everything? It's not like anyone actually wants to watch us eating breakfast. Can you imagine if this is what they broadcast?" Lili looked around the room. "Even international superstar Dominic Moore wouldn't be enough to keep that from being boring."

"You'll get used to it." He kept holding her hand, right there on top of the table, in plain view of the local news and anyone else who wanted to look.

No shit, this was really a relationship.

The local reporter spotted Dom and raised her eyebrows at the sight of those braided fingers. She whispered something to her cameraman, and he instantly shifted positions.

Lili held her head high, straightening her shoulders as she wondered how much she hated that snooty reporter bitch on a scale of one to ten.

What started as a two or so was at a six by the time the reporter was three feet from Lili, only coming over because of their hand-holding, though the professional liar still pretended like she cared about what Lili might say.

"How are you enjoying the competition so far?"

"It's great!" Lili exclaimed.

"We're having a wonderful time," added Dom, with what sounded like the minimum required amount of emotion.

"The Upper Crust Challenge is in Wyndham County for the first time ever, and everyone's watching. I hear that after a rough start yesterday, the two of you bounced back, showing a lot of confidence in the second half."

The reporter held the mic in front of her as the camera zoomed in. Lili pretended to enjoy both things instead of totally hating them.

"It was just the first little bit that was off," she felt like defending herself. When the mic wouldn't leave its new home just inches from her lips, she added, "It's easy to feel confident when you have a great partner."

Dom mugged for the camera. "I'm lucky to be working with the best baker in Mountain View."

"How confident are you in your strategy?"

"A hundred-percent." Dom nodded with confidence and grinned for his punchline. "Our win is in the oven."

"I also hear that the Challenge will be doing something they've never done, in a category that hasn't been announced. How can you be so sure?"

Lili flinched, hoping the reporter had it wrong and wrapped an arm around her partner. "My teammate is great at running the numbers."

The reporter smiled, too wide for the moment. Or so Lili thought.

"I've heard." The reporter smiled again. "I'm sure that will help you in your new role as a commentator on SportsBar."

Lili felt a shadow of confusion drift over her, worsened by the sensation of Dom physically stiffening under her arm.

"That position hasn't been confirmed." He clearly tried to cover his nerves with a laugh.

"SportsBar made an announcement this morning. You and Altruence Brown will be co-hosting a daily roundtable—"

"I honestly just heard the news from my agent." Dom killed her report with an awkward smile. "I'm really not aware of the details." Then looking like he just remembered something, he added, "But I couldn't be more excited about the position."

And another awkward laugh.

What the hell? Lili was freaking out inside while trying to hold her smile.

She'd been so stupid. Dom was moving. Of course he was moving. SportsBar was in Chicago, and scandal or no scandal, he apparently cared more about buckets of money than he did about her.

Which meant that last night hadn't been the tectonic shift for him that it had been for her. She wanted to run from the room. But that's the girl she had been yesterday, and she wasn't willing to be that girl two days in a row anymore.

Dom droned on in the background, after the reporter had apparently warmed him up, she heard him warble something about how excited he was for this next phase of his career, then about how it always seemed that when one door closed, another one opened, plus a couple of other clichés that made her want to strangle him after she'd made the gargantuan mistake of confessing her love, having no idea that she would get frozen in this nightmarish parody of glee for two full minutes that felt like an eternity, until the camera's unflinching gaze finally left her.

Lili was desperate to prove she could stay rooted.

But her need to flee was overwhelming.

She was out of her seat and racing toward the empty sound stage, making it to where the kitchens were prepped and awaiting a new day's attention.

Lili went to Stan, grabbed her mixer, and told him exactly what she was feeling.

"We need to get the hell—"

Dom

"—out of here," Dom heard Lili mutter to himself as he stepped onto the sound stage.

He looked over at the counter where they had made their cake mountain together just one day before. But instead of the unrestrained glee he had seen on Lili's face in flow, baking like she'd been born to do, her expression now was fully harrowed, the corners of her mouth drooping in an unrelenting frown, her big eyes brimming with tears she proudly refused to lose.

She kept violently tugging at Stan's cord, but it had been worked into the tabletop to obscure it from view and wasn't budging. Dom walked over to her, trying to make his manner match the calm in his voice.

"Be careful—" he gave her a smile she didn't want to see "—you don't want to hurt poor Stan."

Lili reeled around and met him with a snarl. "It's just a stupid mixer."

But of course it wasn't.

"I'm sorry," he tried.

"When did you find out?" She didn't want to hear his apology. "When did you know that you got that job, Dom?"

"My agent called last night, after you fell asleep."

"I don't know what's worse, knowing that you would leave when you got the job and still going through with last night, or finding out afterward and then still saying yes."

She shook her head, refusing the first tear from falling down her cheek.

"I didn't—"

"Were you just using me, or what?"

"No! Of course not. I had no idea that the job would come through — my agent said it was a long shot from the beginning — and even if I got the gig, I had no idea that you and I would be a … thing."

"A thing. Thanks. I appreciate you clarifying what we were." A second tear threatened in the other eye, but she refused that one too. "I'm glad to know it's a thing."

"That's not fair, Lili. We—"

"You will *always* be chasing something bigger and better. And I *never* would have been enough for you because I live a small-town life, and Mountain View is just a little too tiny for you."

"That's not—"

"You're famous and I'm not, so it never would have worked anyway. It's just as well that this happened now. Before anyone got hurt."

Lili seemed injured already, and that stabbing pain in his stomach wasn't exactly a picnic for Dom.

"That's not fair," he tried for the third time. "We were—"

"You're right, Dom. It's not fair. This is all really, grossly, massively *un*fair."

He waited for her to stop, then listened to the heavy breathing as Lili slowly reset herself, maybe waiting to hear what Dom might say next or perhaps champing at the bit to cut him off yet again.

When the silence finally felt oppressive enough that he could no longer stand it, Dom broke their stalemate.

"Can you please just get over all of this already?"

"GET OVER IT?"

Maybe it was the wrong thing to say … Lili's cheeks went from blushing to crimson. She gritted her teeth tight enough to sink through a metal plate. "You want me to just *get over my feelings?*"

"No." He shook his head, tweaking the message. "You have every right to your feelings, and I would never want you to 'get over them.' But I do think we should move past these …" He had to be careful. "These *misconceptions.*"

Dom stole a breath.

Lili stared, waiting for him to continue.

"We're two people, but you won't stop seeing me as *just* a football player." Another pause, and it really felt like Lili was listening. "But the truth is, you're not in love with me. You're in love with the *idea of me.*"

Too far. It looked like Dom had just slapped her.

"I'm sorry." He tried to backpedal.

"You've said that. A few times now. Too bad everything else you're saying proves the opposite."

Dom didn't reply. He had to think about his words. He really was trying, even if his results had been disastrous so far. He needed to ease this situation but wasn't sure how. He felt torn. Of course, he cared about Lili — more than he had ever cared about any woman ever.

"Last night *was* special but I still need a job, and the only thing I've ever been truly great at in my entire life is football. This is a good gig for me and—"

"Maybe you've only been great at football because you've never tried anything else! You just keep doing what's in front of you instead of *deciding* what to do. That's—"

"How are you any better?" Dom snapped, finally losing some of the composure he had been working so hard to level. "All you ever do is wait for that perfect moment when you can finally achieve some magical dream! Waiting for fairies to sprinkle pixie dust all over your life, letting it pass you by when you could be living it instead!"

"Well, isn't that just—"

Lili stopped as the door opened, and Diana entered the room with an awkward smile.

"I'm so sorry, but this room is still mic'ed for the show," she told them.

Dom and Lili traded a look of alarm.

"Nothing was recorded," Diana assured them with another awkward smile. "But this might not be the best place to continue this conversation." She glanced at Stan. "Did you need some help with that ... or would you like us to bring another mixer out?"

"I just need help getting this out of here." Lili was still near tears but she'd regained her composure. "I'm leaving, and I need to take it with me."

"Woah. Wait a minute." Diana shook her head. "You can't leave. Filming starts in less than an hour."

"I wish you all the best of luck on today's show, but I won't be a part of it," Lili insisted.

"But you're one of the two finalists!" Diana clearly couldn't believe she was having this argument. "You could win everything today."

"I don't care." Lili yanked at Stan's cord, still to no avail.

"I'm *really sorry*, Lil, but please, don't ruin this because of me. Louise didn't let you down, I did. You can't—"

"I can, Dom, and I need to. Just—"

"Even if you forget about my grandma, think about yourself! Don't you understand what kind of doors winning the Upper Crust Challenge could open for you if you're just willing to see it through?"

"He's right," Diana added.

But Lili ignored her. "Like you even care."

She yanked on Stan's cord again. This time it came flying out of the socket, but the end caught on the counter and with a rip Stan's wiring came right out of the bottom of the little red mixer that could.

Lili hugged her fallen comrade to her chest like she was about to make her exodus with him, one lone tear finally making a track down her cheek, but then she set Stan back on the counter and started toward the door empty-handed.

"Where are you going?" Diana called after her. "You can't just—"

"I'm going to hair and makeup!" Lili shouted as she turned back at the door. "Let's get this farce over and done with."

Lili

Are you still mad?

Submissions <submissions@mansplanations.mvdaily.org>
To: Annabelle Lyons <a.lyons@mountainviewuniversity.edu>

Hello?

Lili felt like Elmer Fudd with an egg frying on top of her head, furious at the rascally rabbit that everyone always loved, chewing on his stupid carrot while giving the hunter that crooked grin.

She scoured her mind but couldn't remember a single time she'd ever been angrier. She was forced into doing something she didn't want to do, with a person she wished she was a continent away from right now, working together in front of a live studio audience.

She wished she could beat this situation to batter and then bake it to ashes.

DAMMIT.

Lili collected her breath. She had to hold this close. Fury eclipsed sorrow, if she let out so much as a drop of her mounting sadness inside, the dam would surely burst entirely. On national television.

So she smiled as the host kickstarted the Upper Crust Challenge, pretending that Dom wasn't standing way too close to her, ignoring the truth that he only cared about himself and that his selfishness was a stink wafting into her nostrils.

"Are you ready for Day Two?" Phoebe Brooke trumpeted to both contestants and audience.

The Kumari sisters, her friends the day before, now looked like a set of bobbleheads standing behind their counter with oversized smiles. Lili could care less about whatever was on Dom's face, but she did her best to appear ebullient.

"People like to say that cooking is more like art, and baking is more like science," Phoebe continued. "But those of you diehard bakers at home know that what we do with our ingredients is different every time, even if we're working from the same recipe. There is definitely an art to this science."

She smiled for the camera. "But sometimes our recipes need an update or a tweak. Every so often, they need to be tossed out entirely ..."

Lili was having a hard time focusing on the host, with most of her attention fixed on wondering what the audience — both the live one in front of her and those at home later, watching the actual event or the clips of her breakdown on YouTube — would think if she shoved Dom off of the stage. He weighed more than her, and was probably used to keeping his body rigid in the face of assault, but a boiling fury inside her had Lili picturing Domicide.

Assuming he broke his neck when she pushed him.

Maybe he didn't deserve to *die*, but Lili would empty her bank account to pay for his public humiliation.

Instead, Dom couldn't stop smiling, proving for the zillionth time that the cameras loved him and wanted to have all of his babies.

A lilt in the host's voice drew Lili's attention.

Her smile seemed almost mischievous as she finished a thought that Lili had missed the beginning of.

"And that's why we decided to shake things up this year ..."

Lili swallowed with a horrible thought: *Does that mean we're not doing chocolate?*

"The judges felt that the Upper Crust Challenge is for true bakers, and as such, they wanted to present a true and fair challenge ..."

Phoebe held her pause to help the audience appreciate the announcement.

"So this year, instead of a general category, our two remaining teams will each be given a specific dessert to create." Another performative beat. "Your final creations will be judged on taste, construction, and overall creativity. Make sure that you add your personal flair."

Phoebe looked at each of the teams in turn. "What about your dessert could only come from the two of you?"

It wasn't a question with an expected answer, but her next one was. "Are you ready?"

"Yes!" they all said together.

Lili loathed the moment in whole but especially hated the way Dom's voice overlapped with hers like a song.

She wished she could elbow him in the ribs right now.

"Are you ready?" That time her question was for the audience.

"YES!" They roared, surely not a single one needing to fake it.

Phoebe pulled a braided cord and parted a curtain.

Then everyone was staring at a giant gameshow-style wheel, neatly lined with simple yet stunning images featuring some of Lili's favorite desserts. She scanned the selection — no cakes but plenty of confections that she knew how to make, including the chocolate bark she and Mr. Spotlight had practiced together. She would have sighed with relief if not for the audience, who would have noted her gesture as obvious.

The furiously clapping crowd had been at it for a while. They started as soon as they saw the wheel and kept getting louder, apparently realizing how much they loved this new twist.

Just when Lili was wondering who would be giving the wheel of her future a whirl, the host answered the question for her.

"Who wants to give this thing a spin?"

A sea of open palms shot from the audience into the air.

But even Lili knew who the host was going to pick. A little sprite, seven years old or so, with actual pigtails.

Lili boiled even hotter as the adorable girl walked up to the stage, strutting in a way that proudly showed off her Disney Princess clogs.

The audience loved it, but Lili loathed her fate in the hands of this child.

Pippy grinned at the roomful of new fans, then stretched up on her toes and gave the wheel a hearty spin.

The crowd fell instantly silent. No clapping or whispers, only the hurried ticking of plastic passing plastic, growing steadily slower and slower …

… and slower …

… and about to land on chocolate bark!

Lili wanted to yip with glee, but then the wheel made one final tick, flopping forward one last space and landing on the lone image that had been making her want to hyperventilate.

"*Croquembouche!*" the host announced.

The declaration was thunder and lighting.

Still smiling, the host explained Lili's nightmare to the audience.

"Croquembouche is a French dessert made from choux pastry puffs, piled into the shape of a cone and finished with a caramel lacquer. This five-star dessert is often served at weddings in Italy and France. Here at the Upper Crust Challenge, we'll be serving croquembouche to see which of these two teams has what it takes to be this year's champion."

Choux pastry. The one thing Lili could never master, and now she had to make a tower of it.

Lili couldn't help but bury her face in her hands.

"Remember the cameras," Dom reminded her with a nudge.

She wanted to nudge him back with her knuckles on his nose. Of course, he never ever ever ever ever forgot about the cameras. He probably had cameras in the bathroom so he could watch himself shower using a picture-in-picture display while reviewing his game footage and red carpet appearances.

Dipti and Rati looked like the host had just announced bonus vacations to Bermuda for anyone who knew how to boil an egg, actually high-fiving on camera while Lili was still being a strong and modern woman by refusing to cry.

She and Dom were thoroughly screwed.

Lili could barely breathe.

The six-hour clock was already ticking, and she had no idea where to start, assuming that running out of the room and rushing right into the nearest ice cream parlor was totally out of the question.

She almost wanted to laugh at the hilarity of yesterday, back when an oblivious version of Liliana Travis had been arrogant enough to think of herself as a professional instead of the amateur she so obviously was.

Not just an amateur, an *idiot*. Because what other kind of person enters a (televised) baking competition when she didn't even know how to make one of the possible desserts?

What had she been thinking?

And what was Dom thinking, erasing their whiteboard and scribbling his dumb ideas all over it. She stood with an open mouth, watching him, unable to move or do anything else as he scrawled:

RASPBERRY AND WHITE CHOCOLATE
ORANGE AND CLOVE
SPRINKLES AND ALMOND FLAKES?

"What are you doing?" Lili asked, even though she knew.

"I'm listing possible fillings. Should we do a buttercream? Yours is—"

"Just STOP." She shook her head. Maybe that would keep it from exploding. "I need to figure this out."

"You're not alone here, Lil, and you don't need to figure it out. I can help."

"Yeah?" she scoffed. "What can you do, magically—"

"I'm actually really good with choux."

Another scoff, followed by a laugh. "You couldn't make snicker-doodles a week ago."

"I made my first batch of snickerdoodles with my mom, right after my dad died, just before she left me." Dom was totally sober, in sharp contrast to her mocking laughter. "I've been baking with my grandma for as long as I can remember. She said you needed to give me baking lessons, so I pretended. For you."

"Why would you do that? And why for me?"

He drizzled some gas on his earlier insult and flicked a lit match onto it. "Because you needed a win."

"*I needed a win?*" she snapped, a little too loud considering the audience. Lili lowered her voice but unleashed her fury. "I don't need any favors from you, and I sure as hell don't need any 'pity lessons.' What a total waste of my time."

He opened his mouth, but Lili wasn't going to let him have it. Not now that what she really meant was bubbling out of her lips. "Is there anything about you that's NOT FAKE?"

Again too loud, but this time she cared even less.

Dom apparently knew there wasn't any right answer to her question, but like a coward, he didn't even try to find one.

"Fine." She couldn't even look at him. "Go on. If you're the expert then—"

"I want to make something really special." In spite of it all he still sounded earnest. "What if we mixed our high school colors in by making light blue macarons to go with the choux in our tower?"

"Now you're just wasting time. Again." She softened her voice. "It's croquembouche. Profiteroles. Just profiteroles. Not buttercream filling, and not macarons."

Dom looked back at her as if searching for words.

"Croquembouche is supposed to be made from profiteroles with pastry cream and caramel. Have you ever made an actual croquembouche?"

"No. But I've made plenty of choux."

"We don't have time for this, Dom. We have time for two things at most, making the classic dessert as best as we possibly can. If we're lucky enough to finish in time, then we can use our extra minutes to pray."

He looked at her, chewing on a thought and still playing the coward.

"Do you have something to—"

Dom

"—say?" Lili glared at him.

He took a deep breath.

Reminded himself of how they got here to settle his emotions.

Yes, Lili was pissed at him. He understood that, and couldn't argue with the root of what she must be going through. But Dom couldn't possibly see how he had done anything to inspire this much ire.

He failed to tell her about a phone call when he should have. Maybe that confession wouldn't have been so hard to make if he hadn't been so worried about her potential reaction. A response that he imagined might be an awful lot like this, at its worst. That's what made it feel like a confession instead of the good news that it was.

And yet, intentionally or not, led her on, making it easy for Lili to believe that they wanted the same things and at the same time.

She had always known he was leaving. He'd made that clear from the start. But maybe she'd thought last night changed that. Maybe he had accidentally made a silent promise he could never have kept.

Of course she was hurt.

"No." He shook his head. "I have nothing to say."

He did his best to appease her further by letting her lead, disregarding his doubts, not around her abilities as a baker, but with a dessert, she had never successfully made, with base components built around what Lili had loudly identified as her culinary kryptonite.

They were back to their first hour from yesterday, with her refusing to collaborate. He stood back until she was clearly stuck in an obvious mistake, and he needed to either insert himself or consign their team to disaster.

Lili's fury while working was unfortunate yet acceptable, but her runny dough was not.

"Can I suggest—"

"No!" she snapped. "I know what I'm doing. I can see that it's runny. I'm going to add flour."

A big mistake if he allowed it to happen, so Dom grabbed the flour from Lili — more of a snatch than he intended after she went to pour it.

"You can't add flour. You have to start from scratch if you've already added the eggs."

"It's just a little," Lili argued.

And he really wanted to give it to her, but that would only make everything worse. "We'll get cracks."

No words as she glared at him.

Or once she was finally done dumping her dough with a vacant expression, dramatically proving that she was now starting over.

Thanks to him.

Her movements turned angry and erratic.

"You should do the flour all at once," Dom told her.

Lili sifted it in slowly while staring at him.

He refused the bait, telling himself that their choux could have a couple of cracks. No big deal. They still had plenty of time to conjure a solution.

He turned the oven on high while Lili finished the dough.

But Dom couldn't even get that right.

"That's way too high for pastry," she said after stomping over.

"The best way to do this is to set it high and change the temperature partway through."

"Right." She nodded. "That is the best way to crack choux."

"I know what I'm talking about here."

"I've always used the low temp slow-bake—"

"And you've never made good choux. That's not me being a shit, Lil. You said so yourself."

Dom was only trying to communicate, but that obviously riled Lili up further.

"You might have been baking with your granny since before she was even born, but you've also clearly been tackled like ten too many times. We need—"

"Sure. Fine. Whatever, Liliana. We'll set it at the lower temperature like you want."

Then he did. "Now everything can take way longer, and the profiteroles won't be cooled, and even the ridiculously delicious caramel that I'm sure you could blow everyone away with if you just decided to try still won't be enough to hold this whole thing together, but at least we'll be able to watch it fall apart while—"

"FINE!" She cranked the knob.

The mood between them was hotter than the oven. Dom thought about the audience and wondered what they were thinking, wondered if they could tell that he and Lili were having a meltdown. Wondered if Lili was wondering if he was wondering about the audience and hated that she probably was. He also hated that she was right and hated all the wondering.

He spotted Diana and Jamal, the show's producers, in intense conversation before Diana stepped forward to guide two more cameramen over to Dom and Lili. They were definitely putting on a show. At least someone was going to benefit from this very public disaster.

The pastry dough ready, Dom helped Lili pipe the pastries and put them in the oven, but even with that problem (sort of) solved, there was already another one added to their bowl.

"I don't want to argue with you about filling, Dom."

"Then don't. Let's decide on something. But we need a flavor. Part of our score is based on creativity."

"I was there for the edge of our seat announcements."

"Can you please stop being a smartass for *one minute*?" Maybe he had something extra pleading in his stare because Lili finally sighed with a hint of surrender, encouraging his finish. "We can't have nothing, so can we please decide on *something*?"

She stared back at him, and Dom had no idea what to think. His frustration was at a ten. It was seriously like she couldn't even hear him anymore.

"Fine. I'll make my own filling," he said.

No response from Lili, so he turned away from her and started on his filling, looking back at the whiteboard to get going.

RASPBERRY AND WHITE CHOCOLATE
ORANGE AND CLOVE
SPRINKLES AND ALMOND FLAKES?

But that didn't help because those pairings all felt off for this moment. Dom could only think about opposites right now. His flavor considerations had to be clashing, or they would feel like a lie.

He settled on a taste that would surely surprise everyone, though its character felt honest to Dom. Strawberry and black pepper. A rare pairing, but he saw the two as a power couple of flavors. Plenty of times while home alone, Dom had made himself an oversized bowl of macerated berries, sprinkling his fruit with vanilla sugar and black pepper. Sometimes, after a rotten day, the concoction was a topping for his ice cream.

He got a mixer that was ten times better than Stan and calmly made his filling while Lili angrily prepared her pastry cream by his side.

Calm as he was, the serenity didn't save Dom from forgetting about lowering the temperature or from assuming that Little Miss I'll Do Everything Myself would be on top of it just to prove him unnecessary.

The beeping oven might as well have been a screaming fire engine.

They traded a look with a full second of shared compassion before Dom and Lili both bolted into action, darting over to the oven as a team, each of them surely knowing it was too late already.

And it was. The choux had cooked too hot, and the balls all cracked. Lili's face was knotted in frustration and defeat.

"At least they aren't too humid?" Dom failed to make her feel better.

Their choux was brittle and hard, without any time to try it again.

The profiteroles cooled in silence, the partners back to their fillings.

They stuffed the pastries with their individual offerings on two sides of a pile, a team only in name. Dom wanted to shrug, but he didn't. He wanted to say, *At least we have two types of filling!* But he didn't do that either. He wanted to acknowledge the inarguable truth that they were going to lose and clearly deserved to, but right now, it seemed that he and Lili could agree on only one thing.

That the best they could do right now was to go through the motions and get to the end of this with a minimum of embarrassment.

Still, he wished she'd quit giving him the silent treatment, breathing next to him like a dragon all out of fire.

Lili

Re: Are we still talking?

Annabelle Lyons <a.lyons@mountainviewuniversity.edu>
To: <submissions@mansplanations.mvdaily.org>

Dear Whoever you are,

The poem was beautiful. The Planck scale is theory.

Since you insist on talking ... let's talk about the major histocompatibility complex (MHC) region. Studies, yes, actual studies, have shown that women, when given a blind smell test, will always prefer the scent with the most different MHC genotype with the p-value being smaller than 0.001.

This means that they are biologically predetermined to be more attracted to those that will create the strongest immune system in any resulting children.

Now, let's dive into the psychology of it. Who you will be attracted to is very likely determined by your brain's wiring. Predisposition to like certain traits is built in.

So the experience of that moment of instant connection, so artfully described in your poem, is a biological response.

The problem with the idea of fate is that there is some force beyond our control guiding us that takes away our agency in our lives.

And the myth of soul mates is flat-out dangerous. If you can't find the same combination of psychologically attractive traits with biologically compatible genetic makeup in more than one person ... the world is a very scary place.

Kind Regards,

Annabelle

MOUNTAIN VIEW
UNIVERSITY

ANNABELLE LYONS
Associate Professor of Psychology
MountainViewUniversity.com

Lili didn't mean to give Don such an icy shoulder, but even her constant deep breaths weren't helping. Cameras were capturing her anger. The best she could do was stop talking to the source of her torment. If she stayed ice-cold, at least she wouldn't be delivering the footage that Diana and Jamal so clearly relished.

She yearned to run out of there, grab an Uber, and trade everything in her bank account for a three-hour drive. She wasn't staying for Dom or even for Louise. Lili was still there because a bajillion cameras would capture her cowardice if she left. Plus all those phones. She would be on YouTube again, as something even worse than Beaver Girl.

The threaded fingers at breakfast, cut with their angry inability to work together, now told the classic tale of a woman scorned.

Hard to believe she confessed her love to this monster who had ruined her life just last night.

She took another deep breath and got started on her caramel.

Lili was excellent at making the stuff, yet still, she questioned her efforts immediately. Everything was off this morning, so of course, her caramel would be terrible.

Her movements met the awkwardness of her thoughts and sent Lili's unthinking hand to the hot pan. She grabbed it by the handle without a potholder, then screamed as caramel flew everywhere.

Don looked panicked and came running over. He took one look at her hand and said, "Your hand—"

"I'm fine."

"You need to have the medical team look at that."

Her burning skin throbbed too much for Lili to argue, so she sat like a mute while her hand was inspected, holding her heavy silence as it got bandaged, forced to watch Dom start on a new batch of caramel.

The blessed relief of not having cameras on her for the few moments with the medic was short-lived because, by the time she was all wrapped up and ready to work again, Dom refused to let her.

"You've gotta be kidding me!" She seriously couldn't believe it.

"You're hurt."

"So what? It's not like I lost my hand. You can't build that tower all by yourself!"

"Watch me." He didn't sound surly so much as defiant. "You can't touch the caramel with your hand."

"This is the part I'm actually good at!"

"I'm sorry, Lil."

Dom was insistent, but that's not what made Lili retreat. Her hand was throbbing even harder than it had been before. She needed to sit.

But Lili only had her rear horizontal for a moment before she was back on her feet in open-mouthed horror, walking over to stop Dom from committing an atrocity upon what was a marginal creation at best.

"What?" He dared her with a look.

"You can't use that." Lili glanced at the styrofoam cone he had just secured from the supply room, her expression surely a parody of disdain.

"Why not?" He asked, while setting it in place.

"Because we'll lose points for not making the tower entirely out of pastry!"

"Well, I don't know how to do that, and you can't help me right now. So if using a cone is what it takes for us to get the job done, then guess what?" Not that he gave her even a second to answer. "That's exactly what I'm going to do."

But Dom was wrong, and the next few minutes proved it. He couldn't build and pour at the same time, so he finally surrendered and asked Lili to "pretty please with sugar on top" take the caramel from him.

It was her absolute pleasure, and even with her incapacitated hand, she managed to assemble the profiteroles into something vaguely tower-like, working around the cone because there wasn't enough time to do things right.

She tried not to let the knowledge that this was all wrong slow her down. And impossibly, they had somehow managed to create something that looked like a croquembouche with two minutes left on the clock.

Still plenty of time to pray. Dom scampered off somewhere — probably to display his abs for the nearest available camera — while Lili stood far enough back from their croquembouche to admire their work.

Not bad. Not bad at—

"What are you doing?" Lili cried out at the sight of Dom's outstretched arm shaking a small bottle over their creation.

"I'm adding a dash of black pepper."

"BLACK PEPPER?"

"It's one of those weird flavor combos. The sweet in the strawberry filling will balance the spice—"

"Last minute!" Phoebe announced.

"If you were going to use black pepper, then it should have gone into the cream filling *with* the strawberry flavor. Sprinkled on top like that—" she shook her head, could barely even say this next bit. "It'll be the first thing that hits their tongue."

"But—"

"But nothing, Dom. Even if black pepper didn't ruin your side of the croquembouche, did you even consider how your little ode to the king of spices would unbalance my pastry cream, which is decidedly not as sweet as your strawberry?"

"It might be my strawberry, but it's *our* croquembouche." Hardly an argument, and now he looked sheepish. "What can we do?"

"We—"

A buzzer sounded with the feeling of a soufflé falling flat.

The Upper Crust Challenge was over.

Lili and Dom traded a look, each of them equally helpless.

This was a total disaster.

Not just the contest but the entirety of Lili's last two days.

They left the stage with two phony smiles and then made their way to the seats with their names printed on them over by the side, sitting as the production team shot all of their closeups of the desserts, one marvelous and the other subpar.

The Kumaris totally killed it, she would have said to Dom if they were talking.

Lili wasn't jealous. She wanted to gush about their sugar-based sorcery with someone, and she had been a better partner to herself than Dom had ever been, so Lili poured some superlatives into her personal bowl and started mixing them round and round to herself.

The Kumaris' pink-colored croquembouche was perfectly conical, without using any sort of base. She counted four shades of pink: rose, blush, powder, and pastel. A complicated confection meticulously assembled with profiteroles and macarons — yes, macarons — mixed with edible flowers to decorate an edifice that was surely watering a roomful of mouths.

Did they really need to sit through the humiliation of judging? Couldn't they just let those two sweet sisters take their victory lap and excuse the losers?

"Are we ready to hear what the judges think of our desserts?" Phoebe's question was for everyone.

"YES!" replied the room. Lili, Dom, and the producers included.

The judges all agreed with Lili: the Kumaris should be made co-empresses of baking and totally get their own show (and that Lili was a total loser, even though none of them actually had the courage to say that).

Specifically, they said:

"Your flavor profile … raspberry and basil … it's just so interesting on the tongue."

"The construction, it's really outstanding. Those of you who have tried to make croquembouche before might appreciate how much you really have going on here." That judge practically whistled with appreciation. "My wife is an architect. I bet she wouldn't know whether to eat your tower or study it!"

"The choux is made to perfection, and the macarons are a *genius* addition."

She felt Dom stiffen beside her with that last one, but he didn't say anything, and the movement might have been because this part of the nightmare was mercifully over.

A full plate of compliments with a side of advice.

"The choux does get a bit soft in the middle," observed the first judge.

As the third added, "You might want to poke each of your prof-iteroles next time to vent the humidity when they're coming out of the oven."

"Sounds like that's going to be a tough dessert to beat!" Phoebe declared as she turned to Lili and Dom. "Let's see what's happening in Mountain View."

She turned her attention to their croquembouche. The judges followed her gaze, and then the audience, as if according to rehearsal.

Lili had always secretly suspected that the universe hated her, and the next second was yet another fine example.

Their entire croquembouche — which had been slowly melting under the lights for a while now, flopped off of the cone, with some of their profiteroles falling onto the table and stopping, though most rolled right onto the floor.

Lili would probably rather have peed herself on TV. The humili-ation was burning her alive. And still, she thought, *At least now no one will have to taste it.*

The host said something that Lili chose not to hear, and it seemed like the judges quickly agreed while the audience held its breath.

Not a soul was surprised when the Kumaris were announced as the winners of that year's Upper Crust Challenge. Lili was grateful for the end of things and the cue required to make her escape from the room.

She ordered an Uber before the door to the room (that she shared with Dom, dammit, she needed to hurry) closed behind her.

She stuffed clothes into her bag even faster, doing her best to ignore his clothes blended with hers on the bed, trying not to remember the way their bodies had been pressed together as if by design, their hearts pounding to make a single beat that she had always longed to hear.

A beat she would probably never stop longing for, even if she taught herself to hate him.

But the worry was unnecessary. Dom didn't interrupt her packing, and Lili didn't run into him in the hallway, or the elevator, or on her way outside the White Dove to where her Uber was already waiting.

Why would he try to stop a good riddance?

She got in the car and closed the door. Finally, alone and almost safe. The driver started to say something, but Lili cut him off.

"Please. Just drive."

The only way to get through this was to see the other side of things. Then she could decide what came next.

Lili had always been so strong. She had learned to hold it in, and over the years, she kept on getting better at it.

But today, she simply didn't have it in her.

Lili sobbed in the car at least half of the way back to Mountain View.

She would have to give this poor driver one hell of a tip.

Dom

Dom had the kind of awful night he was terrific at having, full of drinking and schmoozing, mindless exchanges with well-wishers and fans that he was already trying to forget.

After Lili scrambled out of the White Dove Hotel when the Kumaris were announced as the winners, he had to do everything in his power to minimize the fallout and execute some precision damage control. Her flight made them both look like sore losers when that wasn't the case at all.

But he couldn't exactly explain all the issues and drag their baggage into the spotlight, so he'd poured in the effort to more than make up for her absence, staying up until well past midnight, despite his exhaustion, not only agreeing to every interview request but shaking every hand and returning every smile, partying hard with the Kumaris, who it turned out could get down a lot harder than Dom had imagined. He wanted them both to know how thrilled he and Lili were for them and that they shouldn't take her flight from the Challenge personally.

"She's totally shook," Dom explained to anyone who asked, along with a multitude of people who demonstrated the opposite. "It was an unexpected and rather urgent family emergency. I don't feel comfortable sharing details without her being here, but believe me, that poor girl was doing her best."

He kept repeating himself, saying the same thing in different ways. Not just to clear Lili's name, alongside his and the good folks in Mountain View, but also because Dom knew exactly how publicity worked, both for better and worse. He also understood how content was created in the editing room. His strategy here was simple: if Dom told his story long enough and loudly enough, the producers would have a difficult, if not impossible, time getting away with an edit that made Lili look like the villain.

Yet, as the night wore on and she still hadn't returned even one of his texts, Dom began to question himself. He wasn't even sure *why* he was protecting Lili's image. She *had* run out at the end, and her flight had definitely left him to handle all of the mess by his lonesome.

And yet, he couldn't help but feel sorry for her, or responsible, or maybe even in love with someone he destroyed. But none of that mattered, not right now or maybe ever again. Even if it was abundantly clear that anything between them had been utterly demolished, Dom still wanted for Lili to get everything she wanted. With him here and her not, that left the duty to him.

Dom did it with the widest smile he could hold on his face.

He schmoozed and dined and drank with the cast and crew. He signed autographs and listened to stories from strangers that he would surely forget before sunrise. He went to battle with Diana, raising his metaphorical sword and shield against the persistent producer, plastering an engaged smile onto his face and holding it long enough to feel certain that despite his gentle yet incessant rejections, she wouldn't be taking them out on Lili.

Dom pretended to be enjoying his night all the way to his room.

The one he had been sharing with Lili just one night before when he had been imagining a life where they might have shared more.

He walked past his bed and crashed onto hers.

The sheets still smelled like Lili.

He looked over at the other bed, pictured the two of them trading stares like they had last night, then found himself nodding off to sleep while thinking he should probably shower.

But then he'd have to leave her scent, and right now, that felt like the last thing in the world he should do, so he embraced the sound of an idle snore as it left him and allowed himself to fall asleep.

Dom opened his eyes to a new day and the rest of his life in front of him, ready to greet the opportunity he had been hoping to land, his most recent dream come true after a short flight to Chicago.

And yet for some reason (he knew the reason), Dom could not have been less excited.

He grabbed his phone and looked at the email from Angelica again, reading over the details of his flight. If he'd gone to Chicago yesterday like both SportsBar and his agent had wanted, he would have enjoyed the intimate luxury of a private jet. Instead, he was flying semi-private. Not really a hardship or anything Dom could ever really complain out loud about, and even thinking it filled him with a rush of guilt and got him imagining what Lili might say about his grumbling.

But Lili didn't understand that someone who lived in the public eye *needed* their privacy in a way that everyday people did not.

Dom didn't see that as better or worse, but it was an indisputable fact.

Like on his semi-private flight to Chicago, where his co-passenger was a football fan. "As big as they get," according to the millionaire wearing a trucker's cap. Unfortunately, the "internet entrepreneur" was a fan of the Raiders, a team full of Dom's mortal enemies. That made for a frustrating flight filled with a riot of ribbing and jokes.

That was the thing Dom probably hated most about being in the NFL. Or about being a celebrity at all. Fame was a bright light that felt nice to stand in, but it could also burn you. He was still healing from the fire of his scandal.

But even before that, Dom had always hated the way fame made it so that people always thought they knew him. As if headlines and talking points could ever reveal who he was to the millions of curious people he counted as neither family nor friends, or tell the story of his life.

Still, that never stopped them. Celebrity made it so that strangers acted like they knew him, as if they owned stock in Dominic Moore as if their opinions on who he was or who they thought he should be had value in the world.

Dom was sick of being told that he was playing for the wrong team, getting the wrong haircut, or making all the wrong decisions in his personal or professional life. He was even sick of the compliments and currently considering an all-donut diet so he'd never hear about his glorious abs—

Poor Dom. It must be SO AWFUL, the way everyone worships you!

And again, he was forced to ignore his inner Lili.

This was exhausting, and Dom couldn't stop missing her.

He looked around the plane with a smile, now thinking about how Lili would probably love to help him brainstorm the twenty-one places they could hide a body in here. She would at least want to joke about killing this guy as much as Dom would.

"Stay out of the tabloids!" Trucker Hat said as they landed, framing his insult as advice.

Dom got into the Escalade, waiting just outside the plane. He liked the driver, a good guy named Javier who made easy conversation when he thought that might be what Dom was wanting, then fell into a comfortable silence when he learned otherwise.

Javier treated Dom like a human.

They were halfway to SportsBar when Dom realized that there was someone else in Chicago who was sure to treat him like a human.

Someone Dom was overdue to see.

He tapped on the glass, and Javier looked back at him.

"Can you take me to Clear Meadows? It's a rehab facility in—"

"I know where it is, boss, but the *big* boss wants me taking you straight to SportsBar."

"I get that. But this is fast. A short detour that'll be well worth your time." Dom showed his driver the cash. "And I promise, we'll still get to SportsBar on schedule."

"Clear Meadows, you said?"

Lili

Re: Re: Are we still talking?

Submissions <submissions@mansplanations.mvdaily.org>
To: Annabelle Lyons <a.lyons@mountainviewuniversity.edu>

A world with only one soulmate would indeed be a scary place ... but only if you didn't believe that fate was guiding you.

With Love,

Mansplanations

Lili surveyed the array of baked goods on her countertop.

For a long string of moments, pure silence cooked the air around her. If she really perked her ears, she could probably hear the flapping wings of a bird outside.

But then it broke, and Lili found herself laughing out loud, a cackling guffaw full of hurt and sorrow and longing infused with a pent-up ambition that had been steeping forever.

She'd found herself driven to bake all through the night without stopping.

Something snapped into place yesterday, right after that courier had appeared on her porch with that package. She opened it up and found Stan, swaddled in bubble wrap, his wiring all back in place. Looking at the mixer that had given Lili some of her sweetest memories, she saw life as it could be instead of life as she knew it — meaning a life she anticipated having one day, instead of one actually lived.

And just like that, Lili was done waiting for life to begin.

She was finished with the anticipation and eager to bake her way into something better. She was ready right now to live in her happy place.

Higher Grounds would reap the benefit, and so would all the people in her life.

Everyone deserved the change, especially Lili.

That simple thought propelled her through an entire night's worth of mixing and baking, and frosting. Her bounty now was almost unbelievable. The only problem was that Lili had just done what Alicia had been telling her to do for years, and now she would probably never hear the end of it from her best friend. Alicia was the Michael Jordan of *I told you so*'s.

Higher Grounds was opening with two carry cases of cupcakes, one case full of brownie squares, a lemon meringue pie, and the best chocolate bark Lili had ever made, not that she had been making it long.

Everything was neatly packed into cake carriers for easy transport. Higher Grounds still didn't have display cases, but her plan accounted for their absence. Lili would set out a sample plate filled with one of everything, so her customers could easily see their choices and stir their cravings. She planned to serve her confections on the teacup saucers that saw little other use.

Was it perfect? Not remotely, but it was forward motion and the momentum she needed.

Lili had not only taken her power back, but she was also moving with an inner strength she had never felt before. Yesterday's Lili would have been dying from exhaustion after a night spent furiously working without sleep, but as she carefully loaded the cake carriers into her Prius, Lili felt powerful.

On her way to Higher Grounds, she felt even stronger, and swinging into her usual parking space, she felt ready to conquer the world.

Summer looked at Lili agog as she opened the door for her. Maybe it was because the boss was trying her best to balance five cake carriers while navigating the door with her foot. It could easily have been because the lack of any sleep or a shower made her look manic (more than dirty). Or, even more likely, Summer was reacting to Lili's televised meltdown, which she had yet to see for herself and had tried hard not to imagine during her flurry of baking.

"Are you okay?" Summer asked Lili, sounding like their cats had both died (neither of them had one).

"I'm great!" Lili exclaimed.

Summer clearly didn't believe it, still staring at her with an expression that said, *Are you sure you're not here to drown yourself in coffee?*

"Really. I couldn't be better. Look at what I baked last night!" Lili set her carriers on the counter, opening them one at a time to show Summer what she had done.

"They look delicious." Translation: *Is there anything I can do to make you feel better?*

Lili pointed at their treasure. "We have cupcakes, brownie squares, a lemon meringue pie, and—"

"Are you sure you don't want to talk about it?"

Lili smiled, not even really annoyed. Of course, Summer was concerned about her. "I appreciate you asking, but really I'm doing great. I promise. I'd rather not talk about it right now, but not because I'm obsessing or anything. I really don't care anymore." She shrugged. "It just doesn't matter."

Summer acted like she might maybe believe her.

They set up the sample plate and got everything ready for opening.

Lili's earliest customers all acted like Summer. Everyone tiptoeing around her, like she was a cookie that might crumble at any moment, asking if Lili was really sure that she didn't want to talk about it, even though they rarely had the courage to use those words. Refusing to listen when she insisted that she was fine, that it didn't matter, that she didn't care anymore.

But everything else was whipped cream and sprinkles. Everything Lili had spent the night baking sold out less than an hour after the OPEN sign got flipped. Customer smiles were even brighter than they shined for her coffee.

And most miraculously, the first hour was usually the worst hour for baked goods, considering that clientele tended to hustle early, more likely to be coming or going from their exercise or watching what they eat. Lili figured she could move three to five times the amount of product once moms started to come in with their babies and toddlers.

She had already seen five strollers maneuver their way into Queen of Tarts across the street, and once she started selling cake her superior coffee would be the draw to pull more customers to her side of Main Street.

And that's when it hit her. The perfect win-win really had been staring her in the face all the time. She would have acted on her instinct that second, but something happening between Annabelle and Marcus was momentarily cementing her in place.

Annabelle was venting to Lili, but Marcus kept looking over, more than curious for obvious reasons.

"The lectures are still going great," Annabelle continued, "and it's almost like this Mansplanations asshat did me a favor. We've been dissecting some of his columns in class, and I've been showing my students how wrong he is."

"Because ..." Marcus finally inserted himself.

Annabelle turned to him. "Because everything he talks about can be explained by science." She laughed. "And he doesn't get the irony."

"Irony is the tool of weak-minded clowns."

"That's—" Annabelle stopped.

She was suddenly thinking hard, and Lili had a pretty good idea of what she must be thinking about.

"How did you hear that quote?" Annabelle asked.

"I ..." Marcus stuttered. "It's ... um ..."

"Oh my God!" Annabelle pointed at him. "It's *you*. You're the Mansplainer!" She shook her head. "I should have known it all along. The flowery writing, the deep belief in soulmates and fate. *Of course*, it's the literature professor writing that nonsense! I didn't peg you as a liar, Marcus."

"I'm not a liar. I—"

"You obscured the truth. That's a—"

"I'm sorry." Marcus shook his head and looked Annabelle right in her eyes. "I am *seriously* sorry. Not about the column or about our email exchanges, but I regret that this is how you found out. I should have told you. You're right about that. But I enjoyed our debate, and your class is fuller than ever. I think a part of you was enjoying it too—"

"You're wrong, Marcus. That was *not* enjoyable for me."

"So, does this mean you're going to stay mad at me?"

"What it means, Marcus is war."

Then Annabelle spun around and stormed out of Higher Grounds.

"Shit," Marcus said. "I really should have told her."

Lili nodded. Shit indeed. "Women don't like learning things in public, and secrets hurt."

"Sounds personal. Are you talking about Dominic?" Marcus knew the truth, even if Lili didn't answer him. So he asked her a question. "How often do you keep a secret from someone you don't care about?"

She still didn't reply, but now Lili was thinking.

"It might be cowardly, and it's definitely stupid, but keeping something from you is actually a sign that he cares."

"Thanks, Marcus." Now her stomach hurt again.

He left, and Lili was pondering some serious thoughts. The first of them circled what Marcus had said about Dominic and his secrets, but then she was back to the win-win waiting for her across the street.

"Where are you going?" Summer asked as Lili doffed her apron.

"I'll tell you the second I'm back!"

And then she was gone.

Dom

Javier pulled up in front of the Clear Meadows entrance and turned to Dom. "I appreciate what you're trying to do, man, but I'm out on a limb, so ..."

"I'll be fast," he promised with a nod, already opening the door and hurrying to the front desk.

"I'm so sorry, but there's no visiting," the receptionist replied in monotone after he asked to see Robbie Lewis. She had a puff of artificially red hair, and the lines in her face dragged low by decades of gravity, maybe eons of working a job she hated. Before he could open his mouth, she added, "No exceptions."

"I've got this, Margaret." A newcomer, rolled into the scene from somewhere just out of view, still sitting on her desk chair. She looked at Dom, then at the human dial tone. "I can assure you, Mr. Samperi would approve."

Margaret grunted, then rolled away.

"Well, hello there." The newcomer took center stage, directly across from Dom. "My name is Grace. Mr. Samperi is my boss and a big Dominic Moore fan, same as my husband. Either one of them would just kill me if I didn't try to help you out here. And if they both found out, I'd be dead for sure!"

She smiled like they usually did.

"Don't mind Margaret. She hates everyone," Grace confided with a roll of her eyes. "You're here to see Robbie Lewis?"

"I am." He nodded.

"Well then, GO TEAM!" She pumped her fist. "Let's get you over there."

Grace led Dom into a room where he spied Robbie right away. Easy enough to do considering the baller's bright red hair, a hundred-percent natural, unlike Margaret's. Robbie was smaller than most of the burly men with lumberjack bodies occupying the room.

To Dom's surprise, or perhaps even his shock, the men were all knitting. He saw a medley of projects, from beanies and scarves to headbands and mittens, all in a spectrum of terrible, mostly vague shapes only teasing their intention. In a few instances, the end result was still a mystery to Dom. His friend's project resembled a misshapen cat.

Robbie saw Dom and proudly displayed the mess while waving him over.

"What is that thing?" asked Dom when he got there.

"It's for the Chicago winter."

Dom shook his head. "That doesn't tell me what it is."

"To hell with you." Robbie chuckled. "It's a hat."

"I bet you own more than a hundred hats. What makes you think that qualifies as a—"

"I said to hell with you," Robbie repeated with another hearty laugh. "Did you come here to knit or to visit me?" He pointed at the biggest lumberjack in the bunch. "Able's the only one of us who knows what he's doing, so ask him if you're down for a lesson."

Dom looked over at Able's impressively intricate scarf.

"DOMINIC!" Able pumped his fist before going back to his knitting.

He grinned at Able, then spoke to Robbie. "I was hoping we could take a walk?"

"You know it." Robbie stood and dropped his misshapen cat hat on the chair. "After you."

They stepped outside into a gray day, but that didn't stop Robbie from radiating brightness.

"You seem great," said Dom.

"I feel great!" Robbie pounded his chest. "No puffery. I've not felt this solid in a while, man. I know you keep telling me not to thank you, but seriously, you saved me."

"I couldn't be happier to hear that."

"I got too caught up in that whole world. You know, you've been there, just not dumb, like the way I was doing things. At least you kicked it solo most of the time. I surrounded myself with *all* the wrong folks."

Robbie laughed at his former idiocy. "People saw me like their real-life meal ticket. *Of course*, they're gonna treat me like a god. If everyone's a *yes* man, then they're gonna do whatever I say, whenever I say it, including scoring me whatever I need to — hell ..." Robbie cut himself off with another thought. "Half the bitches in my circle were pushing."

"I've seen it plenty, but you're out of that now."

"Damn right. Not like I didn't know it before, but this place made me stare at the consequences. I feel real again. That doesn't mean I'm ready to leave, but I know there's more to life than football when I do, even as much as I love the game."

"Like knitting?"

Robbie laughed. "Guess what you're getting for Christmas this year."

"Is it better than the nothing you got me last year? Do they offer any other hobbies here? Or did you actually *choose* to—"

"I also paint. And you should see my pottery. Point is, none of that matters, man. It doesn't have to be knitting or painting or pottery, but I've gotta find something that takes me beyond the world of football. You know?"

"I know," Dom nodded without really thinking about it.

"Do you, though?" A challenging grin. "Because I sure hope you can find that. Especially now, after—"

"I wouldn't even know where to start."

"You don't need to know where to start. You saw my hat in there. You just have to *start*. Being here in this place and meeting all of these people, I'm telling you, man, it's reminded me that there's an entire world waiting to be lived in. Spend too much time in one pin on the map, and you're missing out on a planet of possibilities."

"Did someone else say that during group, and you memorized it for this moment right now?"

"To hell with you." Robbie laughed again.

Dom spotted Javier, standing in the doorway with folded hands. He gave him a nod and turned back to Robbie. "Until next time?"

"That mean you're jetting?"

"I've gotta go. I'm expected at SportsBar. We're running tight, but I really wanted to stop by."

"Thank you, brother. Not just for saving me from scandal, but for saving my life."

"Maybe we saved each other."

They hugged then Dom followed Javier to the Escalade.

He climbed in the back, thinking, wondering if maybe taking the fall for Robbie really did save him in a way, helping him break free from the world of football, but if that was true …

Then right now, his driver was taking Dom in the wrong direction.

Lili

ili's spirits were sprinting, with her efforts close behind.

Summer wouldn't understand, or maybe Lili was sick of explaining herself. Either way, this trek across the street to plant a flag in the new life she wanted was only making her feel more powerful by the step.

She kept turning the idea in her head, adoring it even more with every new tumble. This was a great plan, Louise was going to love it, and Lili was ready to make her case.

But all of that boldness began to drain right out of her the second she opened the door to Queen of Tarts. A current of cooked sugar rolled toward Lili in a wave. The scent was thick with remembrance, and that rush of memories made her smile. But mostly, it was the sight of Louise herself that seemed to burgle the bravado right out of her.

Dom might have failed to be the man she had dreamed him to be, but his grandmother was still a remarkable woman. One of the best Lili had ever met. She needed to remind herself that this proposal might be perfect for them both. Louise wouldn't need convincing so much as—

But suddenly, it was Lili who needed convincing.

Louise started clapping the second she saw her. "Perfect timing!"

Lili was confused. "Perfect timing for what?"

"For hopping behind the counter and helping me make some of those fancy-pants coffee drinks that everyone in town seems to love. My coffee is scaring the customers, and this lull is only going to last another minute."

"You're not a coffee drinker yourself, are you?"

"Can't stand the stuff." Louise made a face. "But I drink tea by the gallon."

"You should make that your specialty, then. You only offer 'tea' on the menu right now, but you could offer a variety of your favorites."

"That's a great idea. Maybe—"

But that's all Louise got before the door opened to a customer.

And then another, and another after that.

Lili got instantly busy, not quite sure how she had been so easily pulled into a shift of free labor but loving where she was nonetheless. She steamed milk and started prepping drinks while looking around. Queen of Tarts had gone from empty to buzzing in just a few minutes, and Lili loved the happy hum of budding commerce around her. Louise's bakery was amazing, and the word was spreading fast in Mountain View.

"It's been like this all morning," she told Lili in between ringing up customers at the register. "I'm pretty sure it's not just locals, either. I think a bunch of folks drove down here after the Upper Crustama-doojie to check us out because Queen of Tarts is apparently now a 'destination bakery.'"

Louise laughed to show that she, too, considered the notion ridiculous.

A couple entered, holding hands, each of them giving Lili a hearty wave with their free one. They came right to the counter and told Lili that they had loved watching her on TV before each getting a cookie and leaving Louise's shop with a $20 tip. Then a little girl asked for Lili's autograph.

Her brush with fame felt weird for sure, but not as unwelcome as she would have imagined.

And really, once she started thinking about it, Lili realized that not only was the attention neither gross nor overwhelming, it came from a place of loving and appreciating Lili for her art.

Deciding that she would sell her own baked goods without waiting to be blessed with a kitchen had flipped a light on inside her head. Now she was ready to shine that light on everything and see her world in a truer illumination.

Life right now felt like a plate of cookies, with her glass-half-full of milk.

Lili hadn't expected an onslaught of customers when she came over to pitch Louise on her idea, and now there was a small line and little to no chance that she would have the chance to pull the proprietor back into the conversation she'd come here to have for a while.

But Lili didn't even care. She was tired of waiting. Lili, now that she was clear on what she wanted, and was willing to actively push those ideas forward instead of anticipating the perfect moment, engaged Louise as best she could between customers.

"Just think about it," Lili continued after ringing up the last three brownies, "we could merge our businesses and become something new. A coffee destination as well as a bakery."

Louise didn't seem sure of what to make of the suggestion, so Lili added sweetener to her argument. "We could call it Sugar Boogie, as an ode to the bakery you had to give up."

"I don't need an ode to anything," said Louise with a laugh once they were in another lull and able to finish the conversation. "Everyone needs to stop thinking about the past so much. I never even wanted to reopen a cafe. Or a bakery. Or anything else."

"You didn't?" Lili could not have been more surprised. Running the Queen of Tarts seemed like something Louise had been waiting forever to do.

"Not really." She shook her head. "Maybe not even at all. But Dom had it in his head that he'd taken away my big dream. That closing Sugar Boogie meant losing something that mattered to me so much more than it did. But really, that was just Dom trying to make himself feel better."

"You don't care that you had to give up Sugar Boogie?"

"Of course, I care, but it's not a regret of mine, no. There was a period in my life when I ran Sugar Boogie, and that time of my life was lovely. But that doesn't mean I was destined to keep the place forever or that I ever should have. *No regrets.* Life is a forward march. The best way to live it is by holding it just enough to direct the flow as best you can. But it's still more important to make the most out of every moment you have and appreciate every day."

It sounded like Louise was revealing a secret that Lili needed to know. She might as well have finished with a wink.

"Why did you open the bakery then? I only have a coffee shop, but I can imagine what a big undertaking it would be to run a place like Queen of Tarts, and I *wanted* to do it."

"It's what my boy needed from me."

Of course. For Louise, her decisions were all made around what it meant for her to be the best grandmother she could possibly be. Or, even more accurately, considering her relationship with Dom, the best possible mom.

"I was having a blast before Domi came to town. Honestly, I would love getting back to some kind of retirement." Louise laughed. "Not that I don't enjoy having my grandson here, but between you and me, getting up and doing this every day is *exhausting.* I'd be much happier baking whatever I wanted to, whenever I wanted to bake it. So once Domi's in the right place, I'll suggest that it might be better to have someone else run the shop while—"

The door opened to a horde of customers, all filing into the bakery at once.

Even more of them recognized her this time, but the energy was still friendly. Happy customers upon entry, seeming even happier as they left, even if the beans were still producing sub-par coffee, no matter Lili's skill in elevating them. Lili was eager for more of her conversation with Louise but thrilled beyond belief about everything else.

Lili never really needed to make her pitch because, in the end, Louise had made it for her. There were still plenty of details to work out, and they were far from refining her raw idea into an ideal solution, but she saw a number of ways to make this happen. They would need to figure out which location to keep, though Queen of Tarts' primo kitchen made the choice rather clear. They would also need to determine the financials, but it was easy to see that a big win for them both in the future.

And Lili could not imagine having a better partner.

Of course, there was still the curdled milk in it all with her connection to Dom. He would be hard, if not impossible, to avoid with Louise as her business partner. But he hadn't come home for years at a time before this, and the former football star would also be so busy with his new Sacre bleu commentating job to stay out of Mountain View until the holidays.

"Football is his Sugar Boogie," said Louise, seeming to read her mind.

But Lili didn't want to admit what she'd thinking about, especially since her thoughts had already drifted from their potential business merger to Dom.

"What do you mean?" asked Lili.

"Domi has always lived in the past. He can't see doing anything differently than what he's always done. But I spent a fair share of my best years raising that boy, and I can tell you that it's always better to let him figure the big things out for himself. He would have eventually realized that Sugar Boogie was a part of my past that didn't need to define my future, and soon enough, he'll figure out that he's done with football."

"How can you know that?"

"Because it's time for his next phase. I wish he was faster, but Domi ..." she shrugged. "You know men. These things take longer."

"I'm not sure that's a gender thing," Lili said, then made her confession. "I'm the opposite, and that's my biggest problem. I'm not thinking about the past. I'm fixated on a future that might never come and probably won't if all I'm ever doing is dreaming about it!"

Lili laughed at herself. "I'm always anticipating, never living in the present."

"You seem to be doing a pretty good job of living in the present right now." Louise gave her a smile and might as well have pinned a blue ribbon on her chest. "Are you going to apply that same principle to your love life?"

"I have a few things to get over first."

Louise scoffed, but she didn't get a chance to explain herself before the door opened to yet another rush of customers. Lili was dying to get back to their conversation, but Louise must have been even more eager than she was.

"Buns and Beans!" she blurted. "That's what we'll call it!"

"Sounds a bit cheeky." Lili grinned.

"There will be lines around the corner."

They kept laughing, on and off, until the bakery was finally empty.

"I've got to get back across the street." Lili felt guilt, bordering panic. "I left Summer all alone over there."

"Of course, dear. This was so much fun!"

"Think about how much more fun it's going to be!" Lili said at the door.

"Does this mean I finally get to know the name of your coffee supplier?"

"Only if you teach me to make perfect choux!"

Lili left Queen of Tarts to the sound of Louise's hearty laughter as the door swung closed with a jingle behind her.

Dom

⌾ ☆ ↩ ☒ ⋮

Re: Re: Re: Are we still talking?

Annabelle Lyons <a.lyons@mountainviewuniversity.edu>
To: <submissions@mansplanations.mvdaily.org>

Asshole.

MOUNTAIN VIEW
UNIVERSITY

ANNABELLE LYONS
Associate Professor of Psychology
MountainViewUniversity.com

The luster was already gone from Dom's new position at SportsBar before the Escalade drove past the gates. He didn't want to be there at the studio, but he had yet to actually hate the experience.

It didn't take long. Everyone at the network felt like they had been cast to play a character of themselves. One designed to make

Dom feel like a god among them. They were just short of bowing and scraping as he made his way through the halls. He missed Mountain View even more than before, now back in a world where people only saw him as a commodity, with no ability to recognize the person he was and always had been.

He wouldn't even be playing the game. He would be commenting like any other armchair quarterback sitting in their living room. He no longer cared that he would be doing it while sitting side by side with an athlete he'd worshipped forever.

Even the great Altruence Brown didn't make this the right move for Dom or keep him from feeling like a piece on the board without a mind of his own.

What if he was consigned to this purgatory forever? Stuck in the tar of his former life, talking about what he could no longer participate in, when he could be building something brand new if he just made the choice.

The thought stuck like caramel in his mind as Dom was rushed through hair and makeup, getting introduced to a blur of people he would never really know because they were like doctors barely making eye contact during a routine checkup, ticking boxes, conversing with coworkers while passing Dom down the line from one plastic smile to the next.

"You can wait here," said a lanky assistant, with a spray of freckles across his nose and an Adam's apple the size of a holiday walnut. His name might have been Melvin.

Dom nodded, but Melvin or whoever was already gone.

He didn't want to scroll on his phone, but he felt naked standing in the hallway. Melvin didn't even tell him why he was waiting or how long that wait would be. Even thinking about social media was enough to fill him with chills. Dom didn't care for the news right now. None of the mindless things he did to kill time when he was all by himself, like checking his email or playing any of the dozen stupid games he'd downloaded on his phone, was enough to distract him from his lonliness. He held the phone out in front of him, staring at the screen while pretending to read.

But the phone went bright with a text from an unknown number in his hand: Bet you won't …

His heart was already racing at the preview.

He clicked to see the rest and got a flush of disappointment, followed by a series of conflicted emotions.

 MESSAGES   now

Unknown
Bet you won't take a risk … you total dumbass.
BTW, this is your resident angry pregnant lady.
AKA Alicia, in case all the bad decisions have
clouded your thinking.

He was glad to hear from Alicia — a flash reminder of Mountain View and how terrific he'd felt there — but disappointed that the text wasn't from Lili. The word *bet* had filled him with hope, which then dried like cracked choux the second he saw that it wasn't her.

In that split second of seeing those words, it felt like everything inside Dom had suddenly woken back up.

He longed to see Lili. To be near her. To touch her. He yearned to tell her all about how totally crappy and asinine this job already was. He wanted to make her laugh as he ridiculed his new opportunity, as he admitted the truth that he thought it was beneath him.

Like everything that wasn't her and Mountain View, he needed to tell her how great Robbie was doing and get lost in conversation as the two of them thought up hilarious objects for that room full of lumberjacks to knit.

He could even—

Dom stopped. Swallowed as he started to sweat with a sudden realization.

He dropped the phone into his pocket, leaning back against the wall and slowly sliding down onto his ass.

Was this what love felt like?

He thought it would feel like passion, and that fire for sure had been burning, but this was something more … the unrelenting sense of needing to fill every second with another person, if not in body than at least in thought.

Dom realized the truth like a strike of lightning: he never wanted Lili to leave him because he was ready to share his life with her.

Alicia was right. Dom just didn't know what he could do about it now. He had a signed contract and a list of responsibilities. Thanks to his mistakes, he also had very few options. This wasn't even about Lili, even though he'd been a coward there. Dom had taken a big risk by protecting Robbie. Sure, he was doing a solid for his buddy after Titus asked him to keep an eye on the kid, but there was more to it than that.

Dom should have seen it earlier, the way he was sabotaging himself by taking the fall. An obvious hint that he didn't really even *want* to play the game anymore, and he'd totally ignored it.

He'd hit a wall. Instead of figuring out what to do next, he drifted without thought into the next football-related opportunity his agent could land for him. He didn't try anything new because Dom didn't think he was qualified to do anything else.

But it was just like Robbie said. Even Lili, if Dom was being honest. Maybe he hadn't ever really tried.

He suffered an onslaught of thoughts all at once. Dom was trying to sort them, but he didn't get far before Melvin interrupted him.

"Are you okay?" The kid's Adam's Apple bobbed up and down like a bird wetting its beak.

"Of course. Why wouldn't I be okay?"

"You're sitting on the ground staring off into space ... it's me, Marvin."

Marvin. "I was just thinking."

"Time to fly. They're ready for you in there."

"Great." Dom smiled, even though it wasn't really great at all. "I guess I'm supposed to follow you then?"

"Right this way." Marvin led him to the set, where Dom was mic'ed then escorted to the new presenter seat beside a boyhood hero.

"How you doing?" Altruence Brown turned to Dom with a hearty handshake. "Missed you yesterday. I was hoping we could spend a day cracking bottles and slapping backs before we got down to business in here. But I guess we'll be jumping right in."

Altruence grinned at him, his smile wide and teeth seeming especially bright under all those lights. His manner was warm, just as friendly as Dom had always imagined.

It should have made everything better, sitting side-by-side with his inspiration, but Dom's entire body bristled with an urgent need to get out of Dodge. Desperate for a quiet place to ponder his newest revelation.

But that wasn't going to happen. Not now, just seconds from showtime.

The producer shouted something to the director, then the director shouted something to Dom and Altruence. Even as foggy as his mind suddenly was, Dom had no doubt whatsoever that the cameras were now rolling.

Altruence was talking, probably saying something about sports, football, almost for sure. But to Dom, the monologue sounded something like this:

"Lili. Lili Lili Lili Lili. Lili Lili Lili. Lili Lili Lili Lili Lili Lili Lili Lili Lili Lili Lili Lili?" A hearty laugh. "Lili Lili Lili Lili Lili. Lili Lili Lili Lili ..."

Dom looked over at the plain sheet cake, just visible behind the cameras at the back of the set. Block red letters were easy enough to read from his spot on the stage: Welcome to SportsBar Dominic Moore!"

"Lili. Lili Lili Lili Lili. Lili Lili Lili. Lili Lili Lili. Right Dom?"

He looked from the cake to the camera in daze. "I'm sorry …"

"We were just …"

But Dom had already stopped listening. This whole thing had been a big mistake. He shouldn't be here and needed to go.

"WHAT DO YOU THINK YOU'RE DOING?" the producer shouted as Dom stood, taking off his mic and walking off the set.

"Sorry," he said again, shaking his head and looking over at Altruence with apologetic eyes. "But there's somewhere I need to be."

Pure chaos, with everyone shouting behind him at once.

Dom couldn't afford to hear them. He kept walking faster, brushing by Marvin as he pulled out his phone, passing the hallway where he'd had his epiphany just a few minutes before, dialing Titus as he walked.

He answered on the first ring. "Holy shit, what happened? You just walked away from Altruence Brown. You shoulda seen his face! They're still rolling with game footage."

"Dude, I need a favor."

"Man, I don't know if I can keep associating with you now. Altruence fucking Brown. "

"There's a McLaren in it for you."

"What do you need?"

Lili

Re: Re: Re: Re: Are we still talking?

Submissions <submissions@mansplanations.mvdaily.org>
To: Annabelle Lyons <a.lyons@mountainviewuniversity.edu>

Jerk.

P.S. Did you get called into the Dean's office too?

Lili pulled her Prius into its usual space, exhausted but happy.

She wished she had more cupcakes this morning, but that lone box required a monumental feat of willpower. It had been pulling teeth to stay awake during dinner last night. Her head might as well have weighed more than a bowling ball the way her chin kept dipping down to point at her plate full of uneaten noodles.

A half-hour passed, and she'd barely done more than move the pile around, so she put it in the fridge, went to bed, and set her alarm for five the next morning.

Because right now, nothing was more important than baking.

What seemed impossible before now felt inevitable. Lili was surviving on momentum, but after she caught up on her rest, she'd be thriving for sure. Now that the hard part of deciding was finally behind her, she wanted to bake and sell as much as she possibly could before her coffee shop merged with Louise's bakery to become the best place in Mountain View to either wake up right or get something sweet.

Whatever she and Louise built together would be incredible. Lili had no doubt about it. But selling her wares here at Higher Grounds had been a personal breakthrough, and she wanted to keep doing it every single day until the doors were closed for good.

Even if that meant setting the alarm an hour early and opening her shop exhausted. Lili unlocked the door and let it swing shut behind her.

She was opening alone this morning. Summer had "prior commitments." Probably a frat party last night with a scheduled hangover this morning. Or a sex party, with the hair of the dog for breakfast. Ew.

Lili had no idea and wished she didn't care, but curiosity was a constant itch and one of the reasons she loved having a coffee shop.

But Lili wouldn't be alone for long, and with Summer indisposed, her day was an upgrade. She would be working with Runa, who eagerly agreed to step in as her number two on this fine Saturday morning, so long as Lili didn't need her to come in "stupid early."

Lili loved working with Runa. She was tidy and efficient, and effervescent. They could laugh and gossip while they worked. Yes, she could sometimes do that while working with Summer, but it was only pretending compared to the way she so easily shared with Runa.

Today Runa surprised her by coming into Higher Grounds just a few minutes after Lili.

"Isn't this considered 'stupid early'?" Lili asked.

"Totally, but I love you, and this will be fun. Also, cupcakes." Runa was already grabbing one and sinking her teeth into it.

"That's for the customers!"

"Omhyeh …?" *Oh yeah?* Runa kept chewing as she pulled a ten out of her purse and chomped another bite. "Hernumacstmr." *Here. Now I'm a customer.*

Lili was dying for a cupcake too. She had baked them and thus knew exactly how amazing they tasted. But she needed to know she could sell them, and Runa didn't count. Lili appreciated that she had paid for her cupcake, but Lili needed to see that same behavior from random customers.

She didn't wake up before the roosters this morning to prove something, and a tiny part of her worried that even burning the candles at both ends might not be enough. Despite her confidence while baking the cupcakes and coming into Higher Grounds this morning, a flicker of doubt kept coming on stronger. Maybe yesterday was a fluke? An exception to the rule? Maybe her customers wouldn't want her baking.

But her worry was absurd. Runa's early grab didn't make a lick of difference. Higher Grounds was out of cupcakes just ten minutes after Lili opened the doors.

"OH MY GAWD!" she cried out to Runa once they were alone. "Can you believe this?"

"Yes. How come you don't care when Alicia wants a cupcake?"

"I don't care when anyone wants a cupcake. But Alicia actually fought a customer for hers."

"I would have fought a customer for mine," Runa assured her. "I was just lucky that there were no customers to fight. Hooray for coming in stupid early."

Alicia had come in with Harvey, managing to snag the last cupcake just a second before an older lady behind her, who clearly had a wizened eye on the cupcake, but unfortunately walked much slower than a toddler dragging mom with a hankering for one of Lili's freshly baked desserts.

"Sorry, but I'm eating for *two*," Alicia explained, thinking she had executed the perfect heist.

But the joke was on Alicia. The old lady started cooing and touching her stomach.

Alicia was pure instinct whenever the intruder alert went off on or around her baby bump. She slapped the woman's hand away.

The old lady swore out loud that she'd never come back to this place.

"Oops!" Alicia "apologized."

Keandre Wilson came in for a hot chocolate and a sympathetic ear a few minutes later. Lili made it with extra whipped cream and then layered the top with chocolate shavings.

"The recruiter could not have made it clearer that I was only being considered for the position so he could come closer to filling their 'diversity gap.'" Keandre shook his head. "I'm telling you, Lili, I *had* to walk out. And you *know* how much I needed that job."

"I do." She nodded, adding one last sprinkle of chocolate onto the top before handing it over. "But don't lose hope. I'm positive that you're going to find the perfect job someday."

Keandre smiled at her. "You're always positive about everything."

That wasn't true, but she smiled back anyway.

After the cupcake commotion had died down and Keandre was sipping on his hot chocolate, customers flowed at a comfortable pace. Lili and Runa were constantly moving, keeping their banter light on account of all the perked ears.

But for the last minute or so, Runa hadn't really been paying attention. She kept glancing over to a nearby table.

Lili followed her eyes to where a couple of girls — decaf cappuccino with coconut milk and a cafe mocha — were deep in a volley of barely audible chatter.

She stopped talking to Runa and strained to hear them.

The words were all mumbles, until a pairing that fully unnerved her: *Dominic Moore.*

Lili swallowed and Runa saw her.

"I'm fine!" Lili snapped before she got started, then perked her ears even harder.

She snatched audible phrases like flies in the air.

He's too famous for his own good. Thinks he ...

Can you believe he did that? There's no way ...

It just goes to show you: total ego overload.

His fanbase is GONE ...

"Lil ... Whatever you—"

"I said I'm fine!" Lili snapped at Runa again, this time a little too loud.

The girls raised their volume, probably to hear themselves over Lili's little outburst, but then they queued her up for a new one.

"Dominic Moore has *no* respect."

Runa sighed as Lili marched over to their table.

"You need to mind your own business!"

The girls turned to Lili in tandem and spoke in a duet. "I'm sorry?"

"Is Dominic Moore a bit full of himself? Yes." Lili nodded. "But guess what, ladies? He's accomplished a *hell of a lot more* than the rest of us here, so doesn't he deserve to believe in himself more than most people? Is there really anything wrong with that?"

The cafe was silent, and most of her customers were staring, but Lili had already started, and there was little point in stopping now. It helped that Runa was looking over at her with such encouraging eyes.

"Did I have sex with him on the video? Yes. Was that the table we did it on?" Lili pointed to a table cloth with tiny yellow ducklings, where Alicia happened to be sitting.

Alicia had been savoring the last of her cupcake, but now she pushed the final bites away from her.

"I'm not ashamed or embarrassed! And I shouldn't be. It was *great sex!* And no, I'm not in a relationship with him now, but who cares? I had a hell of a lot of fun with Dominic while it lasted."

Lili laughed at the obnoxious truth leaving her lips right now. "I've done more living in the last two weeks than I have in the last six years."

She shook her head in disbelief at the realization. "Sure, Dominic Moore left Mountain View, but is that any reason to rag on him? He did it to pursue his dream, and is there any one of us in here that could honestly say they wouldn't at least consider doing the same thing?"

She answered her own question. "Most of us are too scared to stare in the face of something unfamiliar. Dominic did both. He went for something new, and then he came back here to Mountain View. And you know what?"

Lili did it again. "He'll always come back, because Dom is still one of us. We're the ones who should be supporting and defending him, not adding to the scandal and gossip."

She finally exhaled.

"Umm …" Latte started. "We were talking about Dominic Moore walking off the set of his show on live TV. Altruence Brown was right there next to him, and Dominic was all like, 'Smell ya' later!' and he just totally walked away. It's all over YouTube, so …"

"It's really awesome that you're the one on that sex tape," Cappuccino gave Lili a … compliment? "You're like, totally famous!"

"You both need to leave."

"But—" They started.

"We're out of coffee. There are termite inspectors coming. A meteor fell in the woods just outside town last night, and there might be radiation."

The girls looked at each other.

Lili added some clarity: "You'll have to go somewhere else."

"You're not seriously kicking us out?" Latte protested.

"You can go across the street to Queen of Tarts. The coffee over there is amazing."

"Don't you think we wanted to go there instead of here?" Cappuccino insulted her.

Then Latte: "Queen of Tarts is closed."

"So are we." Lili went around behind Latte's chair and started dragging it toward the exit.

Latte jumped off of the seat and walked toward the door, with Cappuccino quickly catching up.

"Whatever, psycho!" Latte yelled as she left.

"That was really cool, on the tape!" Cappuccino called out to her, pumping her fist to celebrate Lili's obvious triumph. "Good for you, girl!"

The door swung shut with a jingle then Higher Grounds exploded in applause.

She took a bow, her face surely redder than a jar of raspberry jam, but whatever. Cake could never be batter again. She walked back behind the counter with confidence, even though every part of her was dying to scurry away.

"What were they talking about ... Dom walking off set ... do you know anything about that?" Lili tried not to pour too much hope into her question.

Runa shrugged. "I think he got sick or something. I just saw the video of him walking off camera. Nothing more to it. You wanna see?"

"That's okay." Her shoulders sagged.

Lili suddenly wanted to sleep for a week.

He probably ate a peppered profiterole after she left. She hoped the judges didn't get sick. Lili hated the thought of being even partly responsible for making anyone ill. Except for Diana, she could totally get copious diarrhea, and that would be fine with Lili.

But not really, and Lili wished she could take back that thought.

She wasn't mean, just sad right now. And sometimes, when she felt like this, it was a little too easy, picturing people who weren't even really her enemies with diarrhea. Despite the highs of selling her baked goods and making a new dream with Louise, she didn't have Dom to tell about her wins, and that dulled the shine from most of them.

She also ached knowing that she never told him what she knew about his scandal and that she really admired him for helping a friend out like he had.

She got out her phone to text him, couldn't think of a single word to write, then dropped it back into her pocket and told herself that she'd try again later.

Lili looked out the window across the street at Queen of Tarts, just in time to see Titus leaving the bakery. Empty-handed.

He could have had any number of reasons for being in there, and not a single one was likely to have much if anything to do with her, but Lili still felt compelled to go over and find out why. Her reasoning was bulletproof.

She was a partner in the business now, despite nothing having been formalized and signed, so it would be thoroughly irresponsible, maybe downright negligent if she didn't check in on her newest endeavor right now.

If Titus just happened to tell her more about why Dom had walked off the set of his big opportunity, that would just be a small (wee, really … one might even say *micro*) side benefit to fulfilling her basic responsibility.

"I'll be right back," Lili told Runa, grabbing a clipboard and running out to nab Titus before he made it to his car.

"What's that for?" Runa nodded at her prop.

"To make me official." Then Lili was outside and running over to Titus.

"Bakery's closed today," he told Lili as she arrived at his trunk.

"Oh." She knew that. "But I had a few things to go over with Louise."

"You might want to call her or stop by her place for tea. I just finished painting, so it's better to stay out of there for now. The fumes are bad inside."

"Shouldn't I have helped to pick out the colors?"

"You know Louise, always keeping us on our toes."

The exchange was dying. Lili resurrected it by blurting out what she really wanted to know. "What happened with Dom? You know, on his show?"

"He got sick," Titus replied without emotion.

And her flicker of hope was snuffed out.

"Thanks for painting." She tried for a smile. "But we might be painting again if I hate the color."

"I'm pretty sure you'll love it." Titus grinned. "Just wait until it's all done."

"Okay." It was all she could think to say.

Lili barely held her head up as she crossed the street and entered Higher Grounds, hoping that Latte and Cappuccino came back in just so she could kick them out of her space again.

Dom

Dom sure hadn't been missing getting up at the crack of dawn like he used to do back when practice was a repressively regular part of his everyday life.

He'd gotten used to sleeping in. The last time he'd set his alarm for Are You Kidding Me O'Clock was when he appeared on that stupid morning show with Phoebe Brooke. The one that reminded him of the day he met Lili. Again.

It was a sweet memory, more sugar than lemons for sure.

Lemons made him think of meringue, which was really only an excuse for his mind to conjure another image of Lili. It kept on doing that. The canvas of his imagination right now was basically an altar to Liliana Travis.

Dom convinced Javier to take him straight to the airport after he walked off of the show. He caught the next flight back to Mountain View. He flew coach and couldn't have cared less. He didn't mind being recognized or that a kid kept kicking the back of his chair for two-thirds of his trip.

Dom's world had returned to its proper axis. Everything finally felt right, even at this ungodly hour.

But it was necessary. Dom was sure that even the trio of Titus, Runa, and Alicia wouldn't be able to hold Lili off for long, and he needed to do this.

It was sort of for her but also sort of for him.

He looked at the pristine counter in the back kitchen at Queen of Tarts and exhaled one last time, steeling himself to get started on the cake he'd risen so early to make.

Dom had been baking for most of his life but never alone. Louise saw her kitchen as the best place to both teach and learn some of life's most important lessons, so there had never been any shortage of time in his life when he and his grandma had done it together.

He was working from muscle memory, starting with his mixing of their wet and dry ingredients, separately, of course. According to Louise, even the best bakers sometimes got ahead of themselves and worked in the order of recipe ingredients, assuming that as long as the measurements were all accurate, everything could get mixed together.

He knew to mix his dry ingredients in one bowl and his wet ingredients in the other before whisking them together.

He looked at *his* mixer — a teal green KitchenAid he'd had Titus buy for him while he'd been in transit back to Mountain View — and decided that he couldn't continue without giving the poor appliance a name. He considered several possibilities before realizing that Lili would almost for sure love the pleasure of bestowing his mixer with a name and saved the job for her.

It was a frivolous thing to be thinking about when he should be concentrating on his newest flavor profile: banana nut cake with vanilla buttercream covered in sprinkles.

Soon, Dom was no longer just baking. He was lost in the movement. In perfect flow. Just like he had been during all of those countless hours spent running up and down the field, throwing and catching, jumping and rolling, his body like an instrument of the universe instead of anything he controlled himself.

Baking was like that now, heating his insides with a needed reminder: the zone he lived in while playing ball could be found in other things. Baking was just the beginning. All the measurements and numbers, it was almost like—

Numbers. Dom wanted to laugh out loud.

A sputtering chuckle bubbled past his lips, and he lost a little baby guffaw anyway. He loved numbers. Always had. Dom loved numbers back when Lili was making fun of him about it back in high school. He loved numbers when his coaches were mapping their game tapes. And he loved numbers right now.

Dom could live in a universe of digits forever.

He finished his cake, popped it into the oven with his pride billowing like a flag, and went out into the front of the bakery to put on a pot of coffee. Louise still hadn't solved the problem of swill in her pantry, but even the worst of her offerings had caffeine.

"How's the baking going?" Louise asked.

His back was turned, and her sudden presence was startling, but Dom quickly recovered. "It's going great!"

"What made you want to go in there and bake something for yourself? I've never seen you do that before."

"A wise friend recently told me that the only way I'm going to find out what I love is if I start trying new things. I already know that I love baking, but I've never really done it by myself. Today seemed like a fine day to start."

"Plus, you wanted to make something for Lili."

He laughed and nodded along with the truth. "And I wanted to make something for Lili."

"What are you going to try next?"

"How about knitting? Can you teach me?"

"I can't tell if you're serious right now." Louise shook her head. "And I don't know how to knit."

"I'm not sure if I'm serious." He laughed again. "Maybe we could learn it together."

"Or you could look at some tutorials on YouTube and keep that little hobby to yourself. I'm not a knitting kind of granny." She hesitated, a look he'd never seen before crossing her face.

"I have something to tell you, Domi."

Ice ran through his veins, and he rushed to her side. "You're sick. Don't worry, I'll get you the best doctors. The best care we can—"

"No, son. That's the point." She looked him in the eye, raising her chin for the next part. "I never was. My blood pressure is perfectly fine. I wanted you and Lili to have your shot."

He couldn't help the laugh. As furious as he was with his grandma, her plan had worked. Sort of. "Just never do that again, okay?"

Louise looked around her bakery. "So, are you really thinking this might be what you'll do with your life?"

"Nope. Baking is fun, but it's definitely not *my thing*. But I'm pretty sure I just figured out what will be perfect ..."

"Well, don't keep an old lady waiting."

"It's numbers. I *love* working with numbers. So I'm thinking I could run the business part. Do the numbers, come up with gimmicks and marketing ideas, and use my playful self to help grow your bakery. Plus, of course, I can help you actually bake."

Louise gave him a pleasant sigh and put a hand on his arm. "I never really wanted a bakery, Domi."

He looked back at her blankly.

"I did this for you, because I knew that you needed something. But I'm ready to move into a smaller role. A much smaller role." Louise laughed. "Besides, you're a little too late. I already have a new business partner."

"What?" Dom was confused.

Especially when looking at the width of her grin. "My partner might be willing to take you on as a rookie accountant, but you'll have to convince her first."

Dom smiled back, finally getting it.

Louise winked. "Good thing you're already making her a cake."

Lili

Okay, this was getting weird, and Lili had to decide how much more of this nonsense she was willing to take. What had started out as slightly strange had steadily grown into something baffling. Annabelle came into Higher Grounds and offered to interview her on a subject Lili was totally unqualified for, and that wasn't even remotely close to the strangest part of her day.

"I'm so sorry for making a scene the other day!" Annabelle had apologized with no other preamble — Lili wasn't even sure if she wanted a coffee. After the professor was finished profusely apologizing, Lili asked didn't even ask, wanting to know about how her class was going instead.

"I don't even know where to start." Annabelle laughed but shook her head like she was lost. "Both of our classes are now over-flowing into the hallways, and our lectures are now just thinly veiled attacks on the other's methodology. We've been called in to see Dean Wilkinson next week, so that can't be good."

"Maybe it will be?" Lili suggested, her eyebrows rising in hope.

"Or maybe I'll be on a sabbatical soon. Public arguments aren't exactly professorial." Annabelle looked around the coffee shop. "Has Marcus come in … you know, since the last time?"

"No." Lili shook her head. "Not that I've seen, and I've been here all day."

"Too bad," Annabelle surprised her. "I was hoping for a sparring partner."

Lili laughed in agreement. "Yes. Sometimes life is a lot more fun when you have someone to argue with."

Annabelle looked at Lili curiously. "Would you ever be willing to let me interview you for my research?"

"About what?"

"About love," Annabelle answered.

Lili laughed. "What do I know about that?"

"Even when love doesn't stick, it always leaves its mark. I'm interested in all perspectives and stories."

"I appreciate the offer, but honestly, love is the last thing I want to talk about right now. Do you have any interest in talking about ways to keep your chocolate from seizing? If so, then I'm definitely your girl."

Lili grinned, but Annabelle didn't take her up on the offer.

"You can always change your mind." She smiled back, then ordered her a small Americano with a dash of half and half, plus one spoonful of foam on top.

Then Annabelle left, and the day got weirder and weirder.

Despite the day being slightly overcast, Alicia threw a fit about how bright it was outside. At first, it was a simple comment, but after Lili objected to her closing all the blinds, Alicia went on a tirade, insisting that the sun was bad for Harvey in such abundance and that if Lili really cared about her little nephew — they weren't blood-related, but that in no way diluted the power in Alicia's argument — she would allow them to be closed.

Definitely strange, though Lili was able to write it off easily enough because Alicia had been moody for several months now.

But Runa actually started crying when Alicia wanted to leave the shop to walk some samples up and down Main Street. Like, with actual tears and everything.

"I'm just feeling really vulnerable right now," she told Lili, without explaining what she was feeling vulnerable about, then suddenly insisting that she needed to run out on an errand "for like ten minutes."

But she still wasn't back. And Lili had been stuck making drinks for customers while simultaneously running the till for nearly an hour now. She knew it was ridiculous, and yet it sure *felt* like her two best friends were tangled in some secret conspiracy against her.

Those ridiculous thoughts only came when she was done making drinks. When pouring and blending, and preparing the various coffees, she could stay focused on the work. But whenever there was a lull, like right now, Lili's thoughts kept turning faster and—

She stopped thinking and listened harder to a noise coming from outside.

She made it halfway to the door before Harvey came running over and started tugging on her skirt. "Aunt Willy, Aunt Willy!"

Lili spent less than a second wondering why Alicia was *still* sitting in Higher Grounds with a toddler all these hours later but was bowled over at hearing her (sort of) name out of Harvey's mouth. She needed to give him a hug. Kneeling to embrace her honorary nephew, Lili turned to Alicia. "Why can he say the second L and not the first?"

"Because teaching him to say Auntie Willy sounded more fun than Auntie Lili. You're welcome," she answered Lili before turning to Harvey. "Mommy's so proud of you!"

Harvey went running over to his mother and jumped into her arms.

Lili heard another nagging noise from outside, then used the distraction to take a break from her apparent warden and escape Higher Grounds.

She opened the door, made it outside, and barreled right into a giant cake with legs.

An almighty crash sent them sprawling on the ground, with what had to be cake (?) flying everywhere in a giant mess.

Lili felt the familiar form of Dom under her on the sidewalk. His face was covered in buttercream, lumps of cake decorating them both.

She found herself flushing, suppressing a desperate urge to lick all the cake from his face.

But even if they weren't supposed to be furious with one another right now, she and Dom weren't alone. They were surrounded by onlookers.

And not just a few. This appeared to be more of a procession. A parade route seemed to have formed, running from Queen of Tarts to Higher Grounds across the street, with Dom in the lead.

Whispers had started a few moments ago, but Lili only heard them now.

"It was four tiers!"

"Did you see the thing on top?

"They call that a dildo!"

"But it was made out of JELL-O or something ..."

"Look! It just splatted into a puddle!"

"Why did Dominic Moore have a dildo cake?"

"Everyone, just back off already!" Dom shouted into the crowd, oblivious to the fact that he was still on the ground with Lili onto of him. "I need a moment with my girl!"

My girl?

The crowd dispersed, scattering away, some of the onlookers shaking their heads and others only falling back a few feet until he shooed them off with an aggressive wave of his hand.

My girl? Lili repeated the words in her head again, though right now, they might as well have been *kung pao chicken with a side of yarn.*

Nothing made sense. She had barely moved, still dazed and gathering her bearings, knocked down hard but cushioned by Dom.

And apparently, he'd been pillowed by that giant cake.

It was four tiers!

A big cake he'd apparently made for "his girl."

Lili looked down at him, desperately trying to figure out what was happening before someone made her feel stupid by spilling the beans.

Runa and Alicia were surely part of this. Where were they right now?

"Hey." Dom's finger drifted toward her and stopped on her cheek. He scooped some buttercream from Lili's skin and popped the finger into his mouth. He sucked the cream off and said, "We've got to stop meeting like this."

"Was that cake for me?"

"It was." He grinned. "But it's probably best if you don't eat it now."

"Are you really here?"

"I'm not going anywhere."

"Are you … okay? I heard you got sick and walked off of your show."

"I was sick of not being with you. I walked off to be here, so now I'm cured. The only place I want to be is here, in Mountain View with you."

They stared into each other's eyes, with Lili aware but not exactly uncomfortable with all the watching eyes, surely including Alicia looking out at the scene from inside Higher Grounds, while Runa did the same, standing beside Louise from behind a window in Queen of Tarts.

Their noses came closer and closer.

For a blink, Lili was sure they would kiss.

But then nothing happened beyond the staring.

"You are *totally* covered in cake," Lili observed, her willpower beaten like a bowl full of eggs.

"Bet you won't kiss me anyway," he said.

Then she did. Liliana and Dominic both melted into it as onlookers captured that memory in real-time, knowing that the town would be talking about this kiss forever now.

He finally pulled away and said the most unexpected thing.

Though, really, it was exactly what Lili should have seen coming.

"So, are you finally going to tell me the name of your supplier?"

"Sure thing." Lili shrugged. "I get all of my coffee at the Come N' Go."

"What?" Dom made several faces at once.

"The brand is called Second Cup. You'll find it in Aisle 3, right side, bottom shelf."

"You have got to be kidding me ..."

"I'm pretty sure the manager ordered the giant bag once by accident, but since I keep on buying the last bag, their system keeps automatically reordering it every time. I tried to convince him to hide it in the back for me, but he insisted that all products need to be out on the floor. But you'll have to beat me to it."

At his stunned look, she added, "I'm not big enough to have my own supplier. Yet."

"*Yet,*" he repeated.

And then they kissed again.

Lili

FOUR MONTHS LATER

Lili looked across the street at her former shop, shuttered, both emotionally and physically, now that she and Dom were sharing the more expansive space across the street. Buns and Beans, a name that celebrated the union of Higher Grounds and Queen of Tarts. Now no one could ever argue about where the best spot for coffee and baked goods in all of Mountain View was.

Even staring at the empty shell didn't feel like a loss. She felt gratitude more than anything. Lili's little shop had been an elemental and unforgettable part of this journey. It was easy to praise this new place, with all of the adorable colors — of course, Lili had picked them all out — and lines constantly snaking out the door.

Not that long lines were a problem with Summer and Keandre working the counter, filling orders, and ringing up sales — whatever it took to keep things moving.

"I'll be right back," Lili told Keandre before heading back to check on Dom in the supply room, where he was meeting with a potential supplier.

Keandre nodded and got right back to rocking the register with Summer.

"—are the kinds of discounts that we'll be able to approve with a standing order," the potential supplier finished delivering what sounded like the end of his sales pitch as Lili entered the room.

Dom glanced her way with an acknowledging nod, then turned back to the conversation in question. "Can you repeat that for me? Just the numbers."

Lili didn't need to hear whatever had come before she got there because she'd seen this same dance with every vendor so far. Each one of them would try to run rings around Dom, assuming that the athlete wasn't the ninja with numerals that he was. Each time she took delight in watching her man cut right through it.

"Great." Dom nodded as the distributor finished. "It sounds like you could knock another five-percent off, and this would still be a great deal for both of us. But we're only interested in the Second Cup. I do understand that the Chilean beans are cheaper and why you'd prefer for us to go with that as our first choice, but Second Cup is my fiancé's favorite brand, and if the five-percent is too steep for—"

Their new distributor smiled. "Five-percent will be fine."

Lili grinned at Dom then returned her attention to the window while he signed for their weekly standing order of Second Cup coffee beans. Her gaze settled on the Range Rover. She didn't love Dom's new SUV as much as he did, but that was only because he loved it a *lot*. Matte black and exactly what he'd wanted. Lili didn't know that he'd never really liked his McLaren, but she had a hard time believing he ever actually hated the race car like he claimed.

No matter how often they had bantered about it, Dom still parked in her old favorite spot, even though it was across the street for them now. That space signified yet another silly little contest that neither party wanted to lose, each of them trying to beat the other one to the spot whenever they didn't drive into work together.

Dom was suddenly behind Lili with his hand on her shoulder as Titus pulled his now-infamous McLaren into an adjacent spot.

"Of course," Dom said with a laugh, watching Louise get out of the passenger seat.

"We should probably help them," Lili said, already on her way to the front of their bakery, meeting Titus and Louise just as they arrived at the door, each with an armload of cakes.

"You know we have a kitchen here," Lili said to Louise. "The one your grandson had built. I keep telling you that you're always welcome to—"

"And I keep telling you that there are three things a woman should never share: a man, a kitchen ... and Mascara."

"Thank God! I thought you were going to say underwear."

"Don't be gross, Domi. Mascara carries bacteria. Nobody wants to get pinkeye."

"Is that what happens when you cross a brown eye with a blue one?"

Louise probably would have ignored her grandson even if Eleanor Boothman hadn't waltzed into Buns and Beans as though she owned the place, walking directly to Dom.

"*Dominic.*" Even the way she said his name was insufferable, though Eleanor was obviously *trying* to be nice. "We can't thank you enough for your donation! The park upgrades are all done, and we're waiting to unveil them."

She clapped, turning to Lili. "And a bunch of us were wondering if the Mountain View Beaver might be willing to make an appearance at the grand opening."

"The Mountain Beaver *might* be willing," Lili replied. "If there's something that Eleanor Boothman could do for the Mountain View Beaver?"

"What's that?" Eleanor asked, clearly suspicious.

"Personally pay for the next six months of her HBOMax subscription."

"Why?" Eleanor looked baffled by the request.

"Because that's what the Beaver wants," Lili answered.

Eleanor agreed to cover Lili's next half-year of HBO, then left Buns and Beans grumbling something under her breath.

Titus had been watching the exchange with amusement but was eager to leave their little huddle after spying Runa sitting at a corner table with Alicia and her new baby, cooing in the stroller in between them.

"I'll be back," he said.

Dom laughed at his buddy. "Do you think he'll ever learn?"

"As long as Runa keeps looking adorable all the time and making him laugh?" Lili shook her head. "No."

"Louise looks so happy." Dom nodded at his grandma, filling the display case with her pastries.

"Of course she does. This is what she always wanted, to bake whatever she wanted without obligations. And now she has a place to sell what she makes instead of just eating it."

"True." Dom laughed. "Hey, Lil?"

"Yeah?"

"Why did you make Eleanor pay for your HBO? Don't we have all the streamers already? And can't we afford—"

"Because that woman deserves to have her comeuppance," Lili cut him off but gave him the smile he loved. "Can't you just let me have this one?"

"Of course, you can." He nodded at the window, gesturing at the kids outside, standing in a cluster and clamoring for the beaver. "It's time for—"

"I know what time it is!" Lili snapped because that's how they played, with her pretending like she didn't really want to don the tail and nose that turned her into the Buns and Beans Beaver at least once a day.

"You look so cute," Dom told her before she went strutting outside.

"Not as cute as you look in your thong." Lili wondered what Eleanor Boothman might say if she knew how often Dominic Moore baked in that and nothing else.

"*You shush,*" he whispered.

"You shush." Why do you keep calling me your fiancé to random people ... like that supplier guy a few minutes ago."

"Because you'll eventually say yes."

"You should really stop counting your chickens, Dom." She shook her head. "Four months is way too early to be talking marriage."

"Then I'll just keep asking every month." He grinned. "I bet you won't—"

"OH NO YOU DON'T!" Lili ran outside before he could finish.

The opening notes of Can't Touch This started playing from the loudspeakers now permanently attached to the Buns and Beans exterior.

Lili started to dance as she heard them, already adept at incorporating her new tail into some old dancing, gracing the street with her signature moves as the growing crowd moved with her.

She saw Dom in the window watching, so she turned her wiggling butt his way, grinning to herself, knowing that she really didn't need to dodge that last bet. *Of course*, she would say yes ... eventually.

Lili just wanted to feel his anticipation a little bit longer.

Epilogue

The Dean was out of his seat, suddenly pacing his office with a widening grin. Marcus and Annabelle looked at each other. *Again.*

"WHAT?" they exclaimed together, no longer able to stand it.

"I have a solution." The Dean nodded, though it looked like the gesture was mostly meant for himself.

"A solution to what?" Annabelle asked.

"This little 'argument' between the two of you has generated more attention and publicity than the University has seen since our fountain fiasco."

That really had been something. Bulk detergent from CostCo had been dumped into every fountain on campus. Bubbles *everywhere*.

The Dean finished his thought. "Students are actually engaged and showing up to class, instead of going to sex parties and sleeping in."

"Well, to be fair, I think they are still going to —"

"We just need a way to corral that energy and use it in a way that benefits the school, and is less … disruptive."

"And?" Marcus leaned forward.

"I'm scheduling you to co-teach the class." It sounded like he was announcing the invention of fire.

"You're going to have to say that again." Marcus looked from the Dean to Annabelle and back.

"You two can share case studies and let your students decide."

"Decide on what?" Annabelle asked.

"The final assignment for each case study will be an essay where students declare which side of the argument they take. Did the relationship follow the formula for love, or is there something deeper at play? Students will articulate their reasoning for a grade."

"No way." Annabelle shook her head. "This is my class. I developed the—"

"You're class isn't working." Wilkinson's words were like nails in a coffin. "It's too popular. But if we divide the class and have two professors, then we can break it into sessions and switch off between you."

"I've gotta be honest ..." Now Marcus was shaking his head as well. "I couldn't possibly hate that idea anymore."

"But don't you see that this is how the two of you can resolve your argument?" It looked like the Dean knew a secret that both Annabelle and Marcus might soon be privy to. "Wouldn't you like to know which one of you is right?"

Marcus looked at Annabelle.

Annabelle looked at Marcus.

Of course, they did.

"So it would be like a giant study ..." Annabelle nodded. "Fate vs. formula."

"Precisely," nodded the Dean.

"It's still irresponsible to call this science," Marcus argued, though his resolve was quickly dissolving. "Figuratively or not. I can't in good conscious co-teach a class called The Science of Love."

"You're absolutely right," agreed the Dean. "That's why we'll be calling it The ABC's of Romance."

CPSIA information can be obtained
at www.ICGtesting.com
Printed in the USA
BVHW082256121022
649333BV00001B/65

9 781955 858137